Advance Praise

"*Cumberland* is a richly imagined tale of family secrets, lies, and unspoken truths that threaten the lives of two sisters. The writing is lyrical and funny in the voice of Ansel whose coming-of-age could bring down the entire family and the town around them. This novel has a mythic undertone that moves the layers of the story with the rush of an incoming tide carrying deeper revelations than the characters are quite able to bear.

Gannon writes with a painter's eye and a poet's ear, and there's no denying that she is bringing an original vision to her readers."

— Jonis Agee, author of *The River Wife* and *The Weight of Dreams*

"Haunting, sensual, and captivating, *Cumberland* reminds me of Joy Williams' work; its story of twin sisters—one of them reaching out toward life while the other struggles with illness—is as poetic and moody as adolescence itself. *Cumberland* is about the restorative powers of art and the sea, and I longed to linger in this world and to learn more from these wise and intuitive girls."

—Timothy Schaffert, author of *The Coffins of Little Hope* and *The Swan Gondola*

"*Cumberland* is a remarkable novel that draws us into the intensely physical mystery of twinness. Fifteen-year-old Ansel comes into the urgency of her adolescent body while her paralyzed sister Isabel floats in an increasingly mystical world of art and longing. In vivid and musical prose, author Megan Gannon delivers mystery, suspense, a most unusual love triangle, and surprises that keep the pages turning as the twins' embattled connection appears to reach the breaking point."

—Mary Helen Stefaniak, author of *The Turk and My Mother* and *The Cailiffs of Baghdad, Georgia*

"*Cumberland* tells the story of twin sisters inhabiting two vastly different worlds. One comes of age, finding her way in love and in her relationship with the world, while the other, trapped in both body and circumstance, finally discovers a way to break the silence that seems to imprison her. In a pitch-perfect duet, Gannon illuminates the place their worlds overlap, how the sisters imagine and intuit their way into the other's inner workings with unbearable intimacy. It's a beautifully wrought tale about how the intricacies of our bonds can lead to the most specific betrayals and how the burden of familial wreckage can play out in our lives whether or not we fully understand it. And it's a story about love and survival in the interdependent dynamic of two souls who were once one.

The story moves in a poet's carriage. Gannon's sentences are so full you'll want to say them out loud just to feel them in your mouth; her poetry is at times nothing short of arresting. *Cumberland* is haunting and surprising. You will miss these girls when the book is done."

—Rebecca Rotert, author of *Last Night at the Blue Angel*

Cumberland

a novel

Cumberland

a novel

Megan Gannon

Apprentice House
Loyola University Maryland
Baltimore, Maryland

First Edition

Printed in the United States of America

Paperback ISBN: 978-1-62720-000-4
Ebook ISBN: 978-1-62720-001-1

Design by Kimberly Babin
Cover photo by Mike Gannon

Published by Apprentice House

Apprentice House
Loyola University Maryland
4501 N. Charles Street
Baltimore, MD 21210
410.617.5265 • 410.617.2198 (fax)
www.ApprenticeHouse.com
info@ApprenticeHouse.com

For Leigh

acombren "obstructing progress," from O.Fr. encombrer, from combre "obstruction, barrier," from V.L. *comboros "that which is carried together."

One

If Izzy sends me, I don't feel guilty loving every step
away from the house and down into town: the sandy
road sliding in and out of my flip-flops, the wide-open
ocean-side light, and air so sharp with salt it stings to
breathe. Then saltbush, tang of scrubby shrubs, musty
bark and the flickering of live oaks as the sand picks
up gravel and hard earth along the curve downhill.
The long turn of the road gathering green and shade,
then the paved road and Red's garage with its smell of
crude and sun-warmed metal, the door into Pauline's
diner that jingles and sticks three-quarters closed. The
barber-shop-turned-library with heavy curtains in the tall
windows where still the spines closest to the glass are
brittle, sun-bleached. The Stop 'n' Shop with its low metal
shelves of dusty cans and detergent and the cooler in the
back that smells of milk-soured ice.

The sunlight gathers dust by passing between sagging
storefronts. Two peeling antique stores hold half the old

toys of Cumberland, Georgia. Down the street, the wide windows of Demeers' department store display a chalky mannequin with tapered fingers and blue eyelids. Today she's wearing a blond bob and tennis skirt, Keds and red sweatbands, her gaze cast over my reflection of skinny arms and eyes that don't blink in the bright street where a car pulls past. It's a station wagon full of kids in new sandals and a mom with sunglasses and trim hips. They buy three bags of groceries from the Stop 'n' Shop, slam the doors and shut their noise in with them, then turn onto the road that leads to the C. Grand Hotel for the few weeks the kids can stand. It's summer, so all my days are half Izzy's. This is my half of the errand.

For Izzy's half, I head to the back of the pharmacy. There's a book on crochet in the crafts section and some soft cotton yarn that fades from sea green to sky blue and back. She's already exhausted *Blooming Beads*, *Cross-Stitch the Proverbs, Advanced Needlework,* and many others that used to fill the empty slots in the rack. Every so often Mr. Jorgen lets me look over his catalogues and pick a new craft project to order in. Sometimes it's half a year before I buy a new one; sometimes I need two in one month. And always inside the big bag is a smaller bag of gauze and gloves and tubing.

At the library I try to memorize everything, knowing Izzy will ask something I haven't noticed. The pattern of book-spines preceding the one I pick out for her: brown, green, blue, green, red. The sounds from this

shelf: sniffle. Cough. The flap, stamp, flap, stamp, of the
librarian checking out books. Rustle of a plastic bag, clip
clop of hard-soled shoes on the floor. Just once I'd like
to trump her or pull off a lie, but she always knows when
I'm bluffing. Today she insisted I follow her instructions:
the biggest book on art I can find, then the eighth section,
eighth row, eighth shelf, eighth book. It turns out to be
The Poems of Emily Dickinson. I'm counting again to
double-check when I feel someone standing behind me.

"It's Ansel, right?"

"What?" I turn around with my finger still touching
book-spine number seven. He's tall, with a long face and
delicate nose—Everett Lloyd, the boy one year ahead
of me who only started school in Fort Harmon last year.
I hardly recognize him in shorts and a ratty blue t-shirt.
Most days he wears dress pants and a vest to school, his
knobby shoulders tensed like he's trying not to be seen.
He doesn't play sports or have rich parents, but none of
the football players beat him up and the girls all watch
him walk past in the halls. Last year we were in the same
mixed-grade homeroom and I'd see him with his nose
always stuck in a book, emotion flickering across his clear,
bright face.

"Yeah, um. Hi. Everett."

He glances at my finger still touching where I stopped
counting and an amused smile flashes across his face.
"What were you doing?"

I clear my throat to find my voice. "I was just...

checking."

He nods. "Do you live here?"

"The library? No." He's staring so intently, the beam of his white-blue eyes rippling my insides, the words tumble out before I can bite them back. "You know, I don't. They have this thing about doing laundry in the bathroom. Pretty unreasonable, really. And it's kind of hard to feel homey someplace when they won't even let you wallpaper."

He doesn't blink.

"It's a joke," I say.

"Oh. But you live in Cumberland? Does the bus come out this far?"

Since it's clear another wisecrack might not go over, I tell him I get a ride into Fort Harmon for school, then pull out the eighth book and flit my fingers across the spines, like *my oh my, what was that other book I was looking for?*

"Kind of slow out here in the summers, huh," he says. A stack of five books balances on his skinny hip. Nietzsche. Camus. Hermann Hesse. Two others I can't see. I can't resist.

"Slow? Nah—you should have been here last summer. Now, *last* summer we were low on cockroaches, and let me tell you, that put a damper on all sorts of activities— flea circus, Fourth of July parade..." His dark eyebrows cinch together and his eyes seem to recede beneath them as he watches my mouth intently. "Yeah, so." I clear my throat. "Are you out at the hotel?"

He shakes his head. "I'm staying with my grandparents this summer—doing some yard work for them, playing a lot of Cribbage." He looks at me sideways and his smile spreads slowly. We're standing in front of the circulation desk that I only dimly remember walking towards as he talked. I shove the books across the counter at Mrs. Hammond, wait for her to check them out, and try to figure out exactly how many steps it is to the door. "I could maybe use someone to show me around," he says. I nod, look away, but I can still feel his eyes on my face.

"The library? It's not that tough. You just—"

"No, not the library. Around town. You know. Show me what I'm missing." His lips hitch to one side in a shy smile. "Surely I'm missing *something*."

I slide the books off the counter as possible excuses run through my head: summer job, impending house arrest, crippled twin sister to tend... He takes the top book from my hands and his eyes brighten. "Oh, wow. Dickinson?"

"Yup. Gotta go." I pluck it from his fingers and stop to take a deep breath when I get to the door. The normal thing to say. "See you around." The street is blinding.

When I walk up to the house after all afternoon noticing everything so hard on Izzy's behalf, I can't stop: farmhouse frame of peeling white clapboards, one dusty window next to a tattered screen door at the top of three rickety wooden steps. The hill it sits on has worn away to an abrupt cliff, so the edge of the house flush against the edge of land seems stories high. Some nights I wake from dreams of a door opening into air or the foundation nibbled to sand, one ear to the ceiling hearing a high tide, the other ear to the floor full of the thud of waking up from deep dream.

Father remembered when there was still a landing you could stand on with your back up against the clapboard. From there, a path curved through the beach grass so steep you half slid down to where the water washes up, shells turning end over end in the disappearing glitter. But now, coming up from the beach, you have to climb the steep twenty feet hand over hand, use the side of the house to pull yourself up onto the crumbling flagstones before winding around to the front door.

I'm thinking about the perfectly symmetrical, sharply carved bones of Everett Lloyd's nose as I walk through the kitchen, hustle through the living room where Grand's staring at the TV, and head straight upstairs. Izzy is watching the ceiling closest to the window and when I walk in her eyes shift over to me with a sneaky smile. She's propped up as I left her, our dog-eared *D'Aulaire's Book of Greek Myths* open on her chest, the bones of her bird body arranged and absolutely still under the thin white bedspread. A juice glass on the night-stand holds a cluster of beaded flowers, all of them clear crystal but each a different improbable shape. Except for the green florist's tape wrapped around their stems, they'd look like tiny ice sculptures.

Izzy leans forward and I fluff the pillows behind her downy hair, then flop the two new books and pharmacy bag on her lap. "Oh, and this for your footboard," I say, pulling from my pocket a curly piece of broken tree root I'd found earlier. She smiles, reaches, for it, runs her fingers over the corkscrew curves, then holds it out towards the collage of scraps and bits of pictures and words she's torn from books and taped on the inside of her footboard over the years. The pictures are scattered, graffitied over, upside down and overlapping: an old etching of twin brothers fused at the chest half covers a colored pencil drawing of Aphrodite bubbling up from the ocean. Scribbled over the pictures are words like "alluvium" and "scrimshaw" and Izzy's spindly pen renderings of constellations and magnified neurons. I get the tape out of the bedside table, pull her towards the foot of her bed, and she tapes the root along the edge of a print of a man's head in profile, his skull labeled in rectangles and trapezoids with words like "loyalty" and "secretiveness."

When I prop her back up at the headboard she squints at the collage, smiles, tilts her pointy-chinned head as she fans the pages of the Dickinson book for a second, then snaps it closed, folds her hands and gives me a prim look like a teacher listening to a cheater making excuses.

"Yeah?"

She grabs the notepad from her bedside table and writes *Carpet color?* in her rounded, whisper-light handwriting.

I squint hard. I've been paying so much attention to the day-to-day incidentals of the library I never noticed the things that stay the same. Then I remember the sounds I'd memorized and let out a little hoot. "There isn't any—just the checkered tile left over from the barber shop."

Her grey eyes light dimly and then turn inward. She writes, *How many books in all?*

This is new—guessing instead of noting, and she's the only one who can change the rules of play. "No fair," I say. "Really, Izzy, if you'd asked me before, I could have checked with the librarian." I pull back the bed sheet, see the drainage bag attached to her thigh is not quite half full, then check the clock and do the math. Four hours, so it can wait another four.

Izzy's looking out the window again when I move her legs so she's lying on her right side for a while. She picks up the pencil and notepad and writes, *Going down to the water?*

"What do you want?"

Some violet. But careful—the tide's still high.

I don't ask how she knows, seeing only sky all day out the window, but when I step off the terrace I see she's right. The tide's so high it doesn't break, just slaps the edge of the cliff so hard I know I'm in for nightmares.

> *Years since I felt myself drifting inside her,*
> *my voice and her voice intermingling and*

all either of us could hear. Now with the dull silence of a whole body to mind, how she can't see the little twitchings of feeling as they register on her skin. The tent-pulled tension at lip corners. The flash-stab of her wrong-doing wrist. How when she's lying her eyes mirror too intentionally or don't meet mine at all, two flies flitting to every light-spot inch of a window trying to find an opening. How she comes in with the heat of the day in her hair, teeth pasty and dry from smiling. Tangy with the dust of some other place, offerings in hand. I take the books and craft projects and tell her, tell me, then listen beyond her speaking, for the voice fluttering behind her eyelids, but no matter how hard I reach towards her thinking, I can't hear. That lost-to-me internal voice drowned out by her noise-making throat.

Two

Since there's no shore to comb and won't be still for hours, I walk around to the other side of the house. The air feels still, poised on the brink of storm, and then a high quick wind twirls the ends of my hair and ruffles water the color of a mirror-back as I follow the cliff-edge out.

A lot of the old timers in town know about Izzy, but I'm not supposed to talk about her, not to out-of-towners, and especially not at school. After the accident, Izzy was in the hospital for so long no one at school over in Fort Harmon even knew I had a sister, and when the hospital released her and she still wouldn't talk, Grand decided it was easier for Izzy to just stay home and every night I'd teach her what I learned that day in class. It's gotten harder and harder. Once I know something it's impossible to trace my brain back through the dark of not knowing, the murk of beginning to understand, then the bright knowing. Most of the time she already knows the things I'm supposed to teach her—I don't know how. But sometimes she doesn't, and these are the things I wait to tell her. She still had a baby's handwriting at the beginning of seventh grade, but when I finally taught her cursive, it didn't take more than a few days for the tilted fence-posts of H's and N's to bloom looping tendrils of climbing vines.

Many other decisions were made by Grand, and by the Carson brothers who live on the other side of town. At first they'd arrive every Friday night under the porch light, hats in hand, shirtsleeves rolled, ready to lift Izzy into the tub so I could scrub her down. Then every two weeks, then less, once I was old enough and strong enough to lift my sister myself. Sometimes I let the tub fill a little, making sure the water level isn't high enough to reach her stoma. She laughs to watch her feet float up and turn out like a ballerina's first position, and we play battleship, sinking her feet with shampoo bottles and big bars of soap. When her feet bob back up we both laugh. "Unbelievable! Certified indestructible Mackenzie craftsmanship! The Navy wants to know, Ms. Izzy, what's your secret ingredient?"

It was Grand's turn to mind Izzy when I was at school, but that didn't last long. I try to imagine Grand tearing herself away from the TV in regular intervals to climb upstairs. One day after a few months, Grand said Izzy must have rung her little bell twenty times an hour, sometimes before Grand was halfway back down the stairs, sometimes when she'd just gotten settled back on the sofa. Izzy got a bladder infection and had to go back in the hospital for a month. After that the little brass bell with the flat-cast canary on top disappeared, and the next time she had an infection the doctor gave me lessons on how to change Izzy's catheter and diaper and how often. Now sometimes I just have to change Izzy's sheets when I get home. If it's only a matter of the bag leaking, Izzy and I make a game of that, too. I lift one edge of the sheet, then the other, rolling her back and forth. "Isabel Ailene! Have you been drinking? Where do you get off rolling around like a drunken sailor?" When the sheets are more than wet, we can't play that game.

I follow the C-shaped cliff around to an outcropping of rocks, then turn for the flat straight-away crowded by big-leafed trees, live oaks and magnolias that drop scorched petals and grenade-shaped cones in the ocean. It's a fifteen-minute walk if I'm walking fast, but I take my time, remembering what it felt like to have a pair of white-blue eyes centered on me and everything outside of me blurring. The other girls at school stand in quiet clumps by their lockers as Everett walks by, oblivious to their stares, and they burst into giggles when he's past. Most of the time they laugh loudly, convincing themselves, *ha ha, he's so weird, ha ha,* but sometimes they stop giggling too soon and keep watching. I try to remember if I've ever seen him with a girl, *a girlfriend*, and then the trees open and I start down the sand dunes on a diagonal towards the hotel.

The air is still sulfurous from last night's fireworks,

the sand littered with the paper casings of the bottle rockets Izzy and I could just barely see exploding from the vantage of our bedroom window. Behind the hotel, the wooden pier is swarming with people, some spilling onto the stretch of beach where young mothers sit under umbrellas. Their children wade at tide line or throw sandwich bits to the gulls that float overhead on updrafts, their shrieks loud in the still air. On really hot days the older kids lie across inner tubes, a rope around one foot tethering them to the dock, but today there's a breeze and the few teenagers are tan, slack bodies laid out on towels, one girl furtively checking the white stripe of skin under her shoulder strap.

I keep walking, up the front stairs to the wide white porch clustered with wicker chairs and low tables where waiters whisk in and out of a propped open, leaded glass door, their trays ting-ing. I find a table that hasn't been cleared yet, pour the teacup dregs out and wipe the rim and insides with a jam-smeared napkin, then top off from the still-warm teapot and loop my legs over one arm of the chair. I make sure I'm laughing loudly behind the comics when a waiter walks up beside me, pauses, then briskly turns back towards the door. I laugh showily the way the only child of rich tourists would laugh. Like any minute my parents will be back from couples' tennis, and dad will have the bill charged to our suite. Like it's just me, just me, and two parents revolving around me, real and dependable as planets.

Violet she calls the nearly magenta rhodo-
dendron she must have just plucked on her
way home. I was waiting, holding myself
inside breathing and willing her coming.
I don't say what I know—how nothing
can be violet while the sun's still up. How
it must have coolness and the scent of
dusky corners clinging to petals. Go to the
same rhododendron now as the shadows
lengthen and bring me a blossom—that's
violet. Timing. Like her gaze. I can't make
her stay.

Three

Saturday, July 6, 1974

32 days

Something is scuttering along the floor and rubbing up against the walls, some somethings so numerous they're everywhere, arching backs and tumbling into one another. Then my bed is drifting in the dark and it's water, my bed is a boat and I'm floating idly. I call out for Izzy but she's in another boat and suddenly there's a bigger tide, I'm doubly dizzy, the boat is sinking beneath me and I'm floating, a double drifting. The water's rising and I scream for Izzy. My boat is turning lazily in the water away from her and I jump and hit water so hot it feels sharp as torn metal. I'm going under when I feel her nightgown waving in the dark water and grab it, following it hand over hand up to her, my fingers screaming like bent wire in the twisted cloth. She is sleeping and her boat is sinking with each breath, so I pull her arms over my shoulders and I try to wrap her loose legs around my waist but she's not waking. I jump again, pushing off from the sinking boat— Izzy's so heavy, she's so heavy—and we're miles out from shore and I know I can't make it with the both of us.

I'm awake before I open my eyes. I lie letting the stillness of my bed solidify against my body as the morning sinks in and wonder if this is what it is like for Izzy, sounds always muffled and far off at the edges while she lies still at the quiet center. I try to relax my every muscle and see if I can stop feeling my feet and legs and waist. No matter how hard I concentrate I can't shake the occasional touch of the sheet against my toes and kneecaps or the weight of my own legs against the mattress. What does she think about? What fresh ideas does she find to run her mind over every day? I practice times' tables and sing through old songs silently. I lie there trying to bear it when Izzy starts chuckling from her bed.

"How'd you know I was awake?" I ask. Her hair is spread across the pillow like petals of a withered sunflower, her head too big for the little stalk of her body. She's staring at me, and then I understand why people sometimes don't like to meet my gaze. With eyebrows and eyelashes pale as a burn victim's and no discernible cheekbones, our faces are smooth, upside down tear-drops tapering to a too-pointy chin.

Izzy gives me a mock-serious stare back, then laughs and shakes her head, raising her hands and flopping them down with a gesture that says, *let's get to it.*

"Oh crap—first Saturday of the month. I have to change your catheter today," I say. She laughs again. I

slide out of bed and tug on my shorts, then pull my arms
inside my shirt and fasten my bra.

"I should take it on the road, huh, Izzy. Only problem
is, you're the only person who thinks I'm so gosh darn
funny." Sliding one arm behind her back, I pull her to a
sitting position, then tug her legs over the edge of the
bed, hook my arms under her armpits and haul her up
so my nose is in her hair, her cheek hot against mine.
Like waltzing with a mannequin, I walk backwards to the
bathroom, then push the door open with my butt and hold
her beside the bathtub. "Okay, right foot first, Izzy," and
she can't stop giggling. "Oh, whoops, that's right," I say,
scooping one leg at a time into the tub, then sliding her
inside. "I just keep forgetting."

I unbutton her nightgown all the way down, lifting
up her right side so she can pull one arm out, then the
other. When Izzy's untangled, lying naked on top of
her nightgown I try to whip it out from under her in one
motion. It never works. Once she got three cuts on her
back where the buttons scraped underneath. This time it
all gets bunched up under her butt. I wrestle the cloth out
from under her, grunting and wheezing and making a show
of it until finally it's balled up in my hand. "Ta-dah! Ladies
and gentlemen, please note, not a fork overturned, not a
drop of wine spilled from the goblets."

I pull her diaper off, trying not to breathe or notice
the sharp box that her hipbones make of her body, the
thin flow of skin over the bones of her legs and what little

muscle is left. Every day my own body gets softer and rounder while Izzy's stays the same from the waist down— or worse, shrinks, grows backwards. Someday maybe she'll have the eight-year-old legs we had when we first came to live here.

I get a wet washcloth and wipe and rinse until she's clean, then clamp the catheter, scrub my hands and fingernails and root around under the sink for a new catheter pack, tape, gloves, and gauze. Laughing like a mad scientist, I snap on the gloves, then creep over to the tub where Izzy's giggling. "Let's seeeeee here," I say, holding the tubing as I pull off the tape and gauze just above her left hipbone and inspect the opening. The skin around the port is red, puffy, and when I dab with a piece of soapy gauze around the plastic cap of the stoma an edge of yogurty liquid peeks out.

"Shit," I say, and Izzy looks at me sharply, then down at her hip where I'm swabbing with a new piece of gauze. Her cheek was hot—a fever? For how long? I smile—she's watching my face—and clear my throat. "Yes, yes, yes, veeery nice," I say. Her eyes are a little bleary, but she hasn't been cranky or lethargic like the last time she had an infection. I finish swabbing the stoma, then snip the old inflation port tubing and wait for the water to drain out, pulling the catheter out slowly. There's a little blood, so I snap on some new gloves, swab the blood up with gauze, then measure out with my fingers how far to slide the tubing in, moving fast to get the new catheter slipped in and the balloon inflated. Then I clean around the stoma again, dab on some Neosporin, and lay the empty bag on the side of the tub.

The water is cold when I turn on the faucet, but by the time it creeps up to where Izzy can feel, it's tolerably warm. I dump in some shampoo for makeshift bubble bath and swish it around with one hand. When there's an inch or two of water I scrub her feet and her legs up to her thighs. She doesn't move, just lays with her eyes closed, waiting for me to wash all her parts. "Izzy." A faint smile creeps onto her lips.

"Izzy, here." I suds the washcloth and drop it in her hand. "Open your eyes." Her chin is lifted to the ceiling and her smile brightens. She snaps her eyes open and gives me a look like, *What?*

"You do it," I say.

She tilts her head into a little shrug and then starts right in on her privates, skipping the tops of her thighs. She shuts her eyes again just to bug me.

"Izzy, it's creepy."

She looks straight at me, furrowing her brow, then finishes and dunks the washcloth. We watch a patch of soap bubbles form on the water and she takes the soap again from my hand. I sit on the toilet and look away when she washes her chest. She wrings the washcloth out and drapes it over the side of the tub, and I pull the stopper, wait for the water to drain. She's staring at me hard like I'm supposed to know what she's thinking, and I don't meet her eye as I dry her off and tape the new tubing down, then attach the new bag to her thigh with elastic bands. When I pull her from the tub and cart her back to the bed I can still feel her eyes on me.

"What, Izzy?" I say, turning back to the bathroom for the thermometer.

She gives me an exasperated look, then rolls her eyes and reaches for the notepad. She writes in big letters, the pencil digging in a little more than usual. *It's not like you. I can't feel it.*

> *Fresh from the hospital, I had to learn my*
> *new body, how fingers traveled to the edge*
> *of feeling skin, blood pumping into dead*
> *toes, and the light inside always pulling*
> *this half of my body back into living. Too*
> *much body over the dead edge, I spent*
> *days concentrating on keeping myself alive.*
> *Teeth clenched, staring at one spot, it took*
> *a lot of pulling until I learned that every new*
> *knowing was ballast on this side. So books*
> *and more books she brings at my bidding*
> *to anchor me here with words and thoughts*
> *and lines. Glutting myself with held-inside*
> *sound, some days I'm so heavy in this world*
> *I'm a rock watching tides without a light-lick*
> *of fear.*

Four

The rain's coming down so hard it's erased any horizon, and when I go downstairs Grand is sitting at the table making one of her lists. Presidents' names, church members, state capitals, the addresses of buildings the Carson brothers built—lists and lists she keeps in a stack on the desk, sometimes duplicating the same lists without looking. I pour myself some coffee, then top off her cup. Rings that must be from a week's worth of breakfasts line the saucer.

She nods sideways at me without looking up. Somehow, she's always reminded me of a scarecrow in a clown's wig—rigid-backed, with grey curls surrounding her flat-faced, round head. Her dark eyes are like two holes punched through paper and I pretend it feels good to have someone's eyes on me when she glances up. "Was there something you needed?"

I get the words out fast. "Izzy has a slight temperature. I think she has an infection."

"Well." Grand crosses out a name on her list and I wait for her to say something else as the rain slows from torrents to a hard fall of thick drops. Over the drumming, one high drip drip drip chimes out, the leak in the gutter at the end of the porch I've yet to fix.

"So... I think we need to call the doctor."

The room is silent as I brace myself—is she so far inside herself she hardly hears me, or just gathering her breath the way a storm gathers clouds? She writes a few more names and sighs. "Did you clean her up?"

"Yes," I say.

"Give her an aspirin?"

"...Not yet."

"Well. Go get her an aspirin and see if that doesn't help." She screws her mouth into a sideways pucker as she prints two more names in exact block letters.

My chest feels fluttery as I pass through the living room to the back bedroom door that's always closed. The blinds in Grand's room are drawn as always, but the faint light that seeps in around the cracks shows rumpled bed-sheets musty with the scent of old coffee grounds and stale perfume. The wardrobe door stands open, overflowing with dresses hanging in clear plastic, and lidless hat-boxes litter the room, one bursting with scarves, another with purses.

I cross to the corner and pull open the bathroom door, turning on the light to see the bathtub with a deep rust stain streaking up the center, the chalky, dank-smelling tile gritty under my bare feet. The toilet has dark rings inside it and I put the lid down to dampen the swampy smell. Lipsticks and hairpins and a round tin of face powder clutter a little doily-draped table beside the sink. I pull open the medicine cabinet and sift through the rows of orange prescription bottles where Grand has always kept the aspirin, pick one and turn the bottle over so I can read the name on the typed prescription label: John Mackenzie.

It's hard to imagine there was ever someone else here trying to shore this old house up against rotting. I glance upstairs, but since she's in a good mood today I walk back into the kitchen and try to ask in a voice so casual she won't even notice she's responding, "What was Granddad like?"

Grand looks up quickly, squints, then puts down her pen and takes a sip of coffee. "Well, it's hard to say. When you live with someone, it's... hard to describe a person." She sets her chin, turning her cup in the groove of the saucer, and clears her throat. "How would you describe Isabel, for instance?"

"I wouldn't," I say, and Grand sees her mistake, since she's the one who forbids me to talk about Izzy. She purses her lips and looks down at her list.

"Well."

"I mean, I wouldn't... know where to begin."

She lifts her cup and blows her coffee, one pink rose showing between her narrow fingernails. "You see," she says, looking at me levelly across the rim.

The rain turns down to a trickle as Grand moves into the den for the day's game shows. I give Izzy two aspirin and tell her I'll be back up in a few hours to check her temperature. I'm sitting at the table playing solitaire when there's a *clomp clomp* on the porch steps and a *tap ta-tap* on the screen door. The tall shadow through the curtain could be one of the Carson brothers, but when I swing the door open Everett Lloyd is standing there in a dripping windbreaker and drenched shorts. He stomps his feet and tousles a hand through his dark hair.

"Hey," he says, grinning. My knees feel shaky and I suddenly fear Izzy's long-gone bell will start ringing like an alarm. I grab the doorknob behind me.

"Hey."

He pulls his windbreaker off and his grey t-shirt is soaked underneath, sticking to the bones of his chest. "Ever been swimming in the rain?" he asks.

"Ever been struck by lightning?"

He smirks and his eyes shift beyond me into the house. I pull the door closer behind me and stare back at him. Smiling, he shakes his head, turns and clomps back down the porch steps. I shoot a quick glance back at the den before latching the door and following him, picking along the gravel walkway in my bare feet around to the flagstone. He's grinning like a game show contestant as he slides sideways, his arms out for balance, down through the loose sand to where the tide washes up.

I slide down after him and he's already pulling off his shoes, laying his sopping socks across them. He pulls off his shirt and I drop my eyes, kick clumps of sand towards the water. The clouds are opening, the air clean and still, and the sound of the ocean is louder for the loss of rain. We have to shout to be heard.

"Well?" he says.

"Well, what?" I say, not looking up.

"You coming?"

"It's freezing. The water's probably freezing." I fold my arms across my chest and squint out at the misty horizon.

"Yeah, so." He leans in and mutters a few inches from my face, "Nobody asked you to get naked." His ears are red before the words are even out of his mouth and he turns, lets out a whoop and runs in, holding up his sagging shorts with one hand as he flops backwards into the ocean. I run a few yards down the beach and plunge in, burying my cheeks in green sea.

He treads water and pushes back into the oncoming waves as they start to crest, then paddles quickly as a swell catches the back of his head, driving him under. He comes up spluttering, grins and waves me over, but I dive like I didn't see and come up close to shore. I swim for a while by myself, treading water and checking the house to make sure none of the curtains are pulled back from the window.

The quiet, dreamy-eyed boy in homeroom—I never would have believed he could be so loud. He shouts and ducks under water, coming up spluttering and laughing, then whoops as a wave gathers and gathers and gathers, paddling hard to catch the edge of the crest. At school he's silent, his elbows tucked close to his body like he's ready to flinch at the slightest movement, but now he spreads his arms wide and flops backwards, his eyes shut with a quiet, beaming smile.

I slog out of the water and pull my legs up to my chest, shivering. Everett rides the wave straight towards shore, his head sticking out like the carved face on the front of a pirate ship as the tide sweeps up to my toes.

"I've gotta go," I say. "I'll catch pneumonia." He flops down on the sand beside me and I inch away.

"Oh, right," he says. "You're never sick."

"What are you talking about?" I'm looking out at the water but I try to put a lot into my voice: You don't know me. This is the first time we've ever even hung out. Dummy. Jerk. What do you know.

"You didn't miss a day of school all year," he says, propping up on his elbows so he's staring straight at me. He's right. My first year of high school (and the three years of junior high before that) my home room teacher gave me a Perfect Attendance certificate on the last day of school.

"How would you know? Been interviewing my friends?"

He lowers his chin and gives me a steady, patient look, as the heat creeps into my face. If he's noticed I never miss school, then he's noticed I don't *have* any friends. In the beginning I got invited to sleepovers but of course I could never go After a while the girls in my class stopped talking to me, and now I sit alone during lunch, rewriting the notes from my morning classes so I'll remember what to tell Izzy. Most of the other kids pretend like I'm not even there.

I clear my throat. "Well, what, been keeping a chart?" This time I look over and he's the one to drop eyes and look out at the water. He sits up and brushes the sand from his shoulder.

"I mean, you're kind of a loner—it *seems* like you're always there."

"Yeah well, what are you, my parole officer? The attendance police?" He walks over to his clothes and shakes out his t-shirt, ducks into it, then grabs his socks and loops his fingers in his shoes.

"I've... gotta go," he mumbles. I watch him scramble up the dunes. The water slaps into me, washes around and behind, then pulls sand out from under me as it recedes. I stop shivering as the light fades from the sky.

There's the problem of getting into the house and changing without Grand or Izzy seeing me soaking. I jog down the drive, down the sloping hill to where the pavement starts, then walk into the gathering dark and jingle into Red's garage. He glances out from the truck he's under as I grab the bathroom key and wave it at him. He nods and I walk around to the side of the painted brick and let myself in. It takes a good fifteen minutes to dry my shirt and shorts under the hand-dryer enough so you can't tell they've been wet. I tiptoe across hot asphalt around to the door, hang up the key and wave to Red again on my way back out.

My feet are raw and prickly by the time I jog back up the porch steps. Grand is sitting in her chair, her face flickering with the light from the TV, so I pull three turkey TV dinners out of the freezer and heat them in the oven. I crimp the aluminum edges back, pull off the cardboard top, then carry Grand's in on a tray as she finishes filing her nails and lays the manicure set on the table beside her. "Here, please," she says, patting the coffee table without taking her eyes from the screen.

I eat my dinner at the table, then carry Izzy's upstairs. She's scribbling in a lineless notebook she keeps under her pillow and when I walk in she stops writing to stare at my still-damp hair. She raises a pale eyebrow at me, then points out the window and makes swimming motions with her arms.

"No—no swimming. It was just still raining when I went for a walk." She scribbles on her notepad and holds it up to me. *I heard shouting down there.*

"Don't know." I shake out the thermometer and stick it in the corner of her mouth. She writes, *Hair's on fire!*, smiling wanly around the thermometer.

"What's that mean?"

She shoots me a mock-withering look and writes, *Liar, liar.*

"It's *pants* on fire."

She laughs. *I like hair better.*

"Yeah, well, you wouldn't know a saying from a..." It's an old game we used to play called "you-say-I-say." One of us would start a sentence and the other had to finish it. If you guessed what the first person had been thinking, you won.

I stare at the second hand on my watch, waiting a full minute for the mercury to climb. Izzy ponders then writes, *Silhouette?*

It's been so long since she's guessed one I can't even remember what it feels like, having someone else know what I'm thinking. I take the thermometer from her mouth and tilt it in the light to read, the thin silver line topping out at 100°. "No, Izzy," I say, swallowing against the fear rising in my chest. "Salt shaker."

Must be something, that someone shouting down at the tide line. She'll give away anything to prove she's not hiding what she's hiding. So long since I last heard her thinking I can't quite guess. Yes, a someone, but someone so new to her, held so slightly inside her, I can't see. So new she hasn't learned how to wear this him or her, hasn't learned how to show herself to her best advantage. A him. Must be. One she hasn't touched, doesn't yet bear a trace of. The image of him so thin inside her she's fighting hard against forgetting, holding onto the memory wisp wrapped tight around her shoulders.

Five

Sunday, July 7, 1974
31 days

By the next morning Izzy's temperature is 101°. I give
her two aspirin then wait by the kitchen window, my
pantyhose *whisk whisking* as I rub my knees together.
The older Carson brother pulls up at 9:20 on the nose,
and Grand walks out of her back bedroom glittering with
silver-dollar-sized clip-on earrings, piled necklaces, two
rhinestone clips holding back the curls over her ears. She
stops short when she sees me and I tug at the hem on my
faded, floral dress, the princess waist riding up high on my
ribs, the fabric pinching my armpits.

"You plan on attending church today?"

"Yeah, I um… thought I'd go," I say, suddenly at a loss
for an excuse.

"Well then. You know what sort of behavior I expect
from you."

"Yes, ma'am." I open the front door just as Mr. Carson
knocks.

"Carl," Grand says, holding out her hand like she has a

ring to kiss.

"Ailene." Mr. Carson is so solid and sturdy he's always reminded me of a metal girder: the perfect line of his hard shoulders, feet always waist-width apart forming one long rectangle. Usually his jeans and pearl-buttoned shirt are dusted with construction site dirt, but this morning his blue button down and brown church pants are as starched and sharply creased as a grocery bag. He takes off his white cowboy hat and gives Grand's fingers a brisk shake, then steps inside and glances towards the stairs.

"And Miss Isabel, she's… situated?"

I squirm and glance towards the stairs. "She's fine," Grand says, breezily waving her hand by her ear. Mr. Carson watches my face as Grand steps briskly out the front door and waits at the top of the stairs.

"Everything all right, Ansel?"

"Well, I think Izzy—"

"Carl, we'll be late," Grand says. Mr. Carson runs one of his big, calloused hands over his forehead and back over his wiry hair, then settles his hat back on before taking two long-legged strides to the door. Outside, he has to baby step to walk beside Grand. He wrenches open the passenger's side of the rusty truck, taking Grand's elbow to help her inside, then leaves the door open for me and walks around to the driver's side. I squeeze in next to Grand and pull the door shut as he cranks the engine, popping the truck in reverse.

We drive down the hill onto Main Street, past the trees

and the silent buildings and the one parked car in front of Pauline's. Though they were open only yesterday, all the stores are dark, dusty, and hunkered so low it's like no one's been in them for years. Mr. Carson takes a left on Hill Street and passes a bar and a photo shop before the buildings give way to scrub brush and palmetto leaves. Then the asphalt runs out again and the truck bumps down onto a sandy road, the trees leaning close, draping the air in dusty tatters.

In this part of town the light feels thin and still, the windows of the few square, flaking houses strung up with faded bed sheets. Mr. Carson brakes hard to miss a squawking chicken that flaps back to where three others are pecking around a sagging porch. The house behind it is silent and a dark hand yanks the thin curtain back into place.

We drive to where the road dead-ends into dense trees and scrubby shrubs, pull up in front of the white clapboard church and park next to a silver Buick. Mr. Carson cuts the engine and I slide out of the truck, tugging my dress down so the hem covers my knees, then climb the concrete steps to pull open the heavy door. Grand takes her time, holding Mr. Carson's arm, looking around the way a queen surveys her royal subjects, though we're the only ones outside. She passes through the shadow of the steeple, then slowly climbs the steps, holding out her hand to Mrs. Jorgen who's standing inside handing out bulletins.

"Good morning, Ailene," Mrs. Jorgen says, stiffly

shaking Grand's hand.

"Inga," Grand says, nodding at her with a droopy-lidded smile. "And how is your charming husband?"

"He's fine, Ailene. Same as always." Mrs. Jorgen exchanges a look with Mr. Carson, who takes off his hat and sets it on the rack above the coats before following Grand into the sanctuary. "Ansel, sweetheart," Mrs. Jorgen calls, ducking behind the back pew and handing me a paper bag. "A little something came into the pharmacy for…" she glances at Grand, who's stopping to shake the hand of the two or three people she passes before settling primly into the front pew. "For you to take home," Mrs. Jorgen says, and there's a new book of knitting stitches and three skeins of multi-colored yarn inside. I thank her, but when I ask her how much it all costs she just waves me away. "We put it on your Grandmother's tab, honey. Not your worry."

"Oh. Okay." Grand is busy rooting around in her pocketbook twelve pews away, so I whisper quickly, "Do you think I could get some antibiotics?"

Mrs. Jorgen tilts her head and glances towards where Grand is holding up a compact, smearing on orangey lipstick. "Is someone sick at your house?"

"I think… maybe."

Mrs. Jorgen blinks quickly, touches her fingers to her mouth and whispers, "Well, Ansel, you need a prescription for antibiotics. Have you called the—"

Grand clears her throat loudly and I turn to see her

staring at me.

"Thanks again," I say loudly.

When I slide into the pew, Grand grabs me by the arm and pulls me down next to her. "What did I say? What kind of behavior do I expect from you?"

"I was just thanking her," I say, holding up the pharmacy bag in my other hand.

"You have no need to thank these people," Grand says, sniffing and picking a piece of lint off of her navy blue dress. "Now sit up straight and act like you're part Calvert."

I stuff the bag under the pew as Mr. Carson scoots in next to me and bows his head. Grand straightens, opens her compact again and fluffs the curls behind her ears with one finger. Light floods us from behind a few more times as the doors open and people come in and take their seats.

Dear God, I pray. *Please watch over Izzy and help her get better and don't let her fever get any higher. Please let our birthday come quickly and please let me get my driver's license on the first try. And God, please let me have one more chance to talk to Everett Lloyd. Amen.*

The organ music starts and Mrs. Jorgen walks up the aisle in front of Reverend Clark to light the candles. Reverend Clark scoots to the front of the church behind his walker and gets his balance long enough to raise his hands in the air as the music stops.

"Let us pray."

After the service we all cross the street to the fellowship hall, a high-ceilinged metal building with no windows that smells of rust and burnt coffee grounds. In the center of the cold, bare room is a card table with a red checked plastic tablecloth, and Grand stands instructing the other old ladies where to lay out the cookies and Styrofoam cups.

I'm standing against a wall in the kitchen when Mrs. Jorgen mutters to Mrs. Sibley, "I swear I've about had it with that woman." I peek around the corner at them as Mrs. Sibley shakes her head.

"We've all about had it. Our whole lives. But I don't see that there's much any of us can do about it."

"Carsons should do something," Mrs. Jorgen mutters.

"How's that? Guilt's a powerful thing."

Mrs. Jorgen picks up a plate of brownie squares and carries it over to the table. When she sets it down Grand says something, so she slides the plate a few inches to the right. Lips tight, she walks back to where Mrs. Sibley is arranging pinwheels on a plate. "Though if anyone feels guilty, it ought to be Ailene," Mrs. Sibley starts up again. "Didn't you say John stopped filling his prescription? Some hoity-toity nurse ought to know how to look after her own husband's health." Mrs. Sibley pauses to glance over her shoulder at Grand then reaches under the counter and digs out some floral napkins, plopping them on the tray next to the Styrofoam cups.

"Not to mention guilt shouldn't cost more than five

hundred dollars a month," Mrs. Jorgen says, pulling the lever on the coffee maker, filling oup aftor cup

"That much?" Mrs. Sibley asks.

"At least. Makes you wonder why she can't pay her grocery bills."

"Ailene Calvert could never pay for another thing in her life and no one in this old town would say squat. Remember that birthday party they had when she turned ten?"

Mrs. Jorgen snorts. "The rash, you mean?"

"The rash, and that God-awful solo." Mrs. Jorgen laughs, presses her fingers to her lips and glances over her shoulder at Grand as Mrs. Sibley continues, "Up on that porch all dolled up in her lace and finery, face blistered as a strawberry, croaking out the Ave Maria while the rest of us stood on the ground below, solemn as church mice, just grateful to be there."

"What was it she had, anyway?"

"Measles. Lord, Inga, you mean to say you didn't catch it?"

"No."

Mrs. Sibley shakes her head. "I don't know how you missed it. They let Ailene pass out the cake, and a week after she coughed all over my slice I about died."

Mrs. Jorgen sighs and fills another cup, puts it on her tray. "Any time I complained about Ailene as a girl my daddy would lecture me on how Cumberland wouldn't exist if it wasn't for that family, blah blah blah. Well, I don't care what her father did for this town—all the good deeds of one generation shouldn't absolve the sins of the next. Honestly, Frances. Has anyone even seen that child since they first brought her home from the hospital?"

"Carsons have seen her."

"Well, she ought to be in school."

Mrs. Sibley clears her throat and around the corner of the kitchen door I can see her tapping her temple with one finger, whispering, and Mrs. Jorgen's eyes widen as she shakes her head. "There's a reason no one asks too many questions, Inga. Let it be," Mrs. Sibley mutters, then picks up the tray and carries it over to just where Grand is pointing.

After fellowship hour Mr. Carson unlocks the passenger side of the truck and helps Grand in, then holds his keys out to me.

"Really?" I ask, my heart fluttering.

"Haven't practiced none since school let out." His face is blank but his eyes are twinkling.

I pluck the keys from his fingers and run around to the driver's side as he squeezes in next to Grand and wrenches the door shut. I have to scoot my butt to the edge of the seat to reach the pedals, and when I turn the key in the ignition the truck roars then stops.

Grand sighs and says, "Carl…" I crank the ignition again, holding it longer this time, and the truck turns over and idles.

"She's got it, Ailene." I take a deep breath and stomp

on the clutch, grinding the gears into reverse. "Mirrors," Mr. Carson says, and I hit the brake as a tan car lurches to a stop right behind us. The driver gives a wave and pulls out so I can back up. Once we're even with the road I stomp the clutch again, joggle the shifter into first and press down on the accelerator, slowly inching us forward. "Give it a little more," Mr. Carson says, and when I press my foot down we pick up enough speed so we're sailing down the sandy road, coasting, light as air, the sun flashing between trees. "Brake," Mr. Carson says, and my feet hop around looking for the right pedal.

I find the brake as we jounce up onto the pavement, and Grand says "Oh!" half wounded, half appalled, like someone's just burped into her champagne glass.

"Sorry."

"Doing just fine, Ansel," Mr. Carson says. I bite my lip and press down on the gas again as we ease forward, creeping to the end of Hill Street until we crawl to a stop. I put the blinker on and look both ways, then ease out onto Main Street, jerking the wheel a little to line us up with the white dotted line. There are a few cars parked on the other side of the street, but none on this side to worry about sideswiping. Truck tires whirring easily over the asphalt, I point us towards the end of the street, only a few blocks to go until the curve in the dirt road leads up the hill home. Next to me, Grand is seething, but I grip the steering wheel harder and lean forward, craning under the windshield until the light reaches my face.

*Must have been a quick hit to the driver's
seat buckling grey matter, or so they all
think. It's the only reason they can figure
why I don't speak. All of them forgetting the
one time I opened my mouth and the words
came out sloshed and tumbled, how the
quick eyes of the doctors caught across the
room. I looked to her to know my thoughts,
explain for me, but she stepped back as
they wheeled me away, stuffed me inside
machines, and then I knew. And the severing
of that line with her thinking was worse than
the severing of my spine. How to explain?
They don't know how speaking scatters
thought like buckshot, or how much thinking
every day you have to do when half of you
is unfeeling, concentrating on anchoring in
place. Like legs dipped in sunlit water, how
I always confuse the real with reflection.
Neither flesh feels, so how can you trust
your eyes to tell? Why I'm in the habit of
looking deeper than looking, to see what's
fleeting and what's taking root. How the
world tries to tear your attention away from
even yourself, it seems. Better to be careful.
Better to stay lip-locked against idle chatter
that untethers.*

Six

Izzy's temperature is down to 100° so I give her two more aspirin then wander town for a few hours, hoping I'll run into Everett. When I finally walk back into the house that evening the first thing I hear is Izzy crying. I bolt upstairs and through the door to where she's bent close over the heavy art book, her tears raising measles on the slick paper. She looks up at me and heaves, the book so heavy it hits the floor beside her bed with a ceiling-rattling shake. Then Grand is calling up the stairs and Izzy's screaming and scribbling on her notepad, tearing pieces off and handing me bits of sentences.

Hiding this from me
You have been telling didn't tell me
All of this for how long years
And years all these long gone dead
They knew how to see beneath
surfaces I thought only I knew
Have to see everything have to now

So far behind hurry hurry

She lets out little shrieks as she writes, and all I can do is take the scraps of paper, watching the snot running into her mouth as she rips and keeps writing, gauzy hair standing out from her scalp, the walls all around us retracting. The book will hardly shut when I pick it up for all the bent and twisted pages, and Izzy holds her hands out so hungrily I shove it at her then take a few steps back.

She flips to a page and jabs her finger at a painting and flips again so fast the pages tear. "This painting, Izzy?" She nods and flips again, jabbing a finger and flipping before I can see and pointing, flipping, pointing, riffling through the pages like she's lost something and then she wraps her arms around the book, hefts it to her chest and rocks. I sit on the edge of her bed and put my arms around her but she pushes me away, then shoves the book off her lap until it crashes to the floor. The house shudders and when I put my arms around her again she's limp in my arms for a second, then starts pinching and scratching and shrieking. "Izzy, calm down—you'll make yourself sick," I say, grabbing her hands and holding her tight until the fight goes out of her and she sags against me. Her hands drop in worn-out heaps and she sobs into my shoulder.

"What on earth is all this racket about?" Grand is in the doorway, her eyes blazing.

"It's okay, Grand—I've got it." She stands there for a

minute as I'm rocking Izzy then flashes me a disgusted look and slams the door to our bedroom. "Izzy, show me again," I say, when she settles into sniffling and deep shuddering breaths. "Can you show me again?"

She sits up and I set the book back in her lap. She wipes her eyes with flat palms, turns through the pages and points at bright lines of ocean-tumble swirling color. "Van Gogh," I say. "Okay, what else." Taking little hiccupping gasps, she flips a few pages deeper into the book and points to more neon noxious color and little light dabbles. "Derain. Got it."

She reaches for her notepad and carefully prints, *And all the other wild beasts.*

"Like who?" She turns the page and jabs her finger at magenta old lady wallpaper and a turquoise window escape. "Matisse." She nods. She keeps flipping and points to Picasso, Braque, Dali, Chagall, then shuts the book and looks at me. "All right, Izzy." I run my hands down her arms. "I'll get everything I can."

I'm thinking she'll smile at me now, but Izzy fixes me with a hard stare like she's trying to bore some sentence into my skull. I wait, and listen, but nothing comes, and Izzy's mouth twists into a grimace. Holding the notepad out to me like a police badge, she's written, *You get everything.*

"Okay, Izzy, I'll do what I can." She shakes her head and shrugs my hands away and suddenly she's still. She's looking at me so dead center I think she might bite. *You get me everything—you owe me all of it.*

I stare at the words *you owe me, you owe me all of it* as Izzy's eyes bore into me. All my days of wandering downtown, breathing sunlight in through the pores of my skin and running, swimming, wandering as far as my legs will carry me, days when I walk and walk against the worry of Izzy's fever climbing higher and higher, stretching the tether between us so thin my chest feels tight with the constriction, all these days rise like an oily bubble beneath my ribs, bob up and lodge in my throat, and I turn, run, pound downstairs and out the door, outside.

All I can think is *keep going farther, past the hotel, farther,* until there's a hidden beach I hardly ever go to, my legs rubbery as I pick down the cliff between sharp rocks to the wide sand. I take off my shirt and shorts and run in, swimming then beating against the water until I'm so far out everything is silent and I can just float, the ocean holding me up so steadily I hardly even feel I have a body.

Sky and black water surround me and my ears fill with rocking waves, with night the color of a hole I can drop down into, and none of it, nothing is with me. I let the dark erase me, push my mind over maps and pictures of far-off places. I'm hovering above the narrow walled streets of some Moorish city but somewhere distantly Izzy's shrieking so I push further into the dark, the old stone permeated with smoke rising off of lit embers, the clank clank of a metal smith echoing between women swaying past in long caftans. Like the eye of the filmstrip I watched

in World Cultures class, I swoop down in between the
women and brush past bolted doors where the sounds
of children bounce around like voices down a well and
I round a corner and swoop up again. Up above the
stacks of square, whitewashed houses, then down to the
cobblestones: smoke, clank clank, language I can't speak.

It's cold and I can't tell where the sky begins and the
water ends. My eyelids, my whole body is heavy so I kick
back towards shore, working against my loose limbs. I
slog a little ways up the sand then drop and roll over, the
moon icing my goose-bumped skin, erasing my brain like
a blind eye.

*Only fitting she should bring this book on
the day she's first riotous inside. Flipping
through the different artists' movements,
classicism and realism—why always this
obsession with what can be touched and
measured, all this silliness of breasts and
beauty and brawn. How they delight in
surfaces—the whisk of fabric, the gloss of
bodies—but never the misty swirlings of
the inner eye. Something here that implies
feeling in Cassatt's little whale-white belly of
a daughter, mother spreading her chubbed
toes to water in the white-bellied bowl. The
silent workings between them, a something
that can't be seen. And here, what they*

called fauvism, vision the eyes alone can't see, sight of deepest speaking, color for a true mood. She wasn't even hang-head or blowing over how she's been keeping all these paintings from me, never telling, never teaching me, she never told me—what her whole body can't know, only I. Cubism, how the seams and turnings in a person, the many seen and hidden versions, overlap— yes, they know, they can see beyond the bodies, these painters. How long ago—fifty, a hundred—I am a hundred years behind.

Seven

Monday, July 8, 1974
30 days

"Don't move." The early sun tilts into my eyes so all I can see is someone standing close over me. There's a *click, click* and the person drops a camera from the dark outline of his face and crouches down to root around in a canvas bag. I'm freezing, curled up on my side in the cold sand. Sun-spots swim across my vision and when I turn my head I see the person is a girl, skinny as a colt, crouched in khaki pants and a black tank-top. "Damn. Didn't you hear me?"

"I haven't moved," I say, shivering, and although my eyes burn with salt and sand, I don't lift a hand to rub them.

"Your hair. I wanted the swirl of it on the sand."

"Oh." I sit up and wrap my arms around my knees. "Sorry."

She shrugs, and even though she's almost as small as me, she's older than I first thought—a grown woman, the corners of her eyes radiating faint lines.

She twists a dark filter off the end of her lens then slots it into a plastic box, all of her movements quick and efficient. "I was pretty much finished for the morning anyway. The kids seem to have picked this beach clean."

"You mean shells? There are never any out here. You have to go up that way." I point back down the beach towards the house. My teeth are chattering, and she turns her dark eyes to look at me, then pulls a windbreaker out of her bag and tosses it over. "Hey," I say, her accent registering. "You're an out-of-towner."

"Hardly the only one." She points with her chin towards the windbreaker and I slide my arms in, pull it over my knees, and the shivers stop. She digs in her bag, pulls out a little brush with a bulb on the end, and starts swiping at the lens.

"Yeah, but you're a yankee."

She lets out a loud, quick "ha!" and grins, sitting down next to me and peering at me from behind a shoulder-length curtain of shaggy brown hair. "What's your name?"

"Ansel."

"After the photographer?"

"After my grandfather."

"I'm Lee. But just call me The Yankee."

I get up, dust the sand from my legs, and my whole face blazes when I realize I'm only wearing a bra and underwear underneath the windbreaker. "I bet I'm not the first person to call you that," I mumble as I scoop my clothes against my body, then scramble behind some big rocks back against the cliff. I strip off my still-damp undies and hastily pull my shirt and shorts on over my raw skin, then shove my damp bra in one back pocket and my panties in the other.

"Maybe not, but you're the first to call me that to my face." She's standing beside the rock now and I see the dark eyelid of her camera blink back at me before I can say anything. I shove the windbreaker at her as I push past and the camera winks at me again.

"Well, I…" but nothing I can think of would sound mature, cool, so I turn and walk slowly away from her. She snorts and starts to laugh as I take off running, up the beach away from her, my feet light on the cold sand.

The clock at the diner says 7:15 and Pauline makes me a hot chocolate, on the house. We're the only two there so she settles on a stool, pulls the ashtray over and smokes, watching me.

"Everything okay at home, Ansel?"

I don't think of Izzy when I shrug and wrap my hands around the cup, the heat not seeping deep enough to warm my bones.

"You look like hell, is all." I stare into my mug and blow and sip as Pauline shakes her head. She looks tired as always, her dyed-red hair faded to a carroty orange, her green eyeliner flakey and smudged into her wrinkles like it's weeks old. "Goddamn small towns," she mutters.

"What do you mean?"

She takes a deep drag and exhales slowly, saying, "I mean the way no one—" but the door jingles open as a trucker in a plaid shirt and suspenders slouches in. Pauline stubs out her cigarette and walks back behind the counter, grabs a mug and fills it with coffee before smacking down a menu in front of the trucker. He asks her what's the forecast, she flicks on the radio, a young couple in bright polos and crisp matching khakis slides into a booth, and Pauline stays busy the rest of the morning. I hold myself in my seat against the dark pull of the house and Izzy anchored there, smoldering with fever, and make a mental list of all the countries and capital cities I can think of. At ten I leave my empty mug on the counter and cross the street.

The library has one coverless paperback on Matisse, a coffee table book on Picasso, and nothing on the rest of them. I spend a few hours sorting through cardboard boxes stacked against the back wall that are full of garage-sale *National Geographics* and cast-off *Redbooks*. Brown veins of crusted dirt branch across the covers where bugs have eaten. I keep digging until I find one *Art Today* with an address for a place that sells art posters and postcards. I tear it out and shove the slip of paper into my sand-filled pocket behind my damp panties.

"You look like crap." Everett Lloyd is standing behind me, not smiling, his light eyes distant, like he's looking out at me from behind dingy glass.

"I—yeah. So I hear. I slept on the beach," I say. He

nods quickly—he hasn't even heard me—and shifts his eyes to the door leading back to the bathroom.

"Watch out for that." His shoulders are cinched up, and as he turns towards the front door I realize these might be the last words he'll say to me all summer.

"Am I covered in sand or what," I call after him, then remember I took my wet bra and underwear off before pulling on my shorts and t-shirt. The air slips inside my clothes so easily my face starts to burn and when I rub my arms sand sprinkles the floor around me.

"Yeah," he says, focusing on me, a tiny smile curling the corners of his lips. "You're a real mess."

"Ansel Mackenzie," Mrs. Hammond calls from the circulation desk. "I hope you're planning on sweeping that up."

We both snort and Everett says, "I've got it, Mrs. Hammond."

"Oh sure," I say, "Make me look like some irresponsible—"

"Well, it's not hard."

"You." I swat his arm and he laughs.

Once I've checked out Izzy's books and we're outside, I'm edgy with thinking of things to say and it's hard to breathe enough to say anything. I scrape the sand off the back of one leg with my other foot and shift the books from one hip to the other. We're both standing very tall on the sidewalk, watching the parked cars. Everett clears his throat.

"Hungry?" He nods across the street to Pauline's.

"I should be getting home," I say, and suddenly all the sun and worry and water and wind of early morning wash over me and I feel thick-headed and wrung out.

"I'll get my bike and give you a ride," Everett says.

"No, it's okay. The road's really sandy and I—"

"To the end of the street, then. You gotta give me that at least." He tilts his chin down so he's aiming his eyes straight at me. My stomach flutters and I swallow.

"Okay." I'm dizzy watching his long frame dash across the street to the meter where his bike is leaning. He wheels across to me and takes the books from my arms, smiling and nodding to himself as he reads the titles, then slots them in one of the messenger bags over his back tire. "How do I..." I say.

"I don't think the seat's big enough for both of us." He gets on and straightens the front wheel, then pats the handlebars. "Try here."

Shakily I boost myself up and try to balance. I can feel the bones in his chest beneath the thin t-shirt as I lean back and his arms make a basket around me. He's very still, his breath hot and shallow in my hair. "Hold on," he says into my ear, then stands up and pushes hard on the pedals as I shut my eyes against the light.

The day my father borrowed a twenty-foot sailboat, Izzy and I stood by the front window in Grand's bedroom, watching how the pelicans floated on the ocean air before tilting and dropping like darts to the water. They came up shaking fish into their beaks, choking them down in thick gulps. Grand and mother were in the kitchen, their hips wrapped in aprons, their voices clipped and polite, walking quickly past the kitchen door when I turned back to look: Grand carrying a plate of cookies from the laundry closet where she kept them out of reach, mother selecting the serrated knife from the rack in the back pantry.

Izzy had her face pressed against the glass, so she was first to see the big green "C" of the hotel insignia on the sail as father's boat drifted into view. "He's here! I see him! He's here!" she shrieked, running into the kitchen and leaping at mother as she wiped her hands, quick to catch Izzy. She propped her on one hip and stood next to me at the window, laughing as father wrestled all the sails and ropes and pulleys. "My mariner." She turned and called over her shoulder, "Ailene, come see."

Grand came to the window and peered over our shoulders, saying, "Well, he is half Calvert. There's nothing a Calvert can't do." Then mother's hands tightened on my shoulders, and when I turned to look her lips had flattened to a thin line.

When we got to the beach mother was still quiet, holding each of us loosely on a hip and staring out at father. He must have liked the idea of riding up to the house like a knight on his steed, but now mother was standing in her nice shorts and tennis shoes helplessly waving and calling to him.

"What about the dinghy?" he called back to her.

"Oh, Adam, we'll get wet," she said, setting us down to shield her eyes from the sun. He smiled, stood on the edge of the boat and tugged the collar of his t-shirt over his head, then dropped head-first into the water.

Izzy and I shrieked. I ran to the tide line screaming, *Daddy!* and mother laughed, caught me before I ran into the waves.

"Annie, baby, he's coming. He's swimming in, see?" Father's head suddenly emerged where she pointed, his sandy hair horribly matted, his obvious struggle against the waves doing little to calm the frantic fluttering of my caught-bird heart. Izzy was sitting on the sand crying, her face slick and red as a beach ball when he dragged himself out of the water, slogging through the tide and wet sand towards us. He scooped mother and me into a big hug and mother screeched and wriggled as father buried his face in her neck and whispered, "You'll dry." When he kissed her, she stopped struggling and loosened her hold on me so I slid to the sand. Izzy was still sniffling, so I patted her head and said, "There, there," like Grand always did when she babysat and we cried.

Once father had the dinghy from the garage, he blew into it a few more breaths to make sure it was nice and tight, then floated it on the shallow shifting water and carried first mother, then Izzy, in. Izzy was big-eyed and pale, clinging like a dying starfish as mother talked into her ear and father swam, pushing the dinghy in front of him out to the boat. Mother slid her sunglasses on, and when she tilted her face to the sun she glinted, her sharp laugh caught by gusts of wind. I waited on the beach with the picnic basket, telling myself over and over what he had said. "Right back, Ansel. Sit tight."

When they got to the boat, mother lifted Izzy in, then flopped awkwardly one leg at a time over the edge. Izzy grabbed onto her again and she stood and waved to me. For the flash of a second I imagined my whole family getting into the boat and sailing away without me. I held on tight to the picnic basket handle until father turned the dinghy and swam back. He lifted me with one arm and the basket with the other, then settled us both inside before wading into the water and kicking towards the boat. Suddenly his head went under, and I screamed, reaching for him. He came up laughing, spitting an arc of water like a statue in a fountain.

And then Izzy and I were fussed into Hotel life preservers, picnic things were shuffled and stowed, father pulled up the anchor as the wind caught us with a sudden jerk and we were all sailing away together, the wind in my hair and in Izzy's, tendrils flapping like tattered flags.

> *I learned adding and subtracting before*
> *counting. Later, when she tried to teach*
> *me the rightful names of numbers, it took*
> *two months to set them straight in my*

head. One bead on my needle was a little girl, eyes closed, sitting in sunlight. Two were streamside under a low-branched blossoming, tearing petals and tossing into water gossamer canoes. Three beads were watching the baby, taking turns. Four were each on a blanket corner playing tea and crawling towards petit fours. Five, the baby in the middle, the color of cakes. I added girls and stories up to ten, then took away. Ten, the day cresting into fading, torn dress turns towards home. Nine catches a glint of her father's boat coming in. Eight drifts farther into dusk, grass where she sat bent and singed.

Eight

When I wake up the light is bright and loose, and the porch steps come slowly into focus. I startle and tip forward as a hand grabs my shoulder to steady me. Then I realize: Everett, his breath in my hair, letting me sleep, standing here straddling the stopped bike. I don't want to move and for a second can't find my voice. "How long was I asleep?" I finally ask.

"A while." His voice is so tender I hold my breath. "I rode all around town, but then my legs got tired and I rode back here. I didn't mean to wake you."

"You didn't wake me."

"Good."

As I glance back at the house, I can almost swear the curtain of the front window swishes. I pitch forward and scramble up the stairs, suddenly sure that Grand has been watching us all this time.

"Ansel." His voice is low and quiet and makes me shiver. He cranes back for my books and holds them out to me, and when I reach for them he stretches out his pointer finger to touch my knuckles before letting go.

"I'll see you later," I say, looking back one more time to see him straddling the bicycle, his long, lanky body loose, relaxed, his gaze steady and intent.

When I bang through the screen door Grand is standing at the stove behind something sizzling. "There you are," she says, not taking her eyes from her skillet. She holds the spatula by the very tip of the handle, prodding at some eggs like she's checking that they're dead. The fact that she's not staring me down means I imagined the curtain—she didn't see anything.

"Sorry—I'll do that." I drop the books on the counter and gingerly take the spatula from Grand's fingers. The eggs are a hard snot-yellow at the edges but still milky and curdled-looking in the middle. I flip the whole yellow mass over, chop it with the spatula and stir it around.

"You were up early," Grand says, sliding into a chair. "Where have you been all morning?"

"It's not lunchtime yet," I hedge, unsure whether she missed me at all last night and only noticed this morning I wasn't home. I can't hear anything from upstairs. I strain for even the tiniest squeak of bedsprings, a sigh, a cough, listening so hard I can practically hear dust settling on the jewel-colored glass animals lining the kitchen windowsill. "I didn't make you miss your date with Bob Barker, did I?"

Grand presses her lips into a tight smile and brusquely swishes the hem of her floral housecoat. I try to imagine

what she looked like when she was my age, and Izzy's.
The earliest picture I've ever seen of her was the one from
her wedding when she wore a tight little sheath dress
and a pillbox hat with a veil. She was unsmiling, her dark
eyes flat as always, and she only came up to Granddad's
bow-tied collar. He was beaming, his hands on both her
shoulders, holding her out to the camera like Grand was a
coat the photographer was about to put on.

I was five when my father showed me that picture and
the rest of the ones in the musty white leather album. He
let me sit on the floor with the album in my lap and turn
the pages, and when we were done I looked up at him.
He was lingering over the last page, intent on this final
picture. I wanted to feel his eyes on me, so I snapped the
album shut, and when I did he kept staring for a minute
at the air where the last picture had been. Then he took
the album from my small hands and slotted it between
encyclopedias on the bookshelf in his mother's room.
When I wrapped my arms around his leg to get him to lift
me, we just stood there behind the light-filled curtains, his
hand on my hair.

Once Grand is parked in front of the TV I make Izzy's
lunch and carry the tray upstairs. She's lying on her side
with her back to the door, the white coverlet messily
tugged up over one shoulder, and the sharp tang of her
leaky urine bag and old diaper makes my lungs catch. Her
back is very still, her hair fluffy and matted at the back of

her neck like lemon cotton candy. I put the tray down on the little desk and my throat flutters, the leaden weight in my stomach twists as I slowly approach the bed.

Izzy jerks and lets out a squeal that dissolves into giggles, turning her shoulders to hold out a cat's cradle of blue yarn latticed between her fingers.

"Izzy, good God, if I have a heart attack, you know you're up a creek," I say, relief rushing into my lungs. She's giggling like a crazy person—she can't stop. I stick my hand through her cat's cradle and with a quick twang she drops fingers and stretches her hands wide, the string still looped across the sides of her hands, her face lit and dazzling. She threads the cat's cradle again, and when I creep my hand up through the taut trap, she holds me for a minute, letting the string pinch my wrist. Her eyes are the color of tarnish, and she stops laughing, holds my gaze for a second, the bite of the string deepening. Then I'm free, and Izzy is holding a loop of blue yarn between her pinkies, looking me square in the eye and laughing again, a sound that smoothes down all the jagged bits in my insides.

> *Both of us know I said the one thing I*
> *shouldn't, wielding a pretend envy against*
> *real guilt she feels. I don't begrudge her*
> *the body she spends so much time running*
> *from, trying to spread herself thin against*
> *a heaving horizon. How most days I'm*

*content to follow my mind's gush and
retreat, the internal turnings and tidoo. I
never know where they'll wash up. But
knowing how the guilt lines her insides,
more silent than a voice I can't hear, I
shouldn't have said it. How she was calm,
absorbing the words, the must-be sharp
slice of them against her all-feeling skin,
then how suddenly she drew up into one
hard edge. How she tried to hold, turned,
fled down the stairs and out, the hurt of my
words catching up in one rush and washing
back like silt in my veins before I could
take them back. How one untruth finds a
trueness in the one whose bruises brought
it on. What I should have—please, I need
them—said.*

Nine

Izzy's temperature is back up to 101° but she's clear-eyed, intent on her books, and she doesn't take her eyes from the pages as she opens her mouth for me to drop in the aspirin and tilt a glass to her lips. The house is dark with late-afternoon shadow when I go downstairs for the sewing scissors Grand keeps in the cabinets behind the kitchen table. I shove past all the old bills and lists and table linens so ancient they're stiff along their creases to pull out the sewing kit. Putting everything back, I notice a stack of ragged-lipped envelopes rubber-banded together, all addressed to Grand with a return address from Carson & Carson Contractors. One of the envelopes has the postmark date June 3, 1974—only a month old, and the memory of Mrs. Jorgen and Mrs. Sibley saying something about the Carson brothers and money nudges me.

I slide the top envelope out from under the rubber band and peek inside. There's half a piece of watermarked green paper with a ragged perforation across the bottom.

At the top it reads "Group term policy for John Mackenzie" and under that "Death benefits paid in the form of annuity" with the date 5/1/74—5/30/74. Next to that is the number 543.56. I pull out another envelope and this one reads 4/1/74—4/31/74 and next to it again, 543.56. They're both signed neatly at the bottom, Carl Carson. I read the words over and over but whatever I'm supposed to catch hovers just above me.

The couch creaks in the other room and I shove all the envelopes back, stacking them in front of some manila folders puffy with crinkled pages and labeled "Medical—John," "Medical—Ansel" and "Medical—Isabel." I shift the phonebook back into place and peek into the den. Grand's still parked in front of the TV, so I go back and flip open the phonebook to the L's. I try "Lloyd" and "Loid" and anything else even close, but there isn't a listing in Cumberland and I wonder what Everett's grandfather does to have an unlisted number. I stand at the sink window where the day's grown sharp with shadows and imagine walking barefoot all the way into town, finding his grandparents' house, tapping on the window… and then what.

Izzy's propped up in the desk intent on the art book, and when I come back in with the scissors she reaches for her notepad.

Canvas, she writes. *How big is it?*

"You mean for painting? It comes in all sizes, I think. My art teacher last year showed us these drippy pictures that were so big they wouldn't fit in this room."

She outlines the shape of the window in the air with her finger then writes me out a shopping list. *Tube acrylics: indigo viridian cadmium onyx violet white and any in-between blues and greens. And grey spelled ey not ay.*

"Your wish is my command, mademoiselle," I say, thinking there's no way Grand will give me money for all of that. "Now if you'll just hold still, I'll have this wretched hobo disguise off of you in a jiffy."

I straighten Izzy's head, measuring her hair out with my fingers, looking for the shortest section to go by. Last summer tending Izzy's hair got to be too much, so Grand had me crop it down short, and now the pieces hang in chunks like one of the cubist paintings Izzy's poring over. I wet the brush in the sink until her hair's all flat and damp, then hold strips of hair between my fingers and snip, the scissors' sharpness kissing the sides of my fingers. When I'm done Izzy's hair looks fuller, almost bouncy, curled under at her chin and tidy as a sailor on a box of salt.

After I make dinner, change Izzy's sheets, take her temperature and tuck her in for the night, I take a deep breath and bring Grand a glass of ice water. Dressed in a filmy sea-green nightgown and matching robe, she sits on the edge of her unmade bed rolling her hair on small plastic rollers, her dingy pink terrycloth slippers dangling from her toes. When I set the water glass on her bedside table she smiles thinly and gives me a little nod of dismissal.

"Grand, I really think Izzy needs a doctor."

She holds up a hand mirror to check her curlers and doesn't meet my eye. "Haven't you been taking care of her?"

"Yes, I've been trying, but she's been running a fever for two days and I think—"

"Give her some aspirin."

"I've been giving her aspirin, but it's only brought her temperature down to 100°."

Grand reaches for another curler and starts to roll the last strand of hair over her left ear. "That isn't very high," she says. "I'm sure she'll be fine."

I sigh, and Grand's flat gaze flicks to my face as her mouth purses. "What did you say?"

"Nothing." She stares at me hard and I can feel her inhaling, dark clouds shifting and settling across her brow. My voice is small in the gathering silence. "I didn't say anything."

Grand smacks the roller down on the bed, the last strand of her hair sticking out in a grey tuft, and snatches me by the arm. "It's hard enough raising two girls without being made to feel guilty all the time," she says, her mouth trembling. "I live on a fixed income. I can't indulge every little whim that flits into your heads."

"This isn't—" I say, and Grand shakes me, cuts me off.

"You want new clothes. Isabel wants to be waited on hand and foot. Well, we all want something. Do you think

I want to make myself sick with worry, alone with you two
in this house all day long?" She spits the words at me, the
dark cinders of her eyes red-rimmed and watery. "I do all
that I can for you girls—all that I can—but it's not enough,
it's never enough." She drops my arm and bolts to her
feet, bumps into me, and shuffles towards the bathroom.
She stops and half turns so I can hear her words. "I should
have just let them take you."

I drop my eyes and back out of the room, my breath
coming quick and short as I shut the door behind me,
then climb upstairs and don't meet Izzy's gaze. I lie on
my bed in the dark, listening to her breathing deepen and
lengthen, her sighs just out of sync with high tide, then
shut my eyes and crowd out Grand's dark, pinhole eyes
with images of Everett's thin, tendony forearms, Everett
standing over his bike, Everett's hairy, gangly legs. I dream
Everett's eyes, dream them closer and closer until I'm
swimming in blue water laced with slants of white sunlight,
sinking deeper and deeper with no need for air.

What goes on outside these walls that
brings her back to me, gasping, teetering
towards tears? This whatever-it-is shouldn't
be her worry. The whole world, and its
whirled versions, and how to reel them all
into this hive of old wallpaper, everything
that could be something to me—which

books, which pictures—how could she
know? The connection severed, she can't
know what I light towards anymore than I
can know who this is she's lit with. The little
tear that pulled apart the accordioned paper
dolls. Now they're two. So you can't tell
which one took the scissors first.

Izzy's breath is measured, her body slack and tangled in the white sheets. Going downstairs, I'm careful to step over the noisy third step and squeeze through the back door before it can open far enough to squeak. The trees are creaking with frogs and crickets and the moon's so bright I don't need a light, just follow the faint glimmer of white sand into town.

When I get to Red's garage I take a right on Cayman Street and realize, walking past the chain-linked yards and tattered screened-in porches, that I still don't know where his house is. What was I thinking? That somehow I'd just sleepwalk there? That something would pull me through the streets, hypnotized, and I'd magically find Everett's grandparents' house and he'd be waiting?

There's a light on in a house at the end of the street where an old man sits in his undershirt in front of the TV's blue flicker. I turn back towards town, cross Main Street, walk along the dark windows of the stores and take a left onto Hill Street towards the blurry sounds of a jukebox, the red glow of a sign reading *Watering Hole*. Someone laughs, a ball cracks, and the voices are muddy and sluggish, slipping over each other like fat eels. I turn back around and catch out of the corner of my eye a red jeep with a New York plate. The Yankee. I duck under the awning of a store so I'm in shadow and watch two men standing across the street outside the bar's open door, bottles held loosely in their hands.

"I don't suppose," one says, taking his hat off, smoothing his hair, and putting it back on.

"I wouldn't know the first thing about one of them kind of women."

"You and me makes two." He chuckles, sticks out his lower lip, tilts the bottle, and takes a long swig. "Might be worth a look-see. You think?"

"You're trouble, you know that? What was it my mama told me the first time you brought your scraggy ass around with a fishing pole and a can of crawdads?"

"Trouble had herself a litter and here comes the runt." They're laughing, and their laughter has too much air behind it and is too loud. "Must be why I'm always looking for something to suckle on."

"Oh, no. No, you don't." The friend of the man in the hat laughs again, leaning against the wall beside the door, then slips a little and falls in a squat against the building.

"Get up, you drunk."

"Just leave me be."

"Get up so you can see how I saunter in there and

sweep that damn Yankee off her barstool." The man in the hat puts his bottle down on the sidewalk and tucks his shirt in, jiggling his belt buckle.

"You'd need one bitch of a broom to sweep her anywhere."

"Come on, you drunk fuck."

"I'm coming." The friend grabs the elbow of the man in the hat and puts his hand out on the wall to steady himself. Then he sticks one foot through the threshold of the bar and puts it down carefully like a toddler stepping onto a boat bobbing against a dock.

I slide down to sit on the sidewalk and pull my t-shirt over my knees. Even across the street the smell seeping out the door is of stale pee and rusty beer cans. The jukebox sounds like it's under water and a woman in a halter-top walks past the door carrying an empty tray, stuffing bills in her apron. Laughter, and the low murmur of voices.

After a while she comes out—Lee, the woman from the beach. In cargo shorts and a green tank top, she doesn't look like she's dressed for a bar. Her hair's in a messy bun and her camera strap is slung diagonally across her chest like a line of ammo, camera bumping at her hip. She's walking fast, but not like she's scared. The man in the hat comes out after her.

"You are never gonna get an opportunity like this again, you know that?"

"Oh, Rusty, I bet you say that to all the girls." She

doesn't turn around as she talks, taking her keys out of her pocket and walking up to the dusty jeep.

"These things we got around here? You can't call them girls." He sidles up behind her and drapes one arm on the window frame, pushes his hat back with his fist. "Not even women. They're just bitches." He puts a finger out to touch her bare shoulder and she fits her key in the door, opens it, swings inside and slams it before he can even get his hand back out of the air.

"Well, I'd hate to think what that makes me," she says, turning the key in the ignition and popping the jeep in reverse. She flashes him a smile that has a little too much teeth then backs up even with the awning I'm crouched under, brakes, and looks at me. "Ansel, right? —Not after the photographer."

"Yeah." I stand up and realize it's pretty cold and the man in the hat is turning to walk back towards the jeep.

She's looking at me with something like laughter in her eyes, but there's an edge to her voice. "If I were you, I'd get in."

"Yeah. Okay." I hustle around to the passenger side and jump in just as the man in the hat makes it to the jeep and Lee floors it. In the rear view mirror the man in the hat stands there, his hands hanging limply at his sides, then spits and heads back towards the bar.

"It's none of my business," she says, glancing at me, one wrist draped over the top of the steering wheel, "But I wouldn't be out alone in this part of town so late if I were you." I watch the dust blow up around the jeep and take my time responding since something in her tone rankles me.

"Except you *were* out alone in this part of town."

"Right. But I'm not you."

"Well, I was looking for someone." She shifts in her seat, pulling her camera around onto her lap, and glances at me again.

"How old are you?"

"Almost sixteen." I'm trying to sound cool but then I realize what a baby I sound like to be rounding up my age.

"Well, I hope to God whoever you were looking for wasn't back there."

"No. I just got lost. Sort of. I was looking for a house."

"What's the address?"

"I don't know."

"Well, what's it look like?"

"I don't know."

Lee lets out a quick "ha!" and leans over to tune the radio wavering between frequencies. She rolls the knob until she finds an oldies station and then pulls the rubber band out of her messy bun, shaking out her dark hair. "You don't know what it looks like? The CIA must be recruiting you already."

I think about the list of skills I'd bring to espionage— cereal making, butt wiping, hair brushing—and I can't help laughing too. "Yeah. Actually, that's what I was doing back there at the bar. Spying, you know. "

"So that whole curled-up-in-the-fetal-position-like-an-abused puppy thing was just part of your cover?"

"Right."

"Good cover."

"Thanks."

She's nice-looking in a skinny, unkempt kind of way. Except for a long, horsey nose, her features are generic as a china-doll's, so balanced and symmetrical they might be pretty if she made an effort, but since she doesn't wear make-up she just looks washed out and plain. Now, with her brown hair down, her plainness is messy enough to seem a little wild, the lines of her cheekbones angling into her small, bow-shaped mouth. The tiniest spark of jealousy simmers in my gut. I look in the rearview mirror and try to imagine my pointy chin, wide forehead, and light-lashed eyes as capable of that kind of fierceness, but I can't see it. I slouch in the seat and fold my arms.

"It's a nice night. I could drive up and down some of these sleepy little streets and you could give a shout if you see the house. The, uh, mystery house." She grins at me.

"Yeah, okay." We don't talk, but the radio is tuned to the kind of music I imagine my parents used to listen to, bobby socks and hair pomade music. I shut my eyes and try to imagine what it felt like to have a reason to touch a boy, to put your hand on the hard curve of his shoulder and feel his arm nestle in against your back, his breath up close. His breath in your hair.

"Shouldn't take long to drive a town that's, what, eight

blocks long and five wide?" She glances at me, and I shrug.

"I've never counted." I try to imagine what a city is like, what New York City is like, and how long it would take to walk from one end to the other. I bet she knows.

"So, do we have anything to go on?" she asks.

"A bike. Probably the only one in town, if he parks it out front."

Lee nods and smiles sideways at me, a knowing glint in her dark eyes. Although it's been years since Cumberland had more than a dusting of late-January snow, all the houses look like they've emerged from a hard winter, the sea air bleaching them tired and wind-scoured. Each street we drive down, a dog barks somewhere inside.

"There." Everett's bike leans against the front porch of a yellow house with a tidy lawn. The windows are dark, but I worry if he looks outside he'll see me craning forward in the seat of the jeep. When Lee slows down, I slouch low, waving her on, and she laughs and guns the engine.

"You get the house number, Ace?"

"316."

"Right. Willow Street. Commit it to memory. Agents don't leave a paper trail."

Ten

Perfect for us the myth of Castor and
Pollux, but which of us is the immortal?
Which of us the boxer Pollux, which the
horse-tamer Castor? Only once before, my
hand under a peach-fuzzed muzzle, the fly-
twitching flank, skin laid thinly over muscle.
Mother holding me up to bottomless eyes,
the smell of hot-animal hay, flat-fingered
careful, wedge of an apple. What she said:
He likes you. So me the mortal, saddled
with flesh. She the everlasting fighter
halving her life with me, but up against what
enemy? Perhaps the pestilence Pandora
let loose: Guilt, gone eyeless, grey lump
of flesh. Lead-winged, it goes nowhere,
sees nowhere to go. Or Accusation, scaled
faceless finger pointing. Or is it, somehow,

secretly sleeping, the serpent-curled,
toothless, moon-eyed Envy. Hardly. Silly
Izzy. Easier to envy a fish flap-flapping on a
dock.

I haven't used much of Izzy's birthday money over the years, so even after I buy the canvas, acrylics, brushes, and lima-bean-shaped painter palette from Millard's hardware store, most of the dollar bills from Grand and crisp twenties the Carson brothers have given us every year are still tucked inside her savings envelope.

I'm crossing onto Main Street when Everett rides up, his hair uncombed, his red t-shirt wrinkled and faded. He doesn't say anything, just takes the paper bag from my hand and rides slowly along beside me. The two of us walking next to each other for all the world to see—the air feels thin in my lungs.

"Where'd you come from?" I ask, shifting the canvas to my other side so it's not between us.

"Home. We're on a corner, so my window overlooks Main Street. I saw you as soon as you walked past the library."

"Oh." He was watching out his window, watching for a reason—watching for me? He didn't even brush his hair.

"So, I knew you read books about artists, but I didn't know you painted."

"I don't... um, tell a lot of people."

He nods, his eyes glowing, and I can't look away.

"So are you going to be busy today? Painting?"

"Oh, these are for later. I'm not busy."

"Good." The slow spread of his smile sweeps across my body like sunlight. I start walking fast and we make it home without saying much or looking at anything but each other and the road. When I take the bag from him, his hand brushes mine, his eyes so still and steady my breath catches. I stick the canvas and paints inside the kitchen door where Grand will maybe see them and take them up, then step back out onto the stoop to find him standing there, hands in his pockets.

"Could I come in?"

"Oh. Well, my grandmother doesn't really like visitors. I was thinking I'd just go for a walk."

"Sure. Good. A walk. Or maybe even a ride?"

This time when I hoist myself up to sit on the handlebars his hands are further in, his thumb knuckles brushing the skin high on my thighs where my shorts stop. I try to sit really still but can't balance and have to shift my weight so I'm leaning back against his chest again. He duck-walks the bike out of the loose sand of the yard to the harder sand of the road. One hand for a second touches fluttery to my waist and squeezes, then he grips the handlebars and pushes off.

"Hold tight," he breathes, and everything in me is clenched, my ribs tight. He curves down the hill and glides past Red's garage and Pauline's and the library and Demeers' and the Stop 'n' Shop, then turns up a side street and follows it to just before it dead-ends into salt brush and sand. He takes the first left and rides up another street and keeps riding to the ends of streets, then cuts across to another. The light flickers between the trees, Everett is telling knock-knock jokes right into my ear, and I'm laughing, breathless from the light and wind and his mouth near my neck.

When he pulls up in front of his grandparents' house I look up at the silent windows and feel a little dizzy to be so close to the bed he's been sleeping in, the shower he's showered in. I follow him up the cement stoop, through the front door into a stuffy, wood-paneled living room filled with heavy upholstered furniture, a console TV in the corner and captain's wheel on the wall. Through another doorway someone calls, "Everett?" and then his grandmother appears—a short, sturdy woman wearing Sears-simple clothes, her white hair cut in a practical bob.

"Oh, and who's this?" Her features are scrunched, her eyes a little too close to her mouth, but her smile is wide open. I give her my hand and let her hold it like something fragile between both of hers.

"This is Ansel. She goes to my school."

"How wonderful! And you thought you'd be the only young person in Cumberland this summer." She puts her soft, thick arm around me and leads me into the kitchen, ushering me to a seat at the Formica table. Everett sits across from me, and she takes four glasses out of the white bamboo-carved cabinets and fills them with ice from tho groon fridge.

"Ansel, are you visiting family too this summer?"

"No ma'am, I live out here." She sets glasses of ice water in front of me and Everett, then two more on the other ends of the square table. She stands by the counter dabbing tuna salad from a big bowl onto white toast with a wooden spoon, drops two more slices in the toaster, and half turns as she talks.

"You don't say. And the bus comes out all this way?"

"No ma'am. The Carson brothers give me a ride. They usually have to go into Fort Harmon every day anyway for their construction business."

"Well, how wonderful." She puts a paper plate in front of me, and I wait until she and Everett are both seated and served before taking a bite out of my pickle wedge. If she knows the Carson brothers she must know my grandmother and maybe my dad when he was little and all about the car crash and Izzy. I glance at Everett to see if he knows something but he's fiddling with a napkin so I look back at his grandmother and clear my throat.

"You... know the Carson brothers?"

She's cutting the last two sandwiches and doesn't turn around when she says, "Well, I've heard of them, of course, honey. But no, Henry and I moved away, oh, a while back, to be nearer Everett and his mom. Maggie moved north when she left high school, and then she had Everett and they were in that big city all alone—living goodness knows how." She says this last bit under her breath as she cuts another sandwich in half.

"The art gallery, Gram. Mom was building her gallery."
Everett picks up his pickle and stares at the seeds. He
won't look at me when I try to catch his eye.

"Yes, honey, I know. But art doesn't put food in little
boys' bellies, and Lord only knows who watched you
when she was out all night." She smiles apologetically at
Everett, then sets the last two sandwiches on the table
and smoothes the hair off his forehead. He picks at his
pickle until she stops petting his hair, puts her hands on
her hips and smiles at me. "But enough of that—we've
only been back here for a few months, so we're still a
little out of the loop, I'm afraid." The tightness in my chest
loosens and I take a deep breath and smile. So that's why
their number wasn't in the phone book.

Mrs. Lloyd takes off her apron, draping it over the back
of a chair, and calls over her shoulder, "Henry!" A gnarled
man in a golf shirt and bermuda shorts scrapes into the
kitchen behind an aluminum walker, all the skin on his face
sagging like melted wax.

"I heard you puttering with lunch, May, it just takes
me a while to get from A to B." Everett gets up to help
him into the chair against the window so I stand too. "Sit
down, sit down, darling," he says, winking at me as he
sinks into the seat. "You're not in anybody's way." He
takes a long drink of water and when he squares his eyes
on Everett I see they're the same starburst blue—less
guarded, more twinkly, but the same shade. "Well now,

Everett, I know you'd find a way to weasel out of Cribbage again. You know I can't resist a game of Euchre If we've got a fourth."

Everett hasn't looked at me much since we came inside, and he seems distant, a little bored when he says, "I don't know if Ansel's staying for cards, Gramps. We might go for a swim later."

"Like hell. You think I'm letting a fourth warm body walk out of this house without at least one round? You like cards, don't you, darling."

"Yes sir."

"See there." Everett's grandfather winks at him, then tucks his napkin into his shirt collar and picks up his sandwich.

Eleven

"You'd better leave the bike here."

Everett cocks an eyebrow at me and lays his bike in the tall grass just off the side of the highway. "I hope this place you're taking me to has food and water," he says, "because if somebody takes my bike we're stranded." I'm trying hard to look annoyed but my stomach's fluttery and I like that he has to trust me. He follows me in among the dense trees and scrub, picking along in his flip-flops and scanning the trees and shrubs with squinty eyes. "'Course, I could always resort to cannibalism," he says as he pinches my waist. I let a branch I was holding for him snap back and whap him in the chest.

It's late, but we have maybe two more hours before the shadows knit together. I've never shown this place to anyone, never mentioned or even hinted to Izzy that there was something, somewhere that was mine and all mine. Every day after school, how I'd give up every detail if Izzy asked the right questions, but in the summer this one thing I've always kept for myself—the fifteen-minute walk towards the hotel, then crossing the two-lane highway and ducking back in among the scrubby brush for another ten minutes. All the days and nights when the only breath among the trees was mine, the highway sounds like a second tide helping to hide me.

"I hate to seem squeamish, but I can't help noticing there's no trace of a trail here, and I was just wondering how confident you felt about finding our way back." He's breathing hard behind me, his flip-flops making sucky noises in the shallow mud.

"Everett, geez, you can still hear the traffic," and then we're out of the trees and in the sandy clearing where the mangroves creep up out of the water. I veer left, up the bank, get down on my hands and knees and start crawling through the branches of bushes I've woven into an opening, clearing here and there to make tunnels inside the green maze of twigs. All the days of tearing my clothes and hacking back branches with the little saw on father's old boy scout knife, hours of dragging the cuttings out into the open, then crawling back in again and again and getting home sweaty and scratched without Grand or Izzy wondering. All those nights I couldn't sleep and walked through the cool night and crawled in, unwrapped the sleeping bag from the tarp I kept it in, and scooped out the shape of my body in the sand to make a bed. Then every summer coming back out and having to reweave here, trim back there, chase off a family of garter snakes, shake out the sleeping bag and leave it to breathe, draped over a tree limb open to the thick, swampy air. All that upkeep, just to have one place that's all mine. And now it won't be.

Everett's breathing hard behind me, and I crawl into the center of the nest, the light a glowing green through the leaves, a circular space big enough to sit up. He's pulling a thorn from the meaty part of his palm and when he looks up his eyes take their fill and widen. He crawls in, sits, and all around us are the slithery marsh sounds of frogs and cicadas and tributary water lapping the shallow shore. When he leans back, lacing his fingers behind his head, his t-shirt rides up, showing a trail of hair below his belly button. I look away.

"I heard the weirdest rumor about you at school," he says, and I can feel his eyes on the back of my neck.

"I can't believe anyone even bothers making up rumors about me," I say, thinking, keep cool—he doesn't know anything. Steady voice, don't look at him.

"This one's so weird I can't help but believe it a little."

I pick up a stick and start drawing in the sand. "Well, maybe your source is really imaginative."

"Liza Seely? I don't think so."

Liza Seely, the cheerleader—one of the girls who always knows what to say, what to wear. One day two years ago, we were all getting dressed for gym class and Liza gasped dramatically behind me. When I turned around all of the girls were looking as she said, slowly, so they could hear every word, "Oh. My. God. Are those *Barbie*?" After that I used my birthday money to buy some new underwear—plain white that fit right, wasn't faded from too many washings and pulling apart at the elastic. Whatever she told him, please don't let it be the Barbie underwear.

He breathes in slowly and says, "She said you had a twin sister."

Oh God. I draw loose hoops in the sand—think, think!—but a lot of time's gone by and I should have laughed right when he said it, should have shot back with something bright and flirty like, "How funny! Are you saying you wish there was more of me, Everett?" Now too much time's passed and I keep hearing his words in my head: *she said you had a twin sister she said you had a twin sister she said you had*—but he said *had,* not *have.*

"She said in the car crash that your mom and dad and sister—she said that you were the only one..."

Let him keep talking, he'll work it all out for himself and I won't have to say anything, let him talk.

"And she said..." He glances at me, falters and then continues on all in a gush. "She said you had a heart attack or something, and they used your sister as a heart donor so now you have a giant scar from the surgery."

The laugh bursts out of me and I can breathe again, I see my way out. "Well, she got some of it right, but geez, Everett!" I laugh and shove him. "Can we say *gullible*? Ever heard of an eight-year-old having a heart attack?"

His eyes widen, he throws away the leaf he's been fiddling with and shoves me back. We're laughing and when I fall backwards onto the sand his hands are on my shoulders. My breath is shallow in my lungs and I hold still, feel myself untether looking into his eyes. His gaze shifts to his fingers as they creep to my collarbone, hook on the neck of my shirt and gently tug it down. He's breathing quick and shallow and I'm not breathing.

"So... no scar," he says. His eyes flicker back up to mine, coming to rest on my mouth and I manage to shake my head. Then his other hand goes to my hair and he leans closer. His breath is on my neck and his mouth is on fire—his lips on my collarbone and my jaw and my ear and his breath in my mouth and his lips.

When I get home the dishes are piled haphazard in the sink, the house dark and silent. It's almost nine. Grand has left a note on the table in her block handwriting: *Ansel Louise Mackenzie. Your sister needs you.* The canvas and paints are still sitting by the back door where I left them, and the flutter in my chest burns into a simmer even though I know, dimly and far-off, that Grand never would have carried them upstairs. I run the plates under the faucet, scrub off the remnants of applesauce, ham loaf, and frozen peas, then slot them dripping in the dishwasher and take my time straightening the hand-towel, sponging the counters. I have to walk sideways to get the canvas up the stairs, the bag of paints swinging from my teeth.

Izzy is lying on her side with her back to the door, and the sharp iodiney smell of all day left alone makes me choke. I drop the art supplies in the corner, grab clean sheets and a new plastic-coated mattress-pad from the bathroom.

"Izzy."

She turns her head slowly and her eyes are expressionless, unblinking as a bird's. Her fingers are twisted together into a strange sort of sideways fan, like she started by crossing the first two fingers and then kept crossing. She holds her hands up to me, and her eyes are blank, blank—like the Izzy inside her has retreated to a back corner and is curled up very small. I tug up her nightgown and pull off her diaper. The skin all over her bottom and the backs of her legs is red and blistered— diaper rash on my teenaged sister. The simmer of anger in my belly turns over, goes cold, and I make my mind a blank.

I don't think about kissing Everett and all the air and sunlight I gorged myself on while the light moved from one end of this room to the other, the hours sliding over Izzy as she lay burning with fever, waiting for the one thing she asked me for. I don't think about spiraling away from my body or becoming only body, his mouth and his hands on my skin and my skin still humming from being touched under my clothes, while Izzy found some way of keeping herself busy. How high did she count before she started over, again and again, as she lay listening, thinking any minute I'd be back with her paints? I don't think about how her nightgown became soaked with sweat or now how she starts to shiver as I get a damp washcloth and the Desitin and wipe her down. As the smell of her stings my eyes they start to water and when I wipe the cloth over her bottom and up her back I can see where her nerve endings start because she flinches.

"Izzy, I'm sorry." The air in my lungs catches, clogging my throat, coming out in hiccups. I gulp and go back to the sink to rinse the washcloth and breathe, my hands shaking. I steady them, draw the air in slowly, thinly, making sure it comes back out whole, and when I turn Izzy on her side she's shivering. She twists her shoulders enough to put her hands on my face but I can't look at her. I squeeze my eyes shut and finally she turns her head back to her pillow, pushes her hands under her hot cheek, and breathes in shallow, hitching sighs.

Anger resides, supposedly, somewhere
under the gut, guttural, somewhere down
in the skin I can't feel. Earlier, clamping
my teeth around screams, something
else—an assertion, a howl, I'm here, I'm
here, someone. But seeing the heat and roil
of the world shuddering out of her, I can't
conjure anything, can't float myself up to
my little bit of feeling skin to lash out at her

*and draw blood. That world, which keeps
her so raw-skinned, sensitive, I don't want
any of it. The shell of this house, and inside
the house the room, and inside the room
the bed and inside the bed the body and
inside the body the air and inside the air the
girl and the girl inside getting smaller and
smaller.*

Once Izzy's ready for bed I sit in the bathroom holding
a washcloth to my face, trying not to make noise. If I've
been keeping too much for myself, then the only thing
to do is give a few days to Izzy. *A few days or a week or
forever, I'll give him up, everything, Izzy, please forgive me.*

I go downstairs to find Dr. Parson's office number
in the phone book and I don't care what Grand will do,
how much she'll scream about doctors' bills and wasting
money, I write down the number to call first thing in the
morning. Then I get some nails and twine from the junk
drawer in the kitchen and string the canvas up like a
screen in front of the window. It's a little taller than the
glass and not as wide, but I think maybe Izzy will want
to peek outside. I position a tall stool with a back and
armrests in front of the canvas, then set up another stool
nearby with a few boards over the arms for a table. I lay
out the palette, the brushes and little tubes of paint fanned
out on top of it in a semi-circle. Izzy is asleep when I finish,

so I sneak back downstairs, scribble the note, shove it in my pocket, and slip out the door.

I don't feel how close and muggy the night air is until I'm standing in front of Everett's house sweating. I tip-toe up the concrete steps and tuck the note halfway into the mail slot. As I'm walking off I hear a window open upstairs, and Everett whispers, "Ansel, I'll be right down." I glance back to see he's not in the window anymore and take off running.

Twelve

Wednesday, July 10, 1974
28 days

It's my birthday and mother is lighting the candles
saying she can't believe her baby is sixteen. It's my
birthday—and somehow that's strange and I try to
remember my other birthdays and Izzy—*where's Izzy?*
Mother looks up. *Who, honey?* she asks, and the candles
are long and thin as coffee stirrers drooping under the
weight of the flame. Mother is singing and father comes
into the room carrying a box big enough to hold a vacuum
cleaner, white kite string wound around and around it like
a cocoon so you can barely see the red paper peeking
out underneath. They're singing and I'm asking, *No,
wait, where's Izzy?* shouting now to be heard above their
voices, *We have to wait for Izzy.* They've finished singing,
they're looking at me, and mother says, *Who?* and I say,
My sister, my twin sister, don't you remember? Father
laughs and pushes the box into my arms and says, *Maybe
this will make you feel better.* I start unwinding the string
around and around, racing against the candles dripping

lower and lower, the waxy purple and green and pink making greasy puddles in the icing, and I get the string all unwound but the paper isn't paper, it's red skin, stretchy as rose petals. Father smiles and takes scissors to it and I scream as the paper bursts apart cleanly. Underneath there's a nesting doll, life-sized and shaped like a bowling pin with a picture of Izzy stretched across the wood, her image blurry and distorted in places and father is smiling but mother's face is sad, so sad. Father says *Is this Izzy?* I scream, *No, not a doll, Izzy, she's real, she's my sister.* Mother turns away and father pulls the nesting doll in half and underneath there's a smaller one just like it. *Is this Izzy?* he asks, and I'm screaming, *No, she's a person, Izzy.* He pulls the nesting doll apart again and there's another one underneath and mother is walking away dripping green and purple wax on the floor and I know it's mother, she's done something, and I'm screaming, *Mother, what did you do? What did you do?*

Izzy is still sleeping on her side when I wake up and crawl across to her, smoothing her hair until she opens her eyes. She squints at me, slowly rising up from deep in dream, smiles, and reaches out a hand to my cheek, looking me straight in the eye gently, gently. I let the butterfly weight of her hand on my cheek sink into my skin, then wipe my eyes and head downstairs. The living room and kitchen are empty, so I hold the air in my lungs and dial the number, keeping my voice low.

"Dr. Parson's office."

"Yes, hi. I need to make an appointment for my sister."

I can hear the secretary flipping through her calendar. "He has an opening next Tuesday."

"Oh." My stomach drops. "I was kind of hoping he could come out sooner. Like, maybe today."

The voice on the other end pauses and says, "*Come out?* I'm afraid I don't understand."

"My sister is paralyzed and Dr. Parson usually comes here to the house—"

"Well, I'm sorry, but Dr. Parson hasn't made house calls for several years now."

That can't be right. How long has it been? Izzy was maybe twelve when she had the bladder infection and Dr. Parson came and taught me how to change her catheter. Three years—my heart starts hammering and I swallow against the lump in my throat.

"Hello, miss? Are you still there?"

"Yes," I say, trying to steady my voice. "It's just—she really needs a doctor. She's had a fever for four days and there was a little pus—"

"If it's an emergency, call 911," the receptionist says, her voice clipped. "I'm sorry, miss, I have another call. Do you want the appointment for next Tuesday?"

"No. Thank you." I hang up and stand looking out the window, then rub the sting in my eyes and find two bowls in the cabinet. When I go back upstairs with breakfast Izzy's pulled herself to a sitting position and points to the canvas with a sneaky little smile.

"Breakfast first, okay?" I say, but she shakes her head and points to the canvas again, so I put the tray on the floor and pull her out of bed. "Okay, but bathroom," and with her body flopped against mine like a drunk dance partner I walk her in and plunk her down on the toilet. I pull open the medicine cabinet and hunt for the old bottle of antibiotics I found a few years ago, left over from when Izzy had her last bladder infection and I was gone on a five-day school trip. Grand was supposed to be watching her but she must have forgotten to give Izzy the rest of her pills. I turn through the orange bottles of grandfather's aspirin until I find the one marked *Isabel Mackenzie*. I pick it up and pause—I should have thrown them out a long time ago, but I didn't and now they're here, and Izzy's fever won't go away—so I unscrew the cap and count nine pills inside. Four and a half days worth. That could be enough.

"Better late than never," I say brightly, and Izzy opens up so I can pop a pill in her mouth. She takes a few swigs of water while her bag is draining and I stick the thermometer in her mouth, then pull off her nightgown and dress her in one of father's old t-shirts I keep in the dresser. "Ally-oop!" I say, singing a waltz-like "da-dum da-dumpty-dum," as I dance her across the floor. She's giggling, and I flop her on the bed, change her diaper, then check the thermometer. 100° still. I force a cheery smile. The antibiotics will start working soon—check her temperature tomorrow and she'll be fine.

I drag Izzy across to the bar stool and strap her in place with a belt. I put the notepad on her lap and say, "You look pleased as..." as she picks up the little tubes of paint, holding them between her fingers like precious jewels. "Izzy."

She gives me a distracted sideways look and scribbles *Punchinello?* She pushes the notepad into my hands and picks up another tube, twists the cap off and squeezes a little cobalt on her finger.

"I was thinking 'pumpkin pie,' but yours is better."

She doesn't even seem to hear me, just reaches out her hand to the canvas and smears the little bit of blue on one corner, ghosting her hand around the canvas in big loops and quick little jags. After a few minutes of this she looks back at me and holds out her hand. I give her back the notepad, but she only wants the pencil. She sketches wisps and lines and almost recognizable shapes: a shoulder curving into a neck, a horse's muzzle, the stacked rectangles of a fist. Like cobwebs drifted onto the canvas in the exact shapes of things they've lived with, her hand breezily traces all the nicks and curves of a body.

"Izzy," I say, but she keeps working like I'm not even there. "Where...? How did you learn to do this?"

Her eyes flicker to the bed, where her notebook peeks out from under her pillow.

"All this time—you've been drawing in there?"

She glances at me quickly, picks up the pencil, then

traces the shape of an eye and below it a mouth screwed up into a sneaky smile.

*What did she think—that I sit here all day
like a dolly dazing away? How my mind
reaches out and pulls in the world she tries
to compass with all her frantic whirrings.
But now the problem of color, how thickly
overlapping, and how each brush holds
the paint. What blue for night sky and how
textured. Gloppy like the deep out-there of
ocean, or thin as the thinnest water slipping
up on shore. What kind of night for us
two, mortal and immortal, body and loose
spirit. Her half thin, my half stacked and
smacky blue-black, heavy as breath. She a
blue showing through the ghostly glow of
skin, and me, thick borders of color where
nothing bleeds. How it might be, but isn't:
knowing the edge of the world and where I
stop against it.*

When I head downstairs later Grand is sitting at the table in her usual spot. I flinch and start to go back upstairs when she says evenly, "Good morning."

Her face is blank, her gaze cold and level, so I cross

the kitchen to the cabinet and pick through the teacups and saucers. I find one of each, pour coffee and take my time picking out a spoon and doling out the sugar, then stir and sip and look out the window over the sink. When I feel Grand's eyes shift from me back to the birdfeeder I sit down at the table across from her and wait.

"Ansel, I'm not going to yell." She stirs her coffee slowly, tapping a few drops off the spoon. "But you were gone all day and Isabel... you have to think of your sister." I swallow and imagine sliding the rose-painted china from between her fingers, flinging it against the wall, watching coffee drip down the floral wallpaper. *You have to think of your sister.* I imagine calmly biting the cup into pieces, chewing it up to dust, but all I can do is nod and swallow coffee. She squints at me, reaches across the table and grips my hand, rubbing her thumb hard over the tendons like she's rubbing off a smudge. "You wouldn't want anything to happen to her." I nod. The finches stab their beaks at the little slits in the feeder. The coffee burns my throat.

Thirteen

While Izzy's working I scoop up all the soiled sheets,
take them down to the laundry closet off the kitchen
and wash them on hot with an extra dash of soap. I'm a
whirlwind, gathering everything I haven't done for months,
erasing all the dust and dirt and guilt and keeping myself
centered here, watching over Izzy. Grand's words—*You
wouldn't want anything to happen to her*—ring in my ears
and I can feel her one floor below us slowly sucking up all
the breathable air.

I sweep all the dust bunnies from under the beds and
rub a sloppy loop of Murphy's oil soap on the wooden
floors around Izzy, then get out the Comet and scrub
the tub, toilet, bathroom tile, sink. The harder I work the
more the tightness in my throat loosens—I can breathe, I
can breathe, I'm here and Izzy's okay. She's humming to
herself and doesn't seem to notice me.

The painting is like two different paintings, one half
washed thin as watercolor, the other half overlapping

thick as mud and all of it seemingly seeping like a stain from the center, the edges of the canvas left blank in a sloppy halo. It's a night scene, the sky airy in the top half, the bottom half solid, chunky as ocean water. Each half is occupied by a figure that looks like Izzy and me, though I can't tell who's who. One is ghostly, just half a face, a shoulder leading into a fist, and one is solid, her body astride a horse laid onto the paint like a paper doll, the lines distinct, scraps of paper with the words *how to tether—a self to this—world—fought against or ridden— into* imbedded in the blue.

I mop the stairs then make bologna sandwiches for lunch. I stand in the doorway to the living room with the tray and Grand pats the couch next to her for me to lay down her plate. The contestants on TV are placing their bids for a can of Folgers. Grand tucks a napkin in the front of her housedress, saying, "Ninety-two cents for instant coffee?" She shakes her head, her eyes glued on the jubilant contestants, and I drop the plate quickly on the cushion next to her and bolt upstairs.

I put Izzy's sandwich on the tray next to the breakfast she never ate and sit on my bed, watching her brush dart between globs of paint, quick as a hummingbird. She dips her brush to the water and wipes it on the palette, then tries a little bit on one corner and fills it in with quick scribbles, testing thickness, the way the colors blend or don't when over-lapped, swooping the paint wispy with a brush or mucking it on with the palette knife. When I finish my sandwich I walk over behind her, then slip the brush from her fingers, unbuckling her from the chair before she can complain. She grunts in surprise but laughs and wraps her arms around my neck as I heft her up, pulling her towards the bathroom.

It's the first time—suddenly I see this and it's so strange—the first time in all these years of lugging her around that she wrapped her arms around me and held on, didn't just flop limp as a rag doll. She's looking me hard in the eye as I drag her across the room, and when I set her on the toilet she grabs my face, kissing me roughly on the lips. Before I can pull away she sticks her tongue in.

"Izzy! What—? God, gross!" She's laughing and I turn on the faucet, swish water in my mouth and spit.

She laughs, wagging her finger at me with an expression that seems to say, *naughty, naughty!,* cackling and smacking her knees.

"Izzy, we're too old for this crap," I say, loading up my toothbrush and scrubbing out every corner of my mouth. When we were little we used to practice kissing, taking turns being the boy. The rules were when you were the girl you had to stand still and let the other one kiss for as long as she wanted, and when you were the boy you had to swoop the other into a big dramatic dip at the end and make up something about how pretty she was. By the time we were seven we figured out there was more involved, but we never got further than the one time Izzy stuck her tongue in my mouth and swooped it around like a toilet brush.

Izzy's tugging on my sleeve making smoochy noises and I don't meet her eye.

"Are we done here?" Izzy laughs and I lean in to close the valve on her drainage bag. She's still shrieking and laughing as I pull her off the toilet, flop her on the bed and put the bologna sandwich in her lap. She picks up the notepad and fills a whole page with *WHO WHO WHO WHO WHO*. I shove the notepad away, saying, "What are you, part owl? Eat, already."

She quiets down and takes a bite, then laughs again, flapping her elbows like wings.

> *So all that excess heat and breath she's*
> *been boiling with is someone, somewhere,*
> *but who who who? One of the many*
> *unknown out there that live in light and are*
> *erased by it. All she told me about school,*
> *the teachers, the essays, the problem sets,*
> *but never other students, never a forgotten*
> *note tucked into a textbook. How her jaw*
> *unhinged without thinking to take a tongue*
> *in, her lips pliant like they never were*
> *before. Someone sometime somewhere.*
> *Yesterday, yes, gone all day—but now? Why*
> *she isn't buzzing as she has been, kinetic*

with the need to get outside, somewhere,
out to him. I lim of the other day swimming
and the damp lawn clippings' scent nestled
in her neck. Him of the brightness her skin
can hardly keep in, the secret caught candle
she tries so hard to hide.

When Izzy's back at the window and Grand is making a list waiting for the news to come on, I step to the back door.

"Ansel?" Grand calls, and I don't turn around.

"I'm just going down to the water for a minute," I say, pulling the door behind me. The air is heavy with salt and sea-wrack, but when the wind shifts there's a clean steeliness that slips in, a hint of ozone, and I know we're in for a good storm. The clouds are gathering, clogging the sky to the north, but the eastern sky is still clear, scudded with pink wisps, and as the sun dips west behind the trees the sky at the edge of ocean seems to brighten. I slide down the hill to the shore, letting the tide wash up to my toes as I kick clumps of wet sand into the waves. I wade in up to my knees and train my eyes on the horizon. All the times when we were little and used to tell father we could see the faint green shore of Ireland, he'd laugh and say, "Wave to your ancestors then, lassies!" holding each of us high on a hip.

Standing there, feeling the water lap at my legs and

watching the sky grow luminous in the late light, the anxious tangle inside me loosens and my breathing comes slow and even. I feel clear-eyed, steady, to be wholly in one place of my own choosing. I can do this. I can take care of her. How the whole world is out there, calling out to me, but I'm keeping myself right here where I'm needed. My arms chill in the evening air, and I feel both bared to the world and impermeable, the far-off tug of someone not Izzy thinking of me, wanting me, and me needing nothing from anyone, air filling every corner of my lungs.

Fourteen

Izzy's taken her last leftover pill and she hasn't had a fever for three days. I've spent the last five fixing the gutter and sagging screens in the porch, weeding and trimming back the bushes and tidying the garage. I'm buffing the last of the wax off of Grand's olive green LTD, wondering how hard it would be to find the keys and get a copy made, when she steps into the garage and silently hands me a list for groceries. We're out of milk, bread, eggs, canned soup, crackers, coffee; I can't say no. I go inside and make sure Izzy's okay, then put on my hooded sweatshirt and resolve to walk straight to the Stop 'n' Shop and back.

It's only ten but already there's a searing brightness to the air, and when I breeze through the automatic doors Mr. Ray is sliding piles of counted change off the counter into the open register. I say good morning and he gives me a two-fingered wave, continues mouthing numbers as I grab a cart and head towards the back cooler. There was no bicycle out front and none in front of the library, so I figure I've got time. I have most of the items on the list and am picking out cans of Campbell's when someone touches my shoulder and whispers, "Hey," close to my ear.

"Geez, Everett, you scared me half to death." I grab six cans of whatever, drop them in the cart and push towards the front, but he's right beside me, smiling and whispering.

"So, did you get sprung early?"

"No—we just needed food and Grand doesn't drive, so... you know. I really can't stop and talk."

"Why'd you get grounded in the first place?"

I keep the cart moving fast enough so I'm always a little in front of him. "That night... I was supposed to be home in time to do some stuff and I guess I forgot." The lie is vague, stilted, but Everett doesn't seem to notice.

"Sorry if I distracted you," he says. He grabs the cart at the end of the aisle, slips a hand to my neck and leans in. I duck but Mr. Ray is busy counting packs of cigarettes in the plastic dispensers over the register. "What is it?"

"Nothing, I just..." My eyes start burning—I need to get out of there. "I'll be in trouble if I don't go." I tug the cart out of his hands and push past him to stack everything on the counter. Mr. Ray punches the prices into the register, enters the total in his accounts book, then bags everything in brown paper.

"Well hello, son," Mr. Ray says. When I glance back, Everett's standing behind me, hands in his pockets, his eyes clear and a little too steady. "How's this old town treating you this summer?"

"Just fine, Mr. Ray, thank you," Everett says, his eyes on me as I load the sacks back in the cart. I can feel Mr. Ray's eyes shift from Everett to me and my cheeks start to burn.

"Well. Glad to see you're finding things to keep you busy."

"Yes, sir."

"Goodbye, Mr. Ray," I say, pushing the cart out to the sidewalk.

"Ansel. Send your grandmother my how-do."

When I get outside I push the groceries around to the side alley where all the other carts are corralled and Everett reaches in to pull out a bag.

"Everett, no, I've got it."

"Tell me what's wrong."

"Nothing's wrong!"

"Then why won't you look at me?" His voice cracks and he's breathing fast. I rake my eyes up his body to his face, trying to aim a gaze at him without really seeing. His hair's rumpled, his eyes so clear and wounded I can't look away, and then his arms are around me and we're kissing right there in the broad daylight. His hands move to my hair and he's telling me how much he's missed me, how he's been going crazy, and I kiss his cheek and nose and mouth and chin and say me too, I'm sorry, me too.

Then someone walks past the alley and we scatter—I grab a bag and Everett grabs the other and we bump into each other, ducking. We crack up, and Everett takes a breath, looking around the corner and gesturing like an army commando hurrying his troops. Then we're scrambling together up the street, still laughing and running and dropping cans out of the bags, tripping over ourselves as we stoop to pick things up.

When we clear the rise to the house we stop giggling and tip-toe around to the flagstones out of sight of the porch. "I can take it from here," I say, shifting my bag to one hip so I can grab Everett's bag with my free hand, but he puts it down on the ground, walks into my empty arm and pulls my face to his shoulder. The whole length of his body is flattened against mine, and I slide my grocery bag to the ground, wrapping my arms around him. I squeeze myself closer and closer so every nook of my body is filled, imagining if I hold him hard enough I'll be able to push myself through to the center of him.

"When can I see you?" he whispers.

"I don't know—we'll get caught—I don't know." He slides his palm to my cheek and kisses me.

"I have to see you, Ansel. I'll put on my camo pants and lie in wait out here in the dunes if I have to. I'll live off seaweed and bury myself in the sand and breathe through a straw—I don't care."

"Okay, okay," I say, and he dips in to steal quick kisses between my smiles. "Come back—sometime—after dark—10 o'clock. Everyone should be asleep."

"Everyone?" He glances toward the house. "Is your

grandmother keeping other innocent young maidens locked away in there?"

I force a laugh. "I just mean... there's no chance the Carson brothers will come by that late or anything." He nods and dips in for another long, soft kiss until I tear my lips away. I stoop to the bags and shoot him a last glance over my shoulder.

"10 o' clock, Ansel. If you're not here I'll just have to lay siege and storm the castle."

Suddenly buzzing again, restless as a moth
batting between windows. How she stands
with ocean eyes at the sill, fingers just
touching lips, cheek, collar bone. More and
more she becomes the nebulous Pollux in
the painting, a collection of separate body
parts to disappear into. More and more me
the Castor tied to the whole picture, the
little bit of body I have left caked flaky with
paint. So long held away from the world,
fixed by these legs in the silence of this
room, how the world outside was always
an idea, a thing foggy from being held
inside. But color is real—a feeling you can
smell and smear, thin or thicken. Not the
far-off scrims of seen objects that shift and
change as the day blazes down. A world,

a felt world flush up against me—smell of
plastics, petroleum, deep ore of an earth
that exists outside memory or vision, a
world so real it smells and can be touched.

Fifteen

Izzy wants to go outside. All those months when they first brought her back and the Carson brothers would stand at the foot of her bed worrying over her intent stare, all the times they tried to heave her from the bed—*the sun will do her good*—and she'd thrash and hit, tear the sheets from the bed, clinging. Week after week, how the Carson brothers would come in and try to lift her, but she'd have none of it, her eyes fixed on a point just over their shoulders, her back and arms rigid against being moved. All those times I was left to build sand castles and moats and whole fragile kingdoms by myself, the ocean crashing over all of it, wiping the beach clean, the heave and tumble heavy as the air in my chest. How I'd sob into her hands, kneeling by her bed, begging her for one look, one flicker of movement, one afternoon when I wouldn't have to balance myself against all that ocean alone—but no. And now she wants to go outside.

"Izzy, no. It's not a good idea." She folds her hands in

her lap, looks at me hard and jerks her head in a stiff nod.

"Izzy, why now? For seven years we haven't been able to budge you from this room and now you want to travel the world? If I take you outside you'll just have to lie there, same as in here."

She balls her fingers into fists and scratches each word into the notepad in big letters. *I WANT OUT.*

"No. Something could happen to you. No way." I turn my back to her and tidy our nightstand, then tug the wrinkles out of her blanket. Someone might see her. *He* might see her. Absolutely not.

She lets out a growl that escalates into a shriek, tears the piece of paper off the notepad and throws it at me. It bounces off my shoulder and I pick it up off the floor without looking at her. "I'm not taking you outside, Izzy. Just forget it." Izzy's eyes blaze; she picks up a book off the nightstand and throws it, then another, and another, letting out little shrieks with each throw.

She grabs the notepad and writes a few words on each page, tearing them off and smacking them down on the bedside table in front of me, one by one. *OUT! I WANT OUT! YOU TAKE ME OUT! YOU TAKE ME! NOW! OUTSIDE! OUT THERE! THE ACTUAL WORLD! YOU DO IT!* I glance at the pages then step away and she wads them up, throwing them one by one without even looking where she's throwing.

"What on earth is going on in here?" Grand is glaring at us from the doorway.

"Nothing, Grand. Izzy's just acting crazy."

A few of the notes are still balled in Izzy's lap and she unwads them, holding them out as Grand stalks over to the bed to read the crumpled scraps of paper. Izzy's quiet now, her eyes welling up, wide and shining, pleading, her hands clenched into prayer and held out to Grand.

"Well, she'll hardly be seen at this time of night. Take her outside for a minute if that's all she wants."

"No. No way. This is crazy! We can't just give in to everything she wants when she wants it. Izzy has to realize that we know what's best for her and sometimes she can't have everything her way and she is *not going outside*. Something could happen—she's safer in here."

Izzy's hands clutch and tear at her hair, and sobbing, gasping, curled into herself, she scribbles again on the notepad, *what's best for her what's best for her what's best best BEST what's best what's best.*

"Ansel Louise Mackenzie, you stop all this noise. You pick her up this instant and take her outside or I'll call the Carson brothers, and once they've finished carting your own twin sister around for you, they can take care of you, too. And don't you go thinking you're too old for a blistered backside, for you most certainly are *not*."

I'm trapped. I can't breathe. The darkness in the pit of my stomach surges, blurring my vision as I pull back the covers, slide her legs over the side, and tug her arms over my shoulders. I flinch past Grand and pause at the top of the stairs, letting the fog clear from my eyes before I take the first step down. Fourteen steps down to the foyer, ten steps across the kitchen to the back door, five steps down the porch to the yard and then I'm half running around the side of the house, Izzy sniffling and letting herself be dragged. I slide down the dunes and slip and fall and drop Izzy, landing hard on top of her legs. She's toppled face over in the sand, so I grab her arms and pull her again onto my back, then stumble the rest of the way down to drop her at the shoreline.

"Here it is, Izzy! Outside—this is where you just *had* to be. How do you like it? Feel all that fresh air on your face? How about all that sky? How's it feel, Izzy? You want me to move you closer to the water?" I look back and she's lying crumpled and awkward, one leg bent and tangled under her, one half of her face covered in sand, her hand at her eye trying to rub it clean. And then the tide washes up and over and under her, picking her up and sliding her back on the beach a few inches until she's spluttering and coughing. I run to her and she's whimpering, keening, hiding in her hands. Her elbow slips up to cover her head with her arms, and when I lean over she scrabbles to latch onto me. I pick her up and start the hard climb back up the dunes.

When we come back in Grand is sitting on the couch swiping red nail polish onto her left hand. She lurches up at the sound of Izzy still crying and takes two quick steps towards me. Izzy is burying into me, clutching my neck, and I say, "She got scared." Grand fixes me with a disgusted scowl and waves us upstairs. Once I get Izzy cleaned up, I put her in bed and she buries her face in her pillow, shoulders shaking, hands clutching at her hair.

I go downstairs and heat three chicken pot pies. I carry one in to Grand and sit at the table to eat mine, looking out the window. At seven I carry the third pot pie upstairs to Izzy, see that she's asleep, leave the tray on the bedside table and go back downstairs. I get out a box of crackers and eat them, staring at the window, until I hear Grand turn off the TV at nine, thump into her bedroom and shut the door. I collect the fork and aluminum tray from the living room, wipe the counters with a kitchen towel, and sit back down at the table.

At ten I go outside to wait on the back steps, knitting my arms across my chest. I listen to the crickets and wait. The moon comes up and I can hear the ocean—always the ocean, sowing and lapping and tumbling under every other sound, uneven as a heart murmur. My throat feels thick but I don't think about it, I don't think about anything, I just pull my knees in and watch the moon rise higher in the sky and nod off with my head on my knees.

When I wake up I go back inside to check the time and see by the glowing hands on the stove clock that it's half past midnight. He isn't coming. The air I'm keeping tamped down in my chest rises to my throat and I know I can't stay here—I shut the door behind me, head out through the bushes and bracken to the highway and watch the headlights approach and pass. When the highway deepens to solid dark I scoot across the asphalt and weave through the bushes until I reach the tunnel and crawl in. The moans of late-night traffic lull me to sleep and then I'm on the highway, a truck roaring over me, a smashed red mess where my waist was, hips glued to the asphalt by guts and gunk, my legs separate from the rest of me, hopping and twitching. I wake up, heart hammering, kick the sleeping bag off my hot legs, close my eyes and drop into sleep where the truck rolls over me again and again, all night flattening me in half.

This body all anchor but out there I could
fall forever upward into bottomless blue
and keep falling, the ground at my back
loosening behind me and this body plum-
meting towards lidless sky. All that water—
random, rhythmless, unleashed, and lashing
out—and no matter how far you are you're
not safe from its salt-sting. Clabber clam-
bering, the crash and slap filling my mind's
reach. How I lost half of myself already to
sudden sound and the world crashing in;
outside, there is no silence secure enough,
settled, or unshaken.

Sixteen

My eyes feel scoured with sand, air hot with the smell of nylon as I roll up the sleeping bag and crawl out of the nest into the too-bright morning. I rake my fingers through my hair, brush off most of the sand, cross the highway towards Willow Street, then climb the concrete steps and knock. There's a squeak and rattle as the door opens and Mr. Lloyd is standing behind his walker staring through the screen.

"Well, good morning, darling. You look a little worse for the wear this a.m."

"Hi, Mr. Lloyd. Is Everett home?" He holds the screen open with one arm and rolls his walker back so I can pass inside.

Mrs. Lloyd pokes her head out from the kitchen and looks at me steadily, saying, "Come in here and have some breakfast, Ansel." When I'm seated with juice and toast Mr. Lloyd settles himself at the table, makes eye contact with Mrs. Lloyd, then clears his throat and rattles open the newspaper. I sit in the silence across from him and swig my orange juice and don't think.

"Predicting some bad storms this summer," he says.

Mrs. Lloyd flips sausage links over with a pair of tongs. "Guess they do every summer," she says, wiping her hands on her apron as she sits across from me at the table. "Do you eat sausage, honey?" I nod and she watches me chew my toast for a minute, then gets back up, fishes out the links. When she carries the plate back over to the table, her eyes are soft and steady. "Everett's mom came and picked him up yesterday evening." I chew, staring at the back of Mr. Lloyd's paper. "We expect he'll be back in a few days, though."

"When she's finished with him," Mr. Lloyd mutters, rattling the paper in half and laying it down so he can attend to his sausage.

"Henry."

"Well May, it's not our fault our daughter turned out the way she did. You might as well call a turd a turd."

"Henry!"

"Everett's gotta dote on his mother and attend to her every whim for a few days is all, darling. Then she'll be back to her parties and artists and good-for-nothings and Everett will be right back here."

Mrs. Lloyd gives an exasperated sigh and smiles warmly at me. "We expect him home soon."

Late morning is quiet at the hotel. Seagulls waddle

between the cleared tables choking down dropped bits of toast as waiters lean in the doorway of the kitchen smoking, their uniforms unbuttoned a few buttons. I spend an hour tossing bits of sticks in the water and writing Everett's name in the sand, then walk around the hotel to the docks where the sails of rented sailboats get smaller and smaller. A young mother walks a little boy in sandals up and down the boardwalk, her free hand resting on the shelf of her belly. I take off my shoes and drop my feet in the water, my mind bleaching blank as the horizon.

A motorboat engine cuts off and a man in ratty khaki shorts calls, "Tie us off, will you, love?" He tosses me a rope and I let the boat drift up against the bumpers before pulling it snug and lashing the rope around the dock cleat. He's sinewy, sun-leathered, his arms bunchy with muscles, and all his movements are long and swinging, a little twitchy. "There we go," he says, hopping out of the boat to lash the back end. "Grown up around boats, have you?" he says, his large hazel irises taking me in.

"A little." He nods, and even the way his hands work seems foreign. "You?"

"Yeah, you know. Commercial fisherman's son over round the northeast end of Scotland. Never did get my land legs." He sits on the edge of the boat, his legs dangling in and shakes a cigarette out of a pack. His long, slightly beakish nose gives his whole face a sad-eyed, hangdog expression, and although his hair is dark and curly his ear-length sideburns are reddish, patchy, the individual hairs curling in different directions. When he holds the cigarettes out to me I stare, then take one, holding it carefully between straight fingers. He strikes his lighter and cups the flame to his mouth, then mine. "Are you sucking in, deary? Every now and again you get one that's no willing." I clench the cigarette harder between my fingers and suck in until the tip crackles. I hold the smoke in my mouth before exhaling slowly, casually, and sit next to him as he flicks ash off into the water.

"So how long have you lived in America?" I ask.

"Forever. Left Scotland when I was sixteen. Haven't been back since."

I cough and he smacks me on the back a few times. I stare at the water and try to make my voice nonchalant.

"You just left? When you were sixteen? And nobody came after you?"

"Well, if anyone had missed me I suppose—"

"Here I am! Sorry, Iain—did you have to wait long?" It's Lee in the same tank-top and hiking boots I saw her in the night of the bar, her torso crisscrossed with the straps of canvas bags hanging from her shoulders. "Oh, Ansel. You coming with us?" Iain takes a last drag on his cigarette and drops it in the water, then steps into the boat and lets Lee hand in her bags.

"If it's alright with you," I say.

"Boat's already going—I don't suppose the skipper will charge us for one more body." Lee sneaks a half-smile at Iain and he blinks, holding out his hand to help her in. All the twitchiness is erased from his movements and he's unsmiling, steady-eyed, suddenly all business.

"Your call," he says.

I toss my cigarette into the water and climb in, take a seat and stretch out, my feet propped up on the side. "When are we coming back?" I ask, thinking, she'll be okay. Just this once, she'll be fine.

"Before dark. I've got to get the film in before closing." Lee's stowing lenses and camera attachments in various bag pockets, and Iain's untying ropes, walking a wide berth around her. She looks up, tilts her head and smiles. "I think your first question should have been 'where are we going,' though."

"Doesn't matter where we're going," I say, unraveling the other rope and dropping it into the boat.

Iain pulls the motor and we roar away from the dock as the little boy in sandals drops his mother's hand, runs to the edge and waves. Lee finishes stowing things, then lays her belly on the side of the boat, reaching far enough to trail her fingers in the water. When I lean over to see, she slaps a handful at me. I splash back but she ducks and the spray catches Iain in the face.

"Oh! Poor Iain," Lee says, handing him a towel and laughing. "Poor little skipper getting soaked by a scallywag." He gives his face one wipe and hands the towel back with a tight smile. Lee tucks the towel behind her head, leans back, and closes her eyes against the sun. Iain watches her, then slides his gaze out over the prow.

As we roar farther and farther away from land the tether anchoring me to Izzy pulls so tight in my chest I can barely breathe. She'll be fine, she's fine. I'm almost sixteen. Soon I'll have my license and somehow, I'll leave this place, I'll get out. I suck air into my stomach, uncinch my shoulders, shake my hair in the hard wind, and point my chin towards the horizon. We're facing blue—wide-open, sun-spangled, view-blurring blue—and as my eyes clear the tightness stretches to a breaking point, then snaps, dissolves, the tether's pull fading like the tug of a far-off magnet. By the time we reach the island I'm dizzy, my head spinning, as light as a kite loosed from its spool.

I laugh out loud, a barking half-shout, and Lee grins at me before jumping down to the sand. Iain throws her a rope and she uses the boat's momentum to haul it further up on the shore. The island is like everyone's idea of where castaways wash up—maybe a mile long, with shallow, pristine beach rising for about twenty yards off the water before dunes and the scrub and trees take over, densely knit. Lee grabs some of her bags from the boat, hauling them far up onto the beach, then sits down on the sand and starts fiddling with her camera. Iain pulls a bottle of yellow beer out of the cooler and points at me. I nod, so he pulls out a second and pops the top.

"Might as well get comfortable, deary. It'll be a while." He contemplates the lip of his bottle for a second before taking a big swig, his other arm draped across the side of the boat. I sit next to him on the bench, sun-warmed, eyes shut, and take my first sip of beer. The taste of metal, of new sewage pipes fills my mouth, scrapes the back of my throat. Choking back a cough, I swallow clean saliva and try again, but when the second sip isn't much better I wedge the bottle behind a seat cushion and jump down to shore.

Lee's tripod handle is hooked over her shoulder, her camera bumping at her hip as she slowly walks the beach, digging every now and then with the toe of her boot, then walking on. Further down the beach she drops to her knees, pulls the tripod open and clips on her camera, fiddling the tripod handle as she peers through the viewfinder.

"You're blocking my light, Ansel."

"Oh. Sorry." I step around behind her, scanning the messy detritus of broken shells to see if I can tell what caught her eye. She moves the tripod over a few inches, adjusts the focus and fiddles with some of the dials on her camera, pressing the button so the timer beeps a slow click. Then she fiddles with some dials and this time the click is quick. I'm still looking at the shells trying to see what I'm missing when she grabs my arm and positions me so I'm blocking the sun again and snaps a few more exposures.

"Wanna see?" She motions me over and I drop down on my knees to look. In the small rectangle of the viewfinder the jumble and clutter of shells seems to snap into place, as if there was a pattern in the chaos and all she had to do was find it. I gasp, and Lee laughs, "You see?" Nodding, still holding my eye to the camera, I move the tripod until the muddle clicks into a new pattern. Lee leans over to look and clicks off a few exposures. "Not bad," she says. "You've got an eye. Maybe you're named after the photographer after all."

She digs in one of her bags, pulls out another camera and hands it to me. "You know how to use one of these?"

"Not really. I know how to push the button."

She pats the sand and we sit next to each other in the bright sunlight as she explains light meter and F-stops and shutter speed, shows me how to zoom in and out and focus.

"I'll keep that telephoto lens on there so you can have some range, but I only brought the one tripod, so you'll need a lot of light and a fast shutter speed if you're zoomed in close on something." She unclips her camera and shoulders her tripod, gives me a little nod. "I think there's about ten more shots on that roll. Knock yourself out."

I head into the trees where the light is filtering in through the branches and turn slowly, the camera held up to my face. Here the trees are a spindly tangle of short trunks and wavering branches, quick scrimshaw lines against a backdrop of white light. When the lines and shapes snap into a pattern I press the button, and the delicate click of the shutter feels like something jagged breaking loose inside me, shifting, and settling into place.

*First author's photo, frontispiece daguerreo-
type of book eight from the eighth section,
eighth shelf, eighth row: how she—poet
of the too-large irises, sharply parted
pulled-back hair and hand holding a blur
of blossoms—how she knew the way into
blooming. How her language slips silently
inside, unlocking thought like a gaseous key
slotting deep in a dark lock. Speech is one
symptom of affection And Silence one—
The perfectist communication Is heard
of none—she writes. Why I'll never stop
casting out for our long-lost line, why I'll
never stop longing for her voice inside my
mind or mine in hers. And why, even now,
away from the doctors, I won't resort to the
thin external whistling of larynx, the clumsy
fumbling of a body making sound. When I
write, when she reads the words I scratch
on paper, she hears my voice sounding
faintly again inside. Her silent reading, my
internal speaking. The closest I can come to
being heard.*

A few hours later I break through to the bright sprawl

of the beach, the twin blues of water and sky so sparkling it's hard to see. Lee's already back at the boat, her bare feet propped up on a seat, a bottle of beer tilted to her lips. Iain sits hunch-shouldered nearby, both hands cradling his bottle, picking at the label. He's talking, and Lee leans over, uses one finger to push up the bill of his cap. I clear my throat as I walk up and he stands quickly, knocking into the cooler before shuffling to the back of the boat.

I swing the camera into the hull, then flop my belly over the edge and wiggle in. Iain's still bent over rustling some bags when Lee tears her eyes from him and smiles at me. "Any luck?"

I shrug. "We'll see."

She tilts the last swallow of beer back and without looking Iain sticks out his hand for the empty bottle. She holds onto it and scoots past him to the trash sack. Iain flinches, stands up straight and steps back a little as Lee brushes past him again and picks up a diving mask. "Fancy a swim?" she asks, in an overdone imitation of his accent.

I nod and look back at Iain, who's crouched again over some bags.

"Take off your shoes and give me a hand pushing the boat out, Ansel." She rolls up her jeans and we drop back down to the beach, shoving hard on the count of three, sliding the boat across the sand until there's enough water underneath and it slips from our hands. We wade quickly

after it and Lee scrambles over the bow, then reaches a
hand down to help me up. She doesn't even glance at Iain
still fiddling with something in the back of the boat before
pulling off her shirt, unbuckling her jeans, and wiggling out
of them. Iain doesn't turn, but he's motionless, quiet, and
I can't bring myself to take off my clothes in front of him.
I just wedge my feet into some flippers, pick up a mask
and wiggle the snorkel into my mouth. When we've drifted
out to where we can't see bottom, Lee slaps around the
boat in her black bra and flippers, then scrambles onto
the side. She stands with her hands on her skinny, boyish
hips, her black panties sagging in the butt, and the boat
bobs when she hops into the water.

"Aren't you coming, Iain?" I ask.

"No, darlin,' I'm on the clock. You two enjoy
yourselves." He doesn't even turn his head.

I take a deep breath and slide in, my lungs seizing and
shrinking against the cold, the water sealing around me
like green glass. In the silent chill distance, through silty
lines of sunlight, the pale blur of Lee swoops into a dive,
her thin arms spread wide like wings. A school of minnows
split and vee around her and she turns quickly, her hair
blossoming. I paddle along at the surface, the sun acidic
on my neck and back, the waves slapping sharp salt over
my head, sputtering into my snorkel. Below me, a white
claw surfaces from the foggy sand, sending up a cloud of
silt before digging deeper in. I paddle until my skin feels
salt-scoured, my eyes stinging in the emerald light while

Lee keeps diving and turning, grabbing at fish as they dart away from her.

When I surface by the boat Iain leans over so I can hand him my mask and flippers. I put my feet on the side of the boat and he pulls me one-handed out of the water as easily as grabbing a beer from the cooler. He wraps a towel around my shoulders, then wipes off his sopping arm and sits down, stretching out the antenna on his little radio and fiddling with the dials.

"How much longer do you think she'll be?" I ask.

He doesn't even have to look around—his eyes rest on her immediately, several yards away, surfaced, fiddling with her face mask. He takes a while to answer. "Couldn't tell you." He shoots me a blank look. "Haven't a clue."

Seventeen

When I walk into the kitchen that evening Grand is pouring coffee into the outstretched cups of the Carson brothers. Surprise registers on both their faces and they glance at each other, shifting in their chairs.

The older brother nods to me. "Ansel." Grand puts the coffee pot back on the stove and walks briskly out of the kitchen. "Have a seat," he says.

"In a minute," I say, my breath in my throat and my heart drumming. "I have to check on Izzy."

"We've tended to her." His eyes are weary as he nods to the empty chair. His hand circles the mouth of the teacup, fingers too thick and calloused to fit inside the handle. Both brothers are perched in their chairs, uncomfortable. I sit down and keep my eye on the older brother's hands.

"Your grandma's been telling us you've been having some trouble out here." The younger Mr. Carson, shorter, plumper, wedged in between his brother and the wall, drains his cup and I flinch when he stands, walks over to the stove for a refill as the silence lengthens. "Why don't you tell us your side, Ansel," he says, sitting back down and squinting at me, his button nose and round face in sharp contrast to the long, deep creases carved in the cheeks of his older brother.

In the easy way he sits back down I can see he's just here to talk to me, they're not going to hurt me, they never have, and my breath comes quick. My eyes well up and I rub the tears away with the heels of my palms. Both brothers drop their grey eyes to their teacups and take several quick swigs. The older brother clears his throat. "It's only... your grandma would like your assurance that you'll help her tend to your sister a little more. She seems to think... well. She seems to think you could be a little more attentive."

I nod and push my fingers into the holes of the doily tablecloth. The younger Mr. Carson leans his squat bulk a little towards me and half-whispers, "You're growing up, Ansel. Even since school let out, anybody can see... well, how you're nearly grown. It doesn't seem right... I mean," he glances at his brother, who's nodding, "I like to think your word will be enough here tonight. Your word that you'll help your grandma a little more."

I nod, and the older Mr. Carson slaps his leg and stands up. "Good. All right then," he says, and steps out on the porch as his brother nods to me and follows quickly behind him. They clomp down the steps and walk, one hunch-shouldered, the other straight-backed with long strides, around to where their pickup is parked by the garage. I carry their cups to the sink, then tear the boxes off of three TV dinners and set the oven to preheat. When I hear the truck doors creak open on their old hinges I turn and then I'm out the door, down the steps, calling, "Mr. Carson."

The older brother looks away and hitches himself up into the driver's seat as the younger Mr. Carson walks back, lays a pudgy-fingered hand on my shoulder. I don't know where to start. I stare at the mud splashed up over the toe of his yellow work boot and we stand there like two people looking for lost change. Then he says, "All right now, go on in," and I turn and walk back into the house as the engine revs.

Thursday morning, Izzy doesn't seem to be concentrating on anything when I pick up her rag-doll body to take her to the bathroom—it's like she's not there at all, like those first few months after the hospital when she stopped talking, wouldn't look at me, just stared, but I knew she was there. She'd furrow her brow, stare harder, even put her hand over my mouth when I'd talk to her. She heard me, but she never answered, no matter how hard I begged.

When I set her breakfast tray over her legs, she looks pointedly at the note she's left me on the bedside table but doesn't move to eat until I'm headed back downstairs.

I shove her note in my back pocket, slip on flip-flops and tell Grand where I'm going.

"I hope you don't plan on going gallivanting," she calls after me.

Feeling the tug of the hotel, I walk straight to the hardware store and pick out two canvases, *pillow-sized*, as Izzy's note says, and more white and blue paint and *a brush the size of baby's teeth.* I'm moving fast, the morning seeming to roll away from me as I work my way down Izzy's list. Walking back, two parked cars tick quietly in the early morning heat outside Demeers', where the mannequin in the window is dolled up for some cotillion Cumberland hasn't held in twenty years. Dressed in a peach slip-dress with a ruffly chiffon overlay, a fabric rose pinned to the left hip, they must be targeting the summer crowd, but her curly red wig and blue eye shadow make her look like she's dressed for a ball at the loony bin.

All around me the day is lengthening and when I get home Grand's nowhere to be found. Upstairs, Izzy's still eating her breakfast, setting her spoon down between bites. I busy myself taking down her old canvas and stringing up a new one until finally, finally, she drops her spoon with a clatter. I strap her into her chair, pull her paints close, and ask if she needs anything else. She ignores me, just keeps drawing, so I take that as a no and go.

Who knows where Grand has gone or for how long, but I have four hours before I have to be back for lunch, so I jog along the beach, the wet sand clumping between my toes. The silvery water is quiet, sneaky as a lapping cat, the sun not shining hard enough to burn off the clouds, and then I turn a bend and the beach umbrellas are in sight, tilted in the far sand like cocktail garnishes. I pound up the empty beach, faster and faster over the blank stretch of sand and up to the hotel where families are still lounging around the breakfast tables. Too cold for swimming, the kids listlessly color paper placemats, their parents hidden behind newspapers.

Lee is at a table by herself, no newspaper, watching the families around her with bright, amused eyes.

"I was about to give up on you," she says, pushing a chair out for me with her foot.

"Sorry. I had some chores to take care of. And I'll need to be back by lunchtime."

Lee nods, pulling a plastic sheet of slides and a hand-held viewer from her bag and flopping them on the table in front of me. "Have a look."

My hands are shaky as I hold the sheet up to the sun, select a slide, and drop it into the viewer. I stare at a jumbled clutter of black and brown lines, the mess and tangle and confusion of scribbled tree branches. My throat constricts as I switch out the image for another picture of blur and scrawl, another of washed out light, and my stomach is lead, my throat acid as I work my way through all ten shots. "I'm sorry I wasted so much of your film," I say.

"What are you talking about?"

I shake my head and hand her back the viewer. "They're not what I wanted—what I saw."

She smiles and scoots forward in her chair. "Which ones."

I can't bear to look through the viewer again, so I tap the tree branch pictures in the plastic sleeve, the wavering lines I saw so clearly just a messy tangle. Lee slots them one by one in the viewer and squints, nodding. "Yeah, you wanted the bark texture, right? But with the sunlight streaming through, the camera metered off of that, so you lost all those great mid- and low-tones. I think these would have been better suited for black and white, anyway."

She looks up at me and I can't find my voice. It's so strange to think that someone I've just met might know how I see the world, that some near-stranger could slip inside my mind after I've lived so long in my head alone. I nod and don't meet her eye. "And—I don't know. I wanted more to get in the picture—the frame to be a little wider, somehow. But I guess you're just stuck with the width of the film."

"Well, you could try a panoramic. But I'm guessing a wide-angle lens might have given you the effect you wanted. Try it." Her camera is equipped with a short, snub lens and when I pan around the lawn at the families eating I see it's exactly what I'd wanted—everything flattened out, stretched at the edges.

I swallow and nod quickly, dropping the camera to my

lap and fiddling the strap.

"So we'll go back. Get the photo you wanted. I'll coo if Iain's busy. Say, tomorrow?" Lee pours a cup of tea and hands it to me, forgetting the saucer, so I pick it up and hold it out to her like a tiny tray. She snorts, setting the cup noisily into the indentation. "Guess I'm a little rusty on my niceties," she says. "Comes from living too long out of the back of a jeep."

"Don't you even have a home?"

She lets out a quick "ha!" and nods, chewing her toast. "I do, I do actually—a studio in New York. But I've got this fellowship to finish the seashore pictures, and the beaches up there are pretty picked over, so I've been cruising the coast all summer."

"You've got a *what*?"

"A fellowship." I look back at her blankly and she smiles. "Rich arty folks give me money to keep being a bohemian."

"Oh. I didn't know you could do that. Just take pictures for a job, I mean."

"Well, sometimes things get lean, but nowadays I can pretty much string together residencies and shows and grants and do okay."

"Wow." A waiter fills our water glasses and looks at me hard when he sets mine down. Trying to remember if he's seen me here freeloading summer after summer, I take a quick forkful of scrambled eggs off of Lee's plate and stare back at him, daring him to say something. "So, people pay you for pictures of seashells? I thought you had to work for a newspaper or something if you wanted to make any money." I'm speaking loudly, waving my empty fork as I talk, and Lee cocks an eyebrow at me, glancing at the waiter as he finally moves on.

"Yeah, well, so did I. Which is why I lived overseas for about five years, working for the Associated Press. But then I couldn't do that anymore, so I came home and regrouped."

"You got fired?"

Lee wipes her mouth and lays her napkin on the table, her hand resting on top of it. She shakes her head. "I was doing a lot of war correspondence?" She looks up at me with flat, weary eyes, but the waiter is circling our table again so I stir my toast in the air like a duchess waving a cigarette holder, urging her to go on.

"I was taking a lot of pictures of people living in shells of bombed-out buildings and dodging bullets and clutching their bleeding loved ones, you know. And one day I was hunkered down behind a burnt-out car with about four other photographers, people getting shot left and right all around us. These photographers, they were clicking away, practically ooh-ing and ah-ing. I had stopped taking pictures and I was just watching them shift and bob like vultures over a carcass. And there was this little boy, probably about five years old, he was huddled across the street in the corner of this building that was getting shelled pretty heavily, and I realized that all these photographers had their lenses trained on him. They were waiting for him to get shot so they could photograph his death. So when there was a pause in the shelling I ran over and grabbed him and carried him back over to where we were, out of range, and all the other photographers were *pissed.* I guess they thought I'd cost them their Pulitzer." She brushes some toast crumbs off the tablecloth and looks up at me with a rueful, washed-out smile. "So after that I started taking pictures of seashells."

I don't know how to get to the boat graveyard by the roads so Lee and I walk along the beach lugging her camera equipment. It takes us two hours to make the thirty-minute walk because she keeps stopping to take pictures of driftwood and seaweed strands. Each time she has to set up her tripod, fiddle with aperture and shutter speed, wait for the light to change or the tide to wash up just right or the wind to pick up or die down. We keep walking and as the shadow of the house passes over us I flinch out of view under the hill.

Lee gives me a questioning squint, and I shrug. "That's where I live."

She looks up at the drooping gables and flaking paint, the cliff edge eating away at the foundation and lets out a low whistle. "Wow. Now *that* has possibilities. But I'll leave those shots for you to root out."

"I don't have a camera."

"What's wrong with mine?" She takes out the one I

was using the other day and sets it heavily in my hands. "I've still got a week before my show. Just as long as you give it back before I leave." I nod. *Thank you* sounds so babyish in my head.

Lee grins a half-smile, nodding with her chin down the shore. "How much farther?"

"Maybe twenty minutes if you don't stop a billion times."

The boats are beached in the dunes, piled half on top of each other pulled back from the water, and when we clear the rise Lee flashes me another grin before half jogging, half sliding down the sand towards them. Most are old speedboats and sailboats, but a few are really old—rowboats and dinghies from when this town was just a fishing village. Once when Izzy and I were still little enough to be summer visitors, we scrambled up here, each of us claiming a house from one of the tipped-over hulls. We clambered under the hard plastic and chased each other and got sun burned until Izzy cut her head on a rusty nail and I had to walk her home with blood dripping down her cheek. But now I see what Lee sees—the way the curves of the hulls and the boards and racing stripes make patterns to be teased out from the tangle. I hold the camera up to my face and turn until the angles shift into place. The click of the camera makes the day stand still.

Lee says if I put my film in our mailbox she'll pick it up and have it developed by tomorrow morning, so I leave her taking pictures of the boats and walk home to make devilled ham sandwiches. Grand is ironing in front of a soap opera, her jaw set, and my breath catches in my lungs. I set down her plate on the coffee table, and after making it upstairs without her saying anything or even looking at me, I can breathe again.

When I open the door to our room Izzy puts her brush down and folds her hands, her eyes lowered like a nun. She's painting a portrait of one of us—it's our grey eyes and thin lips and a few wisps of blond hair framing the face—but the rest of the hair is still unpainted, drawn curling into sinister serpentine swirls. I try not to look too hard as I unbuckle Izzy and drag her between the bathroom and the bed. When I lay the plate on her lap she just sits there, staring at the lines on her palm as the seconds tick on. The air in the room is thick, unbreathable, so I leave Izzy and creep back downstairs. The living room is empty again, the door to Grand's bedroom closed, and I pause to scan the kitchen through the viewfinder of Lee's camera.

Sliding the lens over all the everyday clutter, I see how a camera gives a person distance from a house and the lives lived in it—distance from the drab sadness of the fruit magnets on the refrigerator holding up yellowed newspaper clippings, from the curled, ragged corners of obituaries and jello salad recipes that seem suddenly pathetic but worth keeping. I adjust the controls and click the button, then shift the camera to the stained-glass squirrel stuck to the window with suction cups. When I move the rainbow a little bit to the left, the suction cup leaves a white stain on the glass where it's hung for so long, and the whole picture looks dustier, drabber, even better. I align the stain with the bottom right corner of the picture where my eye seems to settle and click the shutter.

I scan the camera across the table clutter, clicking on the condiment caddy of salt and pepper, paper napkins, plastic pillbox with its seven windows, each day marked by a letter and a cluster of raised, transparent dots. Then I zoom in close on the knit tops of the dishtowels buttoned around the oven handle, and again on the dusty blown-glass figurines on the windowsill next to the broken outdoor thermometer.

I turn and scan the stack of envelopes, then set the camera on the table and pull open the envelope marked "Medical—John." It's full of receipts from Jorgen's pharmacy, letters from the doctor, and in the back is one type-written note advising grandfather of the danger of letting his prescription lapse, how it is *imperative to refill his prescription immediately*. Other than that, there are no hospital charts, no doctor's reports, no hint of what the medicine was for.

The envelope with my name on it is thin, just a few reports on tests and x-rays, followed by discharge papers dated two days after I was checked in. Izzy's envelope is the largest, bulging with paperwork, maybe thirty pages of reports on surgeries and various medications, on physical therapy and visits from a psychologist. Flipping to the back, to the discharge papers, I read the words "recommend 24-hour supervision" and "released to her grandmother's care."

Her grandmother's care. Somewhere at the center of my insides is a dark space full of images I don't let anyone see, and for one second light slips in with a click.

Every time I anger, so much less of me left
and so little to begin with. Better if I don't
allow her inside me at all, if I let her dissolve
into the light of out-there the way she wants
to. Better if I don't think how what I paint will
touch her, hurt her, singe a little what remains
of the us of us. How my hand finds lines
I didn't know it knew. How my dreamings
uncoil in paint-slick shapes to see the world
with. It isn't fair—not quite hers, these sins I
spackle on canvas—our story and who hurt
whom too faceted for a single frame. Today
the Medusa she's seeming, her angel face
framed with snakes, headless, and at each
writhing end another something she's kept
hidden hissing itself into the stagnant air to
be seen. Tomorrow, me the Pandora, and
all the error this dead half unhinges. Each of
us bounded now, bordered, kept to our own
canvas.

Cumberland

Eighteen

Friday, July 19, 1974

19 days

Friday morning I make lots of noise brushing my teeth and flushing the toilet trying to wake up Izzy. When I feel her eyes on me for the first time in days, she tilts her head with a puzzled smile. I set her breakfast tray down and say, "It's not nice to stare, Izzy."

She grins around her mouthful of cereal, milk dribbling down her chin, and writes, *Or keep secrets.* Her gaze makes me feel naked after going so long unlooked-at, but the air in my lungs expands a little, and my heart seems to slow. I walk around to the dresser, pull out clean clothes, and don't turn around when I say, "It's only a secret because you can't guess." Dropping the shirt I slept in next to the dresser and stepping out of my dirty undies, I can still feel her gaze crawling my skin when I turn away: starting at my head, sliding down my back, taking stock. Bite after bite of cereal, she doesn't take her eyes from me.

Fluttery, but not so outside-herself dreamy. Less airy, arrowed towards something, some possibility inside her, a jittery stillness, the hard chrysalis cracking. Nothing to do with this mysterious him. This new eagerness is all her own doing, tight-fisted, some inclination wriggling towards a will. Guess, she says. As if I could. How if I had control of all my parts I'd move these mornings, straining towards the rest of the day's canvas and the mystery of what's inside I can't speak, can't know until my hand touches brush to canvas. All I can't yet see pressing out against my skin, blustery with the wind of pent-up vision.

Once Izzy's safely belted into her chair and the house around her is silent I set off running, the screen door cracking behind me like a shot fired into the morning. I duck and weave and hop through the tangle of trees and reach the hotel as the waiters are snapping open the table cloths. As I walk past the front desk a skinny man with a brass nametag calls out, "Good morning—may I help you, miss?"

"I'm just meeting a friend," I say, pointing through the lobby to the grand curving staircase that leads upstairs.

"Which room, please?"

"She's expecting me."

He scans my ratty t-shirt and flip-flops. "*Which room.*"

"423."

"Allow me to call ahead for you." He dials, keeping an eye trained on me.

"Yes, there's a young lady who says she's here to see you? Thank you." He sets the phone down, shuffling some papers on his desk. "She's expecting you."

"That's what I said." I shoot him my most scornful glance and try to inject confidence and good breeding into my stride as I walk off. Upstairs, I tiptoe through one huge parlor after another with soaring ceilings, chandeliers and chairs grouped around fireplaces or tables. Underneath each tall window is a small writing desk supplied with the large embossed C of the hotel letterhead, as if anyone could just sit down and make herself cozy in one of these enormous rooms. I reach the hallway and climb the stairs to the fourth floor where a dark-skinned maid in a black uniform with a little white apron—the kind I thought they only wear in the board game Clue—is pushing her cart of soaps and pillow mints down the hallway. I knock on 423, and Lee cracks the door, her body hidden behind the wood, her hair rumpled.

"Jesus, Ansel." I slip inside and she pads over to the bed in her underwear and tank top, flopping face first, not even bothering to slip her legs under the covers. "When I said 'early' I meant... normal people." Her voice is muffled by her pillow and then she rolls over, grinning up at me. "So, did they fingerprint you?"

"Practically." Her room is decorated in the same gardenia wallpaper as the hallways, the large blossoms bright yellow, the old, sturdy-looking furniture painted white. The other twin banister bed is covered with camera equipment, and at the far end of the room a writing desk rests under one of the breezy curtains. At the room's center, two green-striped wing back chairs flank a table bearing an elaborate fruit basket, the gathered cellophane tied off with a white bow.

"Too bad they didn't know about your espionage work. You should have told them how all your vital stats are on file at Langley—could have saved them some time." I try to smile, standing just inside the doorway feeling like any minute someone's going to appear and drag me away. "Don't let them get to you, Ansel. If the southern genteel that frequent this place aren't treated with enough disdain they don't feel like they're getting their money's worth."

I nod, and she rubs her eyes, groans, pulls a pillow over her face. I feel weird standing there staring at her in her underwear, so I shuffle through the photo envelopes on the table. "Did you get my kitchen pictures back?" She grunts but doesn't move. Holding the plastic sheets of slides one by one up to the light, I find mine and arrange the slides side by side on an empty row of the light easel. They're exactly what I'd wanted, the colors jaundiced in the kitchen's fluorescent lights, the little knick-knacks and clusters of plastic taking on a kind of pathetic importance in their little rectangular frames. Lee turns back over so she's facing me and shoots me a weak, sleepy smile.

"Yeah, they're good." She slides an arm across the bed and smacks me on the back of the head. "They're really good. You bitch."

"They turned out even better than I thought... kind of sad and funny and depressing and touching. This one — the magnets — I didn't even notice how the grapes were upside down, but it makes it even better doesn't it — like an arrow pointing to nowhere." Lee smirks at me across her pillow, groans, swings her legs over the side of the bed, and shuffles into the bathroom.

"No getting rid of you now, I guess." I hear her peeing, the sink running, and then she pads out smelling like bar soap and toothpaste. The belt on her jeans jingles as she yanks them off the back of a chair, steps into them, then sits on the bed, her elbows hitched up beside her head as the tugs her hair into a messy ponytail. "Yeah, the magnets are killer. And this one." She taps the plastic frame of the suction cup slide with her fingernail.

I nod, unable to hide my smile, and Lee cuffs me on the side of the head again. "All right. Let's go see if there's more where these came from."

On the way to breakfast we stop by Lee's jeep for an extra tripod. Then, since I'm antsy, she goes to the door of the kitchen and talks a waiter into bringing out two steaming Styrofoam cups and some croissants in a grease-speckled paper bag. I follow her past the hotel to where the beach gets swampy, dank with sticky mud, around to a squat cabin tucked under the Spanish moss. Lee hands me one of the coffees and knocks on the door. We wait and wait, and when I ask if we should knock again the door cracks open and she holds out one Styrofoam cup. "Room service."

Iain is standing in the doorway in light blue boxer shorts, his face ashen and crushed like a soda can, and my cheeks go hot as I back away and stare at the ground. He takes the cup then shuts the door in Lee's face, and she smiles, sits down on the rickety bench by the door. She hums some folky lullaby as she takes out her camera and slowly wipes the lens with a packet of wispy tissue papers. Then the door opens and Iain throws out a pair of boots in front of him. He jangles a key into the lock and sits on the stoop to lace up.

"Wasn't expecting you quite this early," he says.

"Yeah, I had a little wakeup call myself this morning."

Iain glances up at me, and my still-hot cheeks burn hotter as an impishness sneaks into his smile. "Caught the photo bug, have you, Ansel?" I look down at my feet, trying to shake the memory of his hairy, muscular chest and farmer's tan.

"I think it's a terminal case. No cure in sight," Lee says, grinning at me.

Iain nods, the light draining from his eyes. "Thanks for the coffee," he says, standing up and stiffly holding out his hand to help Lee up from the bench. She tilts her head at him, grinning as she stands, then shrugs past his outstretched hand and clomps down the porch step ahead of him. His hand hangs in the air before he pockets it and shuffles after her and I follow.

Lee and I wait on the dock nibbling croissants until the whir of a motor approaches and Iain pulls the boat up against the foam bumpers of the dock. Lee doesn't even wait for the boat to come to a full stop before stepping onto the edge and hopping in. Iain's face is expressionless, slightly hardened as he fiddles with the motor and gives a little nod.

"All ready then?" He looks at me, his face blank as a basset hound's, nods again, then revs the motor, steering us away from the dock. I pick my way carefully to the prow and stick my face into the wind, my lungs expanding with light and air and all the images that lie ahead of me, waiting for me to find and frame and freeze them forever.

Nineteen

I try not to look as I take down Izzy's first finished pillow-sized painting and string up her next canvas. It's me, then, this Medusa—her far-off, caged expression so clearly mine, with tiny scenes Izzy must imagine I've lived without her budding like a head at the end of each hair-snake. I try not to read the words imbedded in the painting, but my eye snags on *envies* and *coiled poisons*. I concentrate on keeping my face still, my gestures breezy, but Izzy's watching me as she eats her sandwich the way a lion watches a wounded gazelle. My hands start to shake so I knit them together and pretend to stretch, concentrating on the blank canvas I'm stringing up against the window. When I take Izzy to the bathroom then strap her back into the stool, her eyes on me are sharp as darts. She doesn't make a move, doesn't even pick up a brush while I'm still in the room.

Grand's in front of the TV filing her nails, her sandwich picked over. When I stop to ask her if she's finished she just tilts her head a little, rubbing her nails back and forth against the now almost gritless emery board. Her silence follows me into the kitchen. I'm rinsing mustard off the last plate, when there's a tiny *tap ta-tap* at the door. I open it and Everett's standing there with a haircut and a huge grin. Before I can say anything or glance behind me he wraps his arms around my waist and pulls me off the porch, kissing me, tiny frantic kisses on my face and neck. I let his mouth devour everything, kisses like little fish just surfaced to jab at a piece of trash. I close my eyes and my mouth finds his cheeks, his neck, shoulders, mouth. He's here, and I'm wanted, everything I don't want to be or think is erased by his breath and the sounds he makes, wanting me, or the me he thinks I am.

We're kissing, and then we're on the ground, his hand finding my waist and the edge of my t-shirt and sliding underneath to skin that's wide open to his touch, every pore like a mouth gasping for breath. I slide my hands under his shirt and he ducks out of it, then slips mine over my head and the length of his skin against mine is like a gasp of cold water I can't gulp enough of. His mouth is searing, dropping to my chest and finding where I'm most tender and I wrap my arms around his head, feel myself spiraling away, holding on and pulling him with me deeper into this double drowning. The sounds from his mouth are vowels and not-quite-my-name, and suddenly I imagine Grand wondering who knocked, getting up from the couch, bustling into the kitchen, and pushing open the door—

"Everett—wait. Wait." I push him off me and his eyelids are half-closed, his mouth soft and raw as he leans back towards me. I pull on my shirt, shove his at him and clamp my hand over his mouth when he lets out a low moan. "She might hear us. Where can—are your grandparents home?"

"Yeah, they're home, they're always home, they never go anywhere—Jesus, Ansel," and when he sweeps a hand up my neck into my hair I shove him off and scramble to standing.

"The fort, then. We can—"

"Too far, Ansel, God—I can't—" but before he can tangle me in his arms again, I grab his hand and pull him away from the porch and down the dunes to the beach. He's kissing me again, the tide lapping our ankles as he tries to pull me down, but I tug loose, glancing up at Izzy's window, and pull him running up the beach, the two of us staggering, running then scrambling up the dunes to the boat graveyard.

At the top of the dune he stops, and I lose his hand as I run down ahead of him. When I turn around he's frozen, scanning the boats, hands dangling at his sides. I walk back to him and he turns, looking at me from a distance behind his eyes.

"You've been here before. Do you—have you—?" He glances down and then I realize what he's thinking. I can't help it—I laugh out loud.

"Oh yeah, all those teenaged studs in town—I've brought them all out here." He looks at me sideways, some of the caution draining from his gaze, and I lace my fingers between his, pulling his hand up to my lips. "Everett. I'd never even kissed anyone before you." I stare at his toes, and he lifts my face, kisses me gently, then follows me down to the boats.

Lines of my Pandora surfacing when sound
from out-there wafts up. My canvas lashed
to half the window and the other half a view
of sandy sprawl, water and sky erasing,
a relentless emptiness. But there the two
all-too-human, who-I-might-have-been
standing in shallows and a boy a full head
taller holding the whole-me up. Beach light
glinting off his lines, the tawny, sun-filled
skin. From here I remember the scent of
him, his cut-grass scent on her neck. Now
a mouth and breath and a whole body felt
against her whole body. The weight of the
world dragging down on their breathless-
ness, his hands and her hands like mouths
devouring.

Everett's asleep, one bent knee winged over my legs,

one hand tucked under his head, the other spent and washed up on my collar bone. Lying under the baking plastic shell of this boat, the setting sun slanting in at an eye-piercing angle, it feels like sand has crept into every crevice of my sweaty skin, my body not wholly mine, and the me inside my skin has retreated a few layers down.

I push Everett off and sit up, pull on my clothes, and he cracks an eye open, winces, drops his face in my lap. The heat of his breath where I'm most sore makes me squirm and I stand up to gather his clothes.

"*There's a certain slant of light...*" he grumbles, holding a hand up to block the sun.

"Yeah?"

"The Dickinson poem." He pulls his white boxers on and looks at me, his head tilted. "You know." I shake out his t-shirt and hand it to him without looking. "Emily Dickinson."

"I'm not sure this is the time to tell me about your other girlfriends."

He snorts. "Yeah, I wish."

I keep my eyes down, my voice steady, and breathe, breathe. "You do?"

He wads up his t-shirt and throws it at me, hitting me in the side of the face. "*Emily Dickinson?* Nineteenth century poet? White-dress-wearing, house-never-leaving, master-letter-writing genius? You've had her book checked out for two weeks—since that first day in the library."

"Oh… right. The poet." Dimly I remember the plain tan cover and how Izzy kept looking up from the book to mouth sections. Everett grabs me around the waist as I walk by and pulls me onto his lap.

"Which one is your favorite?" He nuzzles my ear and trails kisses down the goose bumps rising on my neck.

"What?"

"Which poem."

"Oh, the one about the, uh… flower—look, Everett, I've gotta go fix dinner." I shove off his lap and smack my flip-flops together to get most of the wet sand off.

"Well, when can I see you again?"

"I don't know, I've got church tomorrow. Monday, maybe. Don't come up to the house—I'll find you."

"Ansel." I'm halfway out from under the boat but I turn enough so I look like I'm listening. He scoots towards me and touches my elbow. "I want to spend the night with you."

My voice snags in my throat. I nod, slip out from under the boat and trudge up the dunes, leaving Everett pulling on his shorts and shouting in a loud, theatrical voice, *"Wild nights—Wild nights! Were I with thee, Wild nights should be Our luxury!"*

Twenty

Sunday, July 21, 1974
17 days

I'm still tender this morning and sit through the church service tilted on one hip. Everyone bows their head to pray, and when Reverend Clark starts to read I think about Izzy sitting ram-rod straight when I came in last night, radiating chill, and how no matter how long I stood in front of the mirror, my body looked the same. And what was there to see? Skin intact, markless, maybe a little red, a little swollen in places. I winced when the water hit my chest and I didn't use soap on the parts that felt raw, just let the water rinse away the sand and heat and sweat and spit.

Grand sniffs beside me and I flush, sit up straighter, concentrating on the words that Reverend Clark is reading: *Upon my bed by night I sought him whom my soul loves; I sought him, but found him not; I called him, but he gave no answer. I will rise now and go about the city, in the streets and in the squares; I will seek whom my soul loves.* I shift my weight, glancing sideways at Grand who's smiling tightly, nodding. Next to her the older Mr. Carson is sitting with his head bowed and his fingers interlaced, rubbing a scab on his knuckle with one finger.

While Reverend Clark talks about how sometimes we have to seek out the love of God, but sometimes we have to be patient and wait for it, I switch hips and look around at the other parishioners, at Mrs. Grady rooting in her nose with a tissue. Then Reverend Clark reads, *My beloved put his hand to the latch, and my heart was thrilled within me,* and I cross my arms tight across my chest. *I arose to open to my beloved, and my hands dripped with myrrh, my fingers with liquid myrrh, upon the handles of the bolt.* The heat in my cheeks spreads quickly down my neck, flooding my chest, and when I shift again Grand shoots me a hard look, whispering, "For heaven's sake, sit still. Act like a Calvert."

After church Mr. Carson lets me drive home, and under my hands the steering wheel starts to turn more smoothly, the gear shifts less jerkily, a slow coasting. Grand is huffy when I pull up in front of the hardware store, but Mr. Carson says it's just fine—no hurry. I dash back to the art supplies aisle and get Izzy's canvas and ten different shades of green and blue. Mr. Millard rings me up, saying, "You must have enough paintings to fill a museum by now, Ansel." I smile, tuck the last of Izzy's birthday money in my pocket, toss the canvas and bag of paints into the back of the truck, then skip around to the driver's side and swing inside. Grand is sitting rigidly, her jaw set, and Mr. Carson has his hand propped up on the window jamb, two large fingers held to his temple.

"Everybody ready?" I ask, grinning, and Grand's jaw tightens as she keeps staring through the windshield.

"Whenever you are, Ansel. Neither of us has anywhere we need to be," Mr. Carson says.

I crank the engine, check the mirrors and back out, pausing at the corner of Main Street. I look left to where the street curves behind the houses to link up with the highway, and for a second the other two people in the car fade and I imagine I'm Lee in her jeep, the wide stretch of light-bathed world sprawling out forever away from the hotel in two directions. I imagine rolling down the window, steering with one wrist draped over the wheel, the wind in my hair, driving and driving and everything in Cumberland—Izzy, Grand, everyone who sees me as just a bored little kid walking up and down the streets of this stupid town—disappearing behind me. How moving always forward in one direction is a way of erasing, and the farther I go the fainter I feel the pull of Izzy, Izzy, Izzy, and every day.

Grand lets out a low, lingering huff, and Mr. Carson leans forward in the seat to look at me. "All clear, Ansel," he says.

"Sorry." I gun the engine and turn right onto the empty street as smoothly as Iain steers his boat around the dock. I drive to the end of Main Street and tap the brake as we bump down onto the dirt, then pound the gas so we don't slow for the climb up the hill. I coast up to the house and cut the engine, the rumbling still burbling in my chest.

As Grand's getting out of her church clothes, I turn the oven on 350° to preheat and Izzy doesn't glance at me when I take her supplies upstairs. This time the painting is of Izzy sitting in a wheelchair she's never had, insects swarming out of her hinged-open belly.

"Well that's cheery, Izzy. Lovely." I'm expecting an almost-giggle, the tiniest crack in her façade, but Izzy just bristles and leans forward, furrowing her brow and pursing her lips.

Downstairs I pop a tuna fish casserole in the oven and slip the plastic sleeve of slides from my beach tote. When the timer on the oven buzzes I grab two crusty pot-holders and spoon out servings on three plates. I take Izzy's upstairs and start to unbuckle her, but she tears my hands away, throwing them aside. I try again and she shrieks, batting my hands away like flies.

"Fine. Starve." I leave Izzy's plate on the bedside table where she can't reach it and go downstairs to eat my casserole at the kitchen table, holding the slides up to the light.

My brush the pitter patter, tap tap, slide
sweep of feet, moving me through internal

rooms blooming at the end of long interior
halls How the paint takes on a movement,
the mistiness of vision, the still tremor of a
body holding breath. Trace a line of water
over the edges and suddenly a gloss, a blur
that's lived-in. What the cubists knew—
how to get in all the views and would-be
versions of a person from one vantage.
But never the worry of how a model might
take it—all the living she's been keeping
obscured by the erasure of action suddenly
made plain. Keep moving in one direction,
she thinks, and you won't ever retread,
retreat, retrace.

Izzy paints all day and into the evening. Every time I try
to unbuckle her to tuck her in for the night she hisses and
bats my hands away. Finally I give up and leave her in her
chair painting, and by the time I get to the hotel it's been
dark for hours.

Although she'd asked me to drop off some images
for printing, after three knocks Lee still doesn't answer
the door of room 423, so I slip the plastic sleeve of slides
under her door, the two slides I liked best checked with
grease pencil. I scoot quickly through the parlors where
women in thin dresses twine among wing chairs sipping
martinis. Outside, the tables are all cleared for the night,

and as I cross to the back of the hotel a low laugh and whispers waft across the lawn. An older woman dripping jewelry steps out from behind a tree with a boy in wait-staff pants trailing behind her, both of their mouths gory with lipstick. I loop around behind the hotel to where the crickets are louder, the dark and smell of sea-wrack thicker, and tiptoe up beside the cabin to peek in the lit window.

Iain's sitting at a table, dinner dishes pushed to the center, his hands slick with oil as he works a piece of machinery. He picks up a screwdriver, the sound of the radio tinny with the nightly newscast, and when I shift so more of the room is in view I see Lee at the other end of the table sifting through prints, looking at them through the magnifier and making marks with a red grease pencil. After a while she stretches and stands up, goes to the stove and pours herself a cup of coffee, then walks over to the table and tops off Iain's mug. He looks up, and she lingers beside him, her hip near his shoulder.

He sets down the piece of machinery and starts to wipe his hands on a rag, but Lee takes it from him and drops it next to the coffee pot. Then she scoots between Iain and the table, hitching her butt up on the scarred wood as she lifts his oil-smeared hands to her neck. Iain holds them there, then slowly slides his fingertips along her collarbone, smearing dark streaks on her skin as he fits his thumb into the hollow at the base of her throat. A teasing smile on her lips, Lee bends forward and

Iain slides his hands down inside the neck of her shirt, thumbing loose buttons until her bra is exposed. He slips his hands beneath the straps and cups her small breasts, rubbing his thumbs where he lowers his mouth. Then he reaches down to her hips, yanks her towards him and, shaky, half standing, buries his face in her shirt, his mouth taking deep gulps, her eyes shut, the smile flickering as she leans down to call his face up to hers and bites his lip. Iain slides a hand under her butt and tugs her against him, reaching behind him to wrap her legs around his waist, then stands up and, kissing, carries her across the room through the darkened doorway at the far side of the house.

I wait and listen, but all I can hear is the deep creaking of the crickets and the radio starting in on some slow jazz number. Shaky-kneed, weak, I rest my cheek against the mildewed clapboards. I know I won't sleep unless I find a mouth to kiss and know just as suddenly where I can find one.

The lights are all out at Everett's house, and since pebbles might crack the glass, I break a stick into little pieces and toss them up at his window. I throw and miss, shivering in the light breeze, and start breaking a thicker stick into pieces when Everett's light comes on and he appears in the bright rectangle, his hand cupped around his eyes. His window slides open and he whispers loudly, "What happened to Monday?"

"I—"

He shushes me and disappears inside. The door to the Lloyd's creaks open and Everett motions me up the stoop, his hand on my waist guiding me through the dark house. I bang my knee on the coffee table and start to giggle, but Everett covers my mouth, hustling me through the living room to the staircase beside the kitchen. I bite one of his fingers and he lets out a little "hey!" as I clamp my hand over his mouth. Eyes glittering in the dark, he grabs my wrist, sticks my finger in his mouth and sucks. My knees give and he grabs me around the waist, half carrying me shaky-legged up the stairs to the triangle of light shining from an open door. He holds his finger to his lips, leads me inside, and slowly, carefully, turns the knob behind us.

Boxes still sealed with packing tape are shoved up against the bare wood-paneled walls, an empty duffle bag folded on top. Under the window, books are stacked two feet high next to a small desk messy with papers, and across the room a twin bed covered in a cowboy comforter is lit by a lamp made of twine and popsicle sticks. Two more stacks of books rise next to the nightstand and a sketch pad lays open to a page smeary with dark pencil in the shape of a face.

My grandparents—are right—across—the hall, Everett mouths, holding his finger again to his lips and pulling me over to the bed. Surrounded by his things in this silent house, I try to think of something sexy and confident to do as he sits on the edge smiling up at me. He slips off his t-shirt and briefs, pulls his skinny, naked legs under the covers, and holds the sheet open for me. I turn my back and tug off my shirt and shorts, watching the door as I crawl in next to him in my bra and panties.

He's chuckling as he pulls the sheet over our heads, but my stomach flutters and I turn on my side with my back to him. I wrap my arms around my knees and squeeze so tight I imagine changing into something else, the way a lump of coal compresses into a diamond. I imagine turning into someone older, someone out in the world all on her own, no one sleeping in the next room, no one depending on her or needing her every few hours in ways she doesn't want to be needed, and the man beside her just one more man she's been with who knows everything or nothing about her, wanting all of her and more. I imagine we're two adults cut adrift in the world, washed up together for one night in an anonymous hotel in an unknown city, lost to everything except each other, and I imagine all of me wants to be here, brazen and bare-skinned and sure of how to use my hands and mouth.

I roll onto my back and Everett lets out a playful growl, curls his body around me. His arm wraps tight around my waist and his hand slides down, pushes inside my panties, his fingers mashing as he breathes hard in my ear. He raises up and leans over me, his mouth sloppy on my shoulder, and when I push the sheet off our heads he rolls on top of me, pulling my bra down on one side so the underwire slices my ribs. His other hand tugs my panties down and when he jabs inside me I gasp with the sting. He grunts, rowing on top of me, rocking and moaning. He shifts a little to the side so his hip bone knocks into me and then he's groaning quietly in my ear, rolling off and curling up with his back to me. I wait, listen until his breathing evens, then reach down and pull up my underwear and adjust my bra. I reach a hand down to check, and my finger touches the raw sting, comes away bloody for the second time in two days.

Twenty-One

Monday, July 22, 1974
16 days

My nightgown is glowing in the moonlight and I open
the window and step out into the bright night weighing
nothing, I'm tissue-light, the air bouncing like a diving
board underneath me as I walk. Close to the ocean the air
starts to thin, dropping me, so I turn back towards town,
the air thickening the farther I get away from the water.
Now I'm walking above the trees and the light from one
yellow house shines up at me as I lean into flying, swoop
down and whip in through the open window. Everett
sits up in bed, his eyes half afraid, and I want to tell him
it's me but I can't speak. Light is pouring out of me and
the fingers that unbutton my nightgown are transparent,
glowing like lampshades. I pull my nightgown open and
my thin-skinned fingers brush a bumpy scar, thick as a
worm and crescent-curved around my left breast. Everett
flinches, raises the sheet to shield his eyes, but then
his gaze catches and he's staring at the light, hot and
throbbing, a faint glowing shape beneath my skin. I step

closer and unzip the skin over my ribs where my heart is nestled, smooth and heavy as a moon rock and painted with flowers and little winged creatures in thick strokes. Everett isn't scared now, he slides forward on the bed and reaches inside my chest to cup my heart and his hand makes the throbbing faster. Weakness slips into my thighs and I'm kissing him, his hand inside my ribs, and I hold his wrist and don't let go, my heart blazing and foreign as an asteroid.

When I open my eyes Everett's shaking my shoulder. It's morning. I fell asleep here, I've been here all night and Izzy... I lunge for my shorts as Everett stumbles free of the sheets, grabs my shirt and shoves it at me, then pulls on his t-shirt and briefs and hurries to the door. It's barely light in his room but I can hear someone creaking around in the hall and then Everett's voice, bright and a little too chipper.

"Morning, Gramps. Gram still sleeping?" I don't hear the response but then Everett's back in the room scooping up my flip-flops and motioning me frantically to the threshold. A door closes across the hall and then Everett scoots out onto the landing, pulling me quickly down the stairs behind him, through the dim living room and out the front door. On the stoop his eyes are glittery and he whispers, "Close one. Want to meet at the boats tonight?"

"I don't know, I—"

There's a creak from upstairs and Everett shoves my

flip-flops at me, slipping back inside. He mouths, "I'll come find you later," grins, and shuts the door.

I hustle into town, past the dark shops and single gleaming light of Pauline's, up the road to home. The dust is so settled it radiates cool, and like footprints on the moon my flip-flops leave quick, neat tracks. I hurry across the still, silent yard and creak in the back door.

Grand is sitting at the table, not in her normal spot, her back to the desk so she sees me the second the door opens. She takes four quick steps across the kitchen, her eyes burning and her mouth screwed up in a grimace. My cheek explodes, and through blurry eyes she raises the other hand and slaps another hard sting across the other cheek. I back away but she grabs my arms and shakes me, her nails digging into my skin and she's yelling, her words just overlapping noise I can't even hear: "—*Leave your sister strapped into that chair all night long lucky she didn't break something heard her fall over and the mess everywhere—you will clean it up and you will not leave this house again for the rest of the summer you hear me you selfish little who knows where you've been all night you get upstairs I don't want to see your face—*"

She yanks me across the kitchen and I scramble upstairs on all fours then burst through the door. Izzy's lying propped up against her headboard, her hands bandaged and her cheek bruised, and she fixes me with a glare of seething chill. Her stool is toppled, the palette turned over and the brushes strewn, paint and pee smeared across the floor.

Feeling Izzy's eyes searing into me, I go to the bathroom and grab a wad of toilet paper and some cleanser, soak up most of the pee, drop it in the toilet, and flush. Then I pry up the palette and see half the paint's dried on the floor so I get a sponge and scrub and scrub, faster and faster, scrub and scrub so hard I can't feel or think about anything but scrubbing, scrubbing, scrub.

It's late morning when someone knocks and I hear Grand step across the kitchen to the door. It's Everett, I know it. I launch myself out of bed, but then Lee's voice drifts up to me, saying, "Oh, what a shame. I'm having a show over at the hotel and Ansel's been helping me with my work. I was hoping she'd be there." Grand mutters a response and I can hear Lee's bright, polite voice, "Yes, of course, I understand. It's important to be firm, isn't it? I wouldn't dream of interfering. It's just that I loaned Ansel my camera and I was hoping before I left to…" Grand says something, and then Lee says, "Yes, that's it. Thank you," and then I hear Grand's footsteps over to the table and back to the door. "Are you sure that wouldn't be an imposition? I don't want to…" After a long pause Lee says, "Thank you so much," and the door shuts and her jeep starts up and drives off. So that's it. The camera's gone. Lee's gone.

I swallow hard and Izzy throws back her covers, reaching down to pull her legs around to the side of the

bed so she's sitting on the edge. She casts her eyes
around the room, then lets out a little squeal of frustration,
bunching up her fists and sticking her arms out like wings,
avoiding my gaze. I walk around, put my hands under her
armpits and, facing me but neither of us meeting eyes, she
lets me drag her to the bathroom. After I drag her back to
the bed and change her, she shoves my hands away and
reaches down to arrange her legs herself.

Downstairs is quiet. Grand must be back in her room,
because the door's closed tight and the TV is silent. I fill a
pot with water and set it on the stove, then notice a piece
of lined notebook paper folded on the table.

Ansel—

*Sorry to hear you're grounded and won't be able to
come to the show. It won't be the same without you. I've
made some killer prints of your slides and I'll put them up
with the rest of my stuff. Is it Mackenzie or McKenzie? I'll
ask your grandmother.*

*I'll send you a post card every now and then. You're
really talented, Ansel. I hope you get your hands on
another camera someday.*

All the best—

Lee

I smooth the note between my fingers, slide it into
my back pocket and walk over to the stove to pour the
oatmeal in, stirring and stirring, oats tumbling over each
other in the fast boil. I spoon a few dollops into each of
three bowls then tap on Grand's door, tell her breakfast's

on the table, and carry Izzy's bowl and mine upstairs. Izzy's expression has settled somewhere between disgust and petulance, and I set her tray on her lap, eat my oatmeal on the edge of my bed. After a while of staring at the wallpaper I hear Izzy's spoon clatter and I carry our bowls back downstairs.

Grand's in her new spot at the table, sitting up tall and tilted over the newspaper. She doesn't look at me as I scrub out the bowls, load them in the dishwasher, then go back upstairs.

Since Izzy's painting is done, I take it down and string up the third pillow-sized canvas and drag her over to the chair. There's a little stripe of blood on her t-shirt where the belt must have cut into her, so I readjust it to sit a little higher and strap her in. I try to arrange the paint tubes on the freshly-washed palette, but Izzy smacks my hand away so I crawl into bed, pull the covers over my shoulder and shut my eyes.

All the burdens of her body, too much
surface to protect and never any of it
retracting. How I hold myself weightless
inside, drawing up the soft parts into
the center of my knowing, too far inside
sometimes for anyone else to touch. But
she's always flush up against her skin, every
touch tender, tindering, setting flesh on fire.

Twenty-Two

Grand won't let me leave my room except to fix meals and by the fourth day of knocking at the back door that goes unanswered someone—Everett, it must be—stops trying. By the time three more days have passed I've scoured the bathroom grout with a toothbrush and cleaned out the medicine cabinet, scrubbing all the who-knows-how-old stains. There's nothing left to clean and it's Monday. Lee's show closes tonight. I make a rectangle with my fingers and frame a piece of the bureau mirror with a section of pink and yellow wallpaper. Draped over the mirror are dusty hair ribbons laddered with the plastic animal barrettes we used to wear, and tucked into the mirror frame is a picture of the four of us at Disneyworld, two mouse-ear-shaped balloons floating above Izzy and me. I get up and shift the picture to hang at more of a diagonal, then go back and check the vantage point from the bed. Now the photograph is too much in line with the diagonal rows of tulips on the wallpaper, so I tilt it the other way, then go back to the bed and see that it's about right. No way to know for sure without the camera.

Izzy is working so intently, her mouth tightened in a line of concentration, she seems to be projecting a force field around her. I take a long bath then pluck Izzy's copy of Emily Dickinson from the bedside table. My eyes run over the words but they're just a jumble of noise in my head, so I mutter two poems aloud to myself. They're still just sounds—does any of this actually make sense to anyone? I slide the book back onto the stack and make both our beds.

All we have in the fridge is half a jar of pickles and a bottle of mustard. I knock on Grand's door and after a long pause she says, "What?"

"Grand, we need groceries." Silence, and then the door opens and Grand strides out in a thick green dress, stockings, ropes of necklaces and heavy heels, her hair fluffed under a white chiffon scarf, her painted nails clutching the patent-leather pocketbook Izzy and I always used for dress-up.

"I'm aware, Ansel. That is precisely why I am going into Fort Harmon today. Carl Carson will be here shortly to pick me up." She brushes past me and I close her bedroom door, following her into the kitchen. She stands at the counter making a list and when I tell her I'm out of toothpaste and sanitary napkins she scowls at me but jots them down. Outside an engine sounds, there's a *clomp clomp* on the porch and a knock and, snapping her shopping list inside her pocketbook, Grand steps to the door. The younger Mr. Carson is standing there holding his hat and Grand tells me with a light smile that Clay will be staying while she's out, to make sure I don't go wandering. He inclines his round head to me sheepishly and steps inside as Grand marches out to the truck.

"Coffee, Mr. Carson?" I ask, as if I've invited him over for a little social call, and he says, yes please. I pour him a cup and go upstairs. The day crawls by with me lying on my bed staring at the ceiling and Izzy mucking around on her canvas. When the clock reads 4:00 I go downstairs to make sandwiches. Mr. Carson is reading the paper, but when I come into the kitchen he folds it over and leans back in his chair, watching me.

"I believe, if you were a boy, you'd resemble John near enough," he says.

"Who?"

"Your grandfather, Ansel. John Mackenzie." He stares at me in surprise, round eyes and a round nose on his round face. "Don't you remember your grandfather?"

"No." Suddenly it seems strange we've never talked about him after all these years of the Carsons driving me to school, but usually the two of them spend the hour-long drive planning the day's schedule, mulling over supply lists and possible jobs. The only times I've been alone with just one brother were the two or three days when the older Mr. Carson let me practice driving in the parking lot at the Fort Harmon mall after school. Mr. Carson scoots into the table and knits his fingers together. I take the jelly out of the fridge, set a knife on the counter, and suddenly I don't care what I say, so I ask. "How did it happen? My grandfather. How did he die?"

Mr. Carson keeps looking at his hands, but his breathing's steady and he strokes a thumb up and down over his finger. He clears his throat and says, "Don't you know that either?" like it's not really a question and he doesn't wait for me to answer before going on. "He had heart problems, Ansel. He had a heart attack one day on the jobsite. There wasn't nothing anybody could do."

"You were there?"

Mr. Carson looks up at me, his round blue eyes steady, expectant. He takes a gulp of coffee, then sits back in his chair and dangles his arms at his sides, like he's making his chest an easy target. "He worked for us." I nod, spreading peanut butter on three slices. "He was our friend. He told us he was taking his pills, but the doctor said he'd stopped. Damn fool. We never would have let him work if we'd of known." The silence stretches on and dimly, somewhere in the back of my mind it feels like a dark door is trying to creak open. I don't like what might be hiding in the quiet so I finish the sandwiches quickly and set one plate in front of him.

"PB & J—nothing fancy," I say. Mr. Carson says thank you, but no, stands up, and strides outside. He kicks the dirt like he's looking for something he dropped, then walks around the side of the house towards the garage.

I carry the sandwiches upstairs and sit down on my
bed to eat. The bandage on Izzy's hand is stained and
even though we have more in the medicine cabinet I go
downstairs and creak through the door to Grand's room.
In the bathroom the extra bandages are shoved in behind
a crusty bottle of cough syrup, beside the rows of identical
orange prescription bottles. A chill starts at the nape of
my neck, spreads across my shoulders, and I shut the
medicine cabinet quickly, walking briskly across the room
and back upstairs.

I keep my back to the canvas Izzy's dabbing at on
purpose, unwrapping the bandage on her right hand and
lightly, carefully, re-bandaging the scrapes where she
must have tried to catch herself when she fell. I stand
there, not ten inches from Izzy's face, smelling her faint
Izzy smell—tangy like urine, orangey and medicinal as
baby aspirin—and she stares past me like I'm not even the
tiniest obstruction, not even a pane of glass between her
and what she's seeing. I sit back down on my bed to finish
my sandwich and the door downstairs creaks open and
closed. Footsteps climb the stairs to our room and when
the door opens, it's Everett.

He's standing there with a triumphant ear-to-ear grin,
and then his gaze shifts from me to Izzy and his smile
freezes as a question crosses his eyes. Izzy turns very
slowly and the iciness she's been blowing at me seems to
evaporate when she looks over her shoulder. The sun is
glinting through the window, glowing in the fluffy cloud of

Izzy's white-blond hair, and Everett stands with his hand on the doorknob, caught in her light. He's wide-eyed, almost terrified, his mouth hanging open around no sound.

Then I'm flying across the room, my hands shoving at his shoulders, *out, get out,* but Everett's eyes have shifted to the painting and he pales and takes a step forward, gaping. I grab him by the shoulders, trying to twist him towards the door, but then I see the painting I've been avoiding seeing and freeze.

It's Everett. It's Everett floating in water with his eyes closed around a smile so beautiful it seems to hold the sun at its center. His brown hair floats in the green-blue water, but then I notice it's just his head, and below him in the blur is the rest of his body somehow severed bloodlessly from his neck, and deeper, blurrier, tangled up among his limbs is me, clinging all over like a leach. In the water behind his head, surfaced further towards the horizon, is the face of a sad-eyed Izzy, her hair wispy in the dusky light of the painting, her body a faint white blur below the water.

"Izzy, how…?" I start to tremble—how dare she, *how dare she?*—but Everett steps forward and Izzy reaches down to unbuckle the belt at her waist, then holds her arms out to him. Everett stares at her, flickers his gaze to me with a question in his eyes, but Izzy stretches further and when he takes a step towards her she reaches her hands up to his neck and pulls herself into his arms. Gaping, he gathers her clumsily, then turns towards me, silently, helplessly. I swallow, my hands shaking, and gesture jerkily towards the bed. Everett carries her over, lays her down, stands staring down at her with his hands on his hips, then tentatively picks up the plate with her sandwich and places it in her lap. Izzy beams a quiet, luminous smile, keeping her eyes on him as she takes a bite and chews and swallows and beams.

My breath jerking out of me in shudders, I can feel myself slowly disappearing behind the two of them, so I grab Everett and pull him towards the door. He cranes to glance back at Izzy as she takes birdy bites from her sandwich, and I drag him downstairs, pushing him towards the back door. The stunned blankness fades from his eyes and as his brow furrows he seems to regain his ability to speak. I'm saying, "Everett, go, just go, get out of here," but he plants his feet and won't budge.

"So, that's your sister, that's—"

"Yes, Izzy, now go, Everett, go."

"But I thought she was—"

"Paralyzed, I take care of her, I mean it, you need to leave." I ball my hands into fists and pound on his chest, trying to back him towards the door, but Everett grabs my hands as his eyes get foggy and far away.

"Izzy," he says, "and I'm in her painting." He flushes, something like awed horror sweeping across his face, and he drags his eyes up to look me right in the eye. "She's the painter?" he asks, and I start crying, hit him hard in the chest, shove him across the kitchen and out the door, shut it, lock it, sink to the floor and shake.

> *Why she kept me a secret and the out-there*
> *a secret from me: because separate, she*
> *can forget at any time one of her worlds.*
> *How at school she must have savored her*
> *singleness, our particular combination of*
> *wide eyes and pointy chin one-of-a-kind,*
> *her flesh only hers, and she a creature of*
> *her own invention. Then here, how she's*
> *always half an answer to an absence. But*
> *now, how his knowing dissolves her half-*
> *scaffolded life—dissolves her. How he sees*
> *through the scrim of her reading, painting*
> *persona—straight through to where I can't*
> *help but be.*

Twenty-Three

There's only one place to go so I go, my legs striding longer and longer beneath me, pounding faster and faster so I can barely get my feet under me I'm running so fast, tripping and stumbling out the door, past the garage where Mr. Carson's standing with his hands held out, then out and out, the dark in my chest gathering like a tide, tumbling and doubling. When I get to the hotel I sink behind a tree and listen to the polite chatter of waiters and hotel guests. I hide my eyes in my arms, breathe, swallow down everything and breathe. When my eyes are clear enough to fake a calm I get shakily to my feet, walk around to the main entrance, and ask the man at the front desk to dial Lee's room. She picks up after three rings.

"Hi. I came to see your show."

"Ansel? I thought you were grounded. Your grandmother seemed like she had you under lock and key—she wouldn't even let me say goodbye."

"I know. I am. Grounded. But I had to come."

Lee chuckles on the other end of the line, "Well, come on up, Houdini."

I hand the phone back to the concierge and walk through the cigar smoke and perfume-scented parlor to room 423. The door opens and Lee smirks at me, stepping aside to let me in. She's wearing a strappy black dress, her hair pulled back in a ballerina bun. All her bags are packed and piled by the door and the room's bare except for some receipts and wrappers on the bedside table, a toothbrush and tube of lipstick on the shelf above the sink.

"Your grandmother's not going to show up and make a scene, is she?" I shake my head. "She'll just wait till you get home and *then* incarcerate you until legal adulthood?"

I nod, avoiding her eye as I scan the emptied room. "So you're… not staying tonight?"

"Nah—I've got another show in New York in a few days, so I need to be there tomorrow to start hanging stuff. I'm leaving right after, driving through the night." She fixes me with a steady, gentle smile and puts a hand on my shoulder while I take deep breaths and concentrate on not crying. Giving my shoulder a squeeze, she says, "I'm guessing you need to borrow something to wear?" Now she's all breezy and efficient and I look down at my ratty t-shirt and flip-flops.

"Is it, you know, black tie?"

Lee laughs, unzips her suitcase, roots around, and pulls out a white sundress. "Hardly. Most people will probably wander through in their bathing suits, but it

simply doesn't do for the artists to look slouchy, dah-ling."
I take the dress from her and change in the bathroom. The
smocked elastic top pulls in enough to fit, and when I walk
back out Lee ties the strap behind my neck. Then she digs
a hairbrush out of her bag, brushes my hair back into a
smooth ponytail and fastens it with a rubber band.

"...The artists?"

"I told you I'd put your pictures up." I stare at her and
she gives me a little shove and smirks, "Just don't go
out-selling me, or we might have to rumble."

At 6:30 I help Lee carry her bags down to the jeep.
She drapes a blanket over all of the expensive camera
equipment and while she's busy in the trunk I quietly
unlock the passenger door. A little before seven we walk
through the dining room to the glassed-in conservatory on
the edge of the hotel. Lee looks like a different person—
smooth and sophisticated in strappy high heels and red
lipstick—and even her bouncy, tomboyish gait seems
streamlined. People are milling around with drinks or
standing in front of her large startling black and whites. I
walk up close to one picture in a corner and marvel at the
sharp lines, the sand like sugar rimming one sharp-focus
shell. Contrary to her bathing suit prediction, everyone is
dressed in sleek summer dresses and sports coats. Lee's
sharp laugh rings out above the low murmurs, and then
she steps across the room towards me, pulling the arm of
a short, balding man in a seersucker suit.

"Ansel Mackenzie, Nigel Fox. Nigel was just asking me about the theory behind your work." Mr. Fox stares at me, looking momentarily baffled, but recovers quickly and shakes my hand.

"Yes, Ms. Mackenzie, I was just asking Ms. Reeser if your work is an indictment of the sixties, evidence that the 'free love' experiment of the last decade was a failure, and that the plight of the modern-day housewife is really no different from that of the 1950s homemaker."

I watch his mouth move as Lee flashes me a mischievous grin, striking a mock quizzical look, the thumb of her fist hooked under her chin. There's a long pause. Lee tilts her head, asking, "Is that what you had in mind, Ansel?" and I say yeah, um—yes, that's about right.

"I'll just leave you two to talk shop," she says, retreating across the room to the entrance where Iain's just walked in. Dressed in a black dinner jacket and jeans, his wet hair brushed back, he looks somehow even more coarse and leathery than usual. As Mr. Fox leads me over to where my pictures are hanging, I crane around to see Lee step close to Iain and twine her fingers briefly in his. He stares at her with a stunned, slightly guarded look as Lee steps closer and whispers into his neck. Then the bodies shift so I can't see them and Lee's standing a few paces away talking to a tall woman with long white hair. Iain's picking out an hors d'oeuvre from an outstretched silver tray, popping one after another into his mouth. The waiter holding the tray is watching the people swirling around them, talking to Iain out of the corner of his mouth.

At ten o'clock the waiters start to clear the empty trays off the buffet table and the last few people trickle out, stopping at the door to chat with Lee. Iain's leaning against the wall behind her, his hands pocketed in his jacket, watching with a wry smile as the guests gush and gesticulate. When the last one leaves, Lee gives lets out a loud "whew!" and shoots me an exasperated look.

"Well, as predicted, Ansel outsold me tonight," she says, rooting in Iain's coat pocket and taking out a wad of bills. She gestures me over, counts out a wad of twenties, and holds it out to me between two fingers.

"What," I say.

"Take it."

"What?"

"Nigel Fox bought two of your prints. I priced them at $200 each—hope that's okay." I stare at the money and Lee shoves it in my hand, then counts out a few more bills and slides them inside Iain's breast pocket.

"What? No you don't, now…" he says, grabbing her hand and holding it.

"Managerial fee," Lee interrupts, "for helping me hang my stuff and take it down and for schlepping me from island to island all summer."

"Lee…" The way he whispers her name is so tender I have to look away.

"I don't want to hear it, Iain." She pulls a frame off the

wall and stacks it on a luggage trolley. Iain lays his fingers on his breast pocket, watching her suddenly brisk and jerky movements, then walks over to the other side of the room and takes down a picture to stack with the others. Lee ended up printing and hanging six of my kitchen pictures, not just the two I'd circled, and there are blank spots on the wall where the two that sold used to hang. I lift the four others off their hanging wires and carry them over to the cart.

"No, you keep them, Ansel. Lord knows this town needs some good art. You might get a chance to have another show someday, you never know." She keeps talking to fill the silence. "And keep the dress. It looks better on you anyway." Lee's voice is overly bright and she doesn't turn to look at me, just keeps taking down pictures and stacking them on the cart.

I don't know what to say. I mumble, "Okay. So, I guess… bye," and stare at my hands. Suddenly Lee sweeps over and squeezes me, planting a quick kiss on my temple before turning her back. I stand there a little longer watching her and, even though I know what I'm about to do, I say with contrived finality, "Thank you. For everything." Lee nods, flashes me a quick smile, and Iain holds out his hand.

"Ansel. Don't be a stranger."

"Oh, right. Yeah. Bye, Iain." I hold on to his hand a second too long and he pats my shoulder and turns, watching Lee shift things and fiddle. Grabbing the plastic sack of my clothes from behind the bar, I stop in the bathroom to change before walking out of the hotel and crossing the clipped lawn to the parking lot. The darkness in my chest expands, pulsing like a dark fog, and I swallow hard against the dizziness that's swirling inside my head. I don't think, just tell my body what to do as I open the passenger door of Lee's jeep and slide over the seatback to the trunk. Shifting her suitcase away from the back of the seat, I prop the four frames of my pictures below the back window, curl up on my side and flop the blanket back over everything, settling in, breathing, breathing, breathing, and not thinking.

After a while I hear voices and the trunk opens as Lee says, "Let's just slide them back here." The bags around me bump and move and then there's a pause. The blanket flips back, and Lee and Iain are blinking at me. "Ansel, what—" Lee says, as Iain lets out a long, low whistle, turns slowly from the jeep and walks away.

"Hi," I say. She stares at me, then reaches through the back to grab my arm and pull me, scrabbling, out of the back of her jeep.

"Hi. *Hi?* Ansel, please tell me, *please tell me* this isn't what it looks like."

I shrug. She gapes at me and mock-shrugs back and sputters.

"Nothing? You just planned on stowing away, letting me haul a minor across state lines without parental consent—*very much* without parental consent—not to mention what in God's name you were planning on doing once we got to New York, and all you've got to say is—" she shrugs.

"I can't stay here. I have to leave." I'm staring at my feet as my eyes well up, and Lee lets out a high scornful laugh.

"You. *You* have to. Ansel, I don't suppose you ever stopped to think about me—what kind of trouble I'd get into or how you'd royally fuck up my life."

I shake my head and know if I say anything the tears will slip out, so I just look at my toes and try not to sniffle. Lee stares, her hands on her hips, and after a minute she gets up, reaches inside the driver's side door and comes back, shoving a tissue at me. I snort, the tears gushing, wipe my nose, hiccup, and don't look at her.

"Jesus." Lee reaches behind me, slams the trunk, and slouches against the bumper. I sit next to her crying into the tissue and she puts her arm around my shoulder, sitting with me until I stop crying enough to talk.

"I'm sorry," I say. "I didn't think. I didn't think it would be a big deal. For you. I just—you don't know what it's like."

Lee wraps her other arm around me and pulls me into her chest. I let the tears jerk out of me, thinking of how Everett's eyes made me feel faceted, sparkling, and how he turned those eyes on Izzy and all the light left me. Thinking how all the wandering around in the world and toilet cleaning and sandwich-making and letting myself be touched has sapped me of some bright center that Izzy beams with and that Everett will see in her, not me. Thinking now all the light Izzy holds inside her leaves a dark hole the same size in my insides. And thinking, the only way to find a light of my own is to go, to get away from here, to run as far and fast as I can, the darkness trailing behind me like locomotive smoke.

When I catch my breath Lee retrieves the whole box of tissues so I can wipe my face. "Ansel, being a teenager… nobody ever said it was easy. I mean, it sucks. You couldn't *pay me* to go back to that time in my life." I can hear the smile in her words as she gives my ponytail a swing. "But you know… even though tonight's little disappearing act probably means you'll be grounded for the rest of the summer, it's not forever."

I nod, realizing suddenly that she hasn't heard what I've said, that she has no idea, can't possibly, no matter how much I want her to, or Izzy… and the thought drops hard into the center of my belly. I'm all alone. I'm all alone and no one can ever really know what any of this is like. Feeling the leaden weight of that idea holding me in place, I hand her back the box of tissues and stand, take a deep breath, wipe my nose and smooth my hair.

"Better?" she asks. I nod. "Okay. Now if you promise not to handcuff yourself to my car, I'll drive you home." She gives my shoulders a squeeze and I get in on the passenger side, buckle my seatbelt, and stare out the windshield. Lee backs up and drives down the service road towards the hotel, then pulls up in front of Iain's house. She puts the car in park, twists the engine off, and pockets the keys.

"I hope you don't know how to hot-wire." Her smile softens as she touches my arm, swings out of the jeep, and clomps up the porch, knocking on Iain's door before going in. The dark and cool seep in through the jeep window and the crickets open and close their squeaky hinges as the stars sharpen. Beyond the trees the waves are sweeping in, gently shushing, and for a second the darkness inside me feels balanced by the darkness outside and everything inside settles and stills.

The door opens and Lee clomps down the stairs. Iain follows her out as far as the threshold, standing in the doorway barefoot and shirtless, just a dark shadow against the light of his house. Lee's eyes are shiny as she gets in and pops the jeep in reverse without looking back. I turn around in my seat and watch Iain's silhouette until I can't see him anymore as Lee drives fast away from the hotel, then takes the sharp left onto the dirt road, bouncing along through the trees until she pulls up in front of the house. She leaves the engine running while I sit there a minute more.

"Okay," I say.

She reaches over and squeezes my arm. "It gets better. I promise." I nod and open the door. "Wait." Lee gets out, roots around in the trunk, and comes around to my side of the car, handing me the bag with the dress in it and leaning my pictures against my legs. When I crouch to pick them up she slips the camera around my neck. "You're on your own for film and developing."

I hold the camera—there's nothing to say. Lee gives me a quick hug, trots around to her side of the jeep, then backs up and turns, bouncing away down the dirt road, her headlights throwing haphazard tree-shadows until the jeep turns left onto the highway.

> *Would she leave me, the speed of her*
> *leaving a comet streaking, burning indis-*
> *criminately? Leave me, and cut any last*
> *thread of duty or affection connecting us,*
> *leave me beached in this bed in this house*
> *with no one to buy materials, no one to*
> *tend the petty demands of the body that,*
> *tended, allow me to hover here, fastening to*
> *canvas? How we can never be anything but*
> *two, now that each of us is shaken at the*
> *center, deadened, our armor cracked, the*
> *arrow of her leaving shot straight through,*
> *quivering in its mark.*

Twenty-Four

Tuesday, July 30, 1974

8 days

Mother is driving as she always does, the windshield
wipers thumping, and Izzy and I are playing I-spy where
you get no clues and only one guess. Father says
something and Mother's laughing, smacking the steering
wheel with the heel of her hand. She's laughing, and
because I know what's going to happen I look up, but
before I can tell her to pay attention the truck in the other
lane swings in front of us too close and clips the front of
the car. We turn in a screeching half circle then crash with
a sudden teeth-jarring smash and we're spinning inside
another squeal as my head knocks forward. The back seat
lifts up like a wave smashing Izzy and me into the front
seat as the horn blares and the whole car buckles. We're
spinning, the sound of metal scraping and sliding, the
smell of hot rubber and I'm screaming, looking, and then
I don't look. Then everything stops and is quiet and I let
myself drop into darkness. I float there for a long time until
voices drift in and someone is reaching over the twisted

metal, carefully lifting Izzy out piece by piece. Like mother and father in the front seat, she's broken neatly, all of them like marionettes—shattered wood, no blood. People are leaning in and plucking out their pieces and then there's silence and I'm trapped in the car all alone. I'm all alone and the silent air around me is so empty I'm screaming, *Don't forget me!* A man in puppet-maker clothes peeks in and looks at me, then shakes his head and ducks back out. *Hey!* I scream, and I can hear him telling someone, *She's all in one piece.* I scramble in my seat, but then a circus van with a red strobe light pulls up and all the broken pieces of mom and dad and Izzy are loaded on and I'm still screaming. *I go with them! Hey! I go with them!* but no one can hear me and the air around me is blank, wide open and I'm sitting in the middle of all that unmappable bright space spilling out around me in every direction, screaming.

It's light out still and the truck has been idling for a while. I hear Grand downstairs opening the back door and then heavy footsteps coming in, the door closing, the truck pulling off, leaving the house quiet. Izzy is staring at me when I open my eyes and I try not to feel the weight of her gaze as I throw my legs out of bed and pull on some shorts. Izzy pushes back her covers and reaches for her notepad, but I haul her to the bathroom, then deliver her back to bed clean and ready for the day before heading downstairs. The older Mr. Carson is standing by the window at the sink drinking a mug of coffee. Next to him, leaning against the cabinet, is a heavy wooden paddle drilled with neat holes and varnished to a hard shine.

A paddle, a paddle with holes, in this house, and the morning so quiet. Mr. Carson turns, but my legs won't move. His eyes meet mine and then he sees where I'm looking and steps in front of the paddle, holding out his hands.

"Now Ansel, that's just for show." His lips move but the words don't mean anything and he puts his cup down on the counter, taking a step towards me. I flinch away—my legs work again—and stumble backwards up the stairs. "Ansel." He's reaching out for me, his eyes locked on mine. "Now listen to me: I am not going to hit you. I will not raise a hand to you." I open my mouth and he steps forward, touches my shoulder. I look into his eyes and they're clear, so clear—he's not lying, he's not lying, please. "Now, my brother's under strict instructions to keep your grandma occupied for one hour. I think that gives us just enough time to go get an ice cream." His eyes are clear and bright as the inside of a drinking glass—no room to hide anything.

Everything goes out of my bones and I sit down hard on the stairs, burying my head in my arms. He stands with his hand on my shoulder, patting awkwardly. "Shoot, Ansel, I'm sorry. Didn't mean to scare you so. I should've left that thing outside, but your grandma, she wouldn't leave well enough alone. Kept calling and yelling about how you'd run off and she couldn't keep you under control no more. I just brought it for her to see—I never had any intention of using it on you. Hell, that wood's never even seen a backside. Clay drilled the holes when we were boys so it'd swing faster—for what I have no idea." I sit doubled over, my ears thundering, until I can breathe again and raise my head. "Now, I don't mean to rush you," Mr. Carson says, "but an hour's hard to come by in a town this size, especially if we're going to get a clear shot at Pauline's." I nod and slip on my flip-flops at the back door, but he's standing at the bottom of the stairs looking up. "Is Isabel attired?"

"Izzy?"

"I mean to take you both." I'm anxious to go now that I know Grand will be back, but Mr. Carson's climbing the first few steps already. I squeeze past him, rush upstairs, pull some shorts out of the dresser, and yank back Izzy's covers, trying not to touch her with my eyes. I hardly ever dress her in normal clothes, just nightgowns and old t-shirts of our father's, and the waist of my shorts float around her stomach. When I pull her to a sitting position, they slip down and hang precariously on her hipbones, the top of her diaper peeking out. I grab the belt off the chair and cinch it around her waist, not bothering with the belt loops, and call down to Mr. Carson. He tap-taps on the door with one knuckle as he comes in.

"We all ready then?" Izzy's been smiling at me like I'm half-crazy the whole time I was dressing her, but now her smile quavers and she turns her eyes to me.

"He's taking us for ice cream," Izzy's smile freezes as she slowly shakes her head. "Izzy's scared of outside," I say, staring hard at the yellow tulips on the wallpaper.

Mr. Carson sighs and steps farther into the room. "But there's nothing to be scared of, Miss Isabel. We're just going to take you to town." Izzy's shaking her head furiously, her eyes starting to well, and when I reach for her she bats my hands away, letting out a sound like a scared rabbit. Mr. Carson sighs, looks at his watch, and rubs his forehead. "Have it your way, then—no time for arguing. Ansel?"

"Just a second," I say, following him downstairs. The dark door in the back of my mind has creaked open a little further and I think I've figured out a way to peek inside. I duck into Grand's bathroom and grab an orange bottle from the medicine cabinet, then carry it with shaking fingers into the kitchen. I open the bottle, pour out two aspirin, set the bottle down on the counter where Mr. Carson can see it, then cross to the cabinet and pour myself a slow glass of water. Mr. Carson picks up the bottle and I stare hard out the window, concentrating on keeping my voice steady. "It looks like a prescription but it's not," I say, glancing back to read his expression. "Grand just keeps the aspirin in these bottles."

I down the aspirin with two hard gulps of water as Mr. Carson tilts his head to one side, turning the bottle over slowly so he can read the label. His brow furrows as he unscrews the cap and pours some aspirin out into his palm.

"These aren't your granddad's old heart pills?"

"I guess they look like them, but no," I say. "Grand says aspirin's the best medicine."

He stares at me for a long beat, then looks down at his hand, tips the pills back in the bottle and twists on the cap. "Where'd you get these from?" My heart is hammering as I take him into the bathroom, open the medicine cabinet and point to the dozen or so bottles lined up side by side. Mr. Carson stares, grabs another bottle at random and pours the pills into his palm, then tilts them back in, twisting the bottle closed and setting it back in its row. Slowly, he turns each bottle so he can read the labels side by side, all exactly the same: *John Mackenzie. Reserpine. .2 mg. Take one tablet orally twice daily.* He stands with his hands on his hips staring at the open cabinet. "And how long has she kept the aspirin in them bottles?"

"Forever," I say. "As long as I can remember."

Mr. Carson nods and palms a bottle. He gently closes the cabinet door, then turns quickly and leaves the house. He's walking so fast I have to jump down the back porch steps to keep up, jogging alongside his long strides, my head airy with realizing it's maybe as bad as I thought— the aspirin—but I want to hear him say it.

"Mr. Carson? You okay?"

He gives a stiff nod, his hand clenched tight around

the bottle. He looks at it again and then shoves it in his pocket

"You ever met a Mr. Barker, Ansel?"

"Mr. Barker?"

"Lawyer-type, big city. Maybe he's been around to see your gramma sometimes, get her to sign some papers?"

"No."

Mr. Carson stops suddenly and looks at me hard. "A Mr. Barker. A Mr. Bob Barker?"

The laugh bursts out of me with all my pent-up nervousness and I catch myself as Mr. Carson's face hardens. "Mr. Carson, I'm sorry but… are you serious?"

"I'm serious as a *heart-attack*, Ansel," and he says the words like they're code. "Your gramma doesn't have a whole lot of papers lying around from a lawyer named Barker?"

"Mr. Carson, um, don't you ever watch TV? Bob Barker is the host of *The Price is Right*. He's not a lawyer—sorry."

Mr. Carson squints at me, shifting his jaw. "So you've never met a lawyer round your gramma's place? She never has any visitors? Never gets any important mail?"

"No, sir. Not that I know of."

Mr. Carson mulls this over, tensing and loosening his jaw, then gives a stiff nod and glances at his watch. "Thirty-nine minutes. Might have to get these cones to go."

We loop down the dirt road and follow the straightaway into town, passing Red's garage. I'm out of breath when we get to Pauline's but Mr. Carson walks right in and steps up to the counter. Pauline brings us two menus and winks at me, but Mr. Carson shakes his head.

"Picking them a little young these days, aren't you Carl?"

"We're in a hurry here, Pauline, so if you could give us three cones to go, hold the humor, I'd appreciate it." He's standing stiffly, his hands hanging at his side. Pauline's eyes widen and she purses her lips as she turns on her heel.

"Well, soooorry. Ansel, come pick out your flavor." I follow Pauline through the swinging waitress doors to the storeroom where the freezer opens with a loud buzz. She hands me a cake cone with a crooked scoop of vanilla, then leans over the cardboard barrel of ice cream, pats another scoop onto a cone and hands it out to me.

"And one chocolate," I say. Pauline nods, dips the scoop into a bucket of water, grabs another cone from the dispenser on the wall and leans in for the chocolate.

"Like it'd kill the man to stop and have a laugh once in a while," she mutters, dropping the scoop back in the water bucket and slapping the freezer lid closed. I hold the shutter door open for her as she hustles out and hands Mr. Carson a cone. The bills are already laid out on the counter and she turns to the register as we head for the door. "Don't you want your change?"

"Don't have time for change," he says, and before the door swings shut I hear her say, "Ain't that the truth."

Mr. Carson trades me the chocolate and takes the other vanilla from me. I'm licking and walking as fast as I can, eating between huffs and puffs. "What'll—happen if Grand—gets home—before us?" I ask between gasps.

"Well, I don't know. Maybe nothing. To tell you the truth, I don't know what's what just now." He takes big bites of his ice cream, his eyes trained on the hill home. "All the same, you make sure to wipe you and Isabel's faces clean, and remember to walk like you've got a hitch in your britches for the next few days." He strides up the hill, his eyes darting the length of the yard, and in a few great strides he's across it, holding the back door open for me. "Same time next week, Ansel?" He hands me up Izzy's cone, his hand sticky with yellow drips.

"Yes sir."

"Fine then. It's a date." We step into the kitchen. I start to take Izzy's cone up to her but I stop and look at him, at his kind eyes the color of sea glass, at the sturdy slope of his wide shoulders.

"Thank you," I say. He flinches, seems to shrink a little, and shrugs. "Wish there was more I could do for you, Ansel, but you see, your Grand, she kinda likes things done her own way. Clay and I told her Isabel needed that home nurse to come back a few years ago and—well. She didn't like it. Told us to stop meddling and stop coming by unless she called, else she'd sick that lawyer of hers on us." He pops the last bite of cone into his mouth, then swipes his dry hand over his lips and wipes it on the seat of his pants.

"Why didn't she like you meddling?"

He shrugs and looks away out the kitchen window, his hands in his pockets. "I don't like to speculate about other people's goings ons. I guess, she being a nurse and all, she figured—"

"Grand? A nurse?" I remember Mrs. Jorgen and Mrs. Sibley saying something about a nurse but I never thought they meant Grand.

"Well sure. Did real well for herself during the war. Your granddad was away fighting and she joined up. None of us could believe it—Ailene Calvert, never so much as a smudge on her gloves and all of a sudden she comes back decorated like a general. Still crisp as a dollar bill in her uniform, not one hair out of place." He's staring at the floor, pushing at a tear in the linoleum with the toe of his boot, and then his brow furrows and he looks up at me. "But you must've known she was a nurse, Ansel. The early years, when she was the one tending your sister, and all the ways she must have taught you to care for Isabel."

"What early years?"

"Why, when you two were fresh out of the hospital."

I shake my head. He swallows, shifts his weight, puts his hands on the small of his back and leans over to look me straight in the eye. "You mean to tell me... well, who's been caring for you two all this time?"

I shrug. "We don't really need much. I always knew how to make sandwiches, and now I can make eggs and soup and all kinds of things."

Mr. Carson is squinting, staring at me hard. "Well, she surely taught you how to…" He shakes his head, looks around, and his voice falters.

"Izzy got an infection once and the doctor showed me how to change her catheter. I don't remember Grand teaching me anything."

At the sudden sound of a motor in the driveway Mr. Carson jerks around, gives me a quick push towards the stairs. "Get that ice cream out of sight, now remember."

"Mr. Carson?"

"What, Ansel?" The truck door slams and I can see through the window as the younger Mr. Carson walks around to Grand's side and opens up.

"Could you get me some rolls of film?"

"Film?"

"For my camera, black and white, thirty-five millimeter." Grand and Mr. Carson are walking towards the house.

"Fine, I'll get you some, now go on."

I scurry upstairs and shut the door behind me. When I hand Izzy the almost all-melted cone of drippy yellow cream she wrinkles her nose and pushes my hand away. I hurry into the bathroom and dump the ice cream in the sink, burying the cone in the garbage and rinsing my face. Downstairs Grand and Mr. Carson are talking.

"—well, Ailene, I'm not gonna paddle that girl again—I don't care what she does. I'll stay with her when you go out, but a girl of almost sixteen—it's not right." I can't hear what Grand says, but the tone is soft and cooing, and then the back door shuts, the truck guns, and the door to Grand's room closes.

How even after the accident we used to
look at each other: matter-of-fact reflection,
gaze that hides nothing. Now her eyes
graze me, harried with hurry, the shame of
my sometimes insufficient tending revealed,
bared to his scrutiny. She has done all she
can, I should tell him. She has done all I'll
allow. I am not this body. I am not the fluids
I ooze with and consume. She allows me
to forget how others see me, allows me to
forget how the out-there and everyone in it
sees only surfaces.

what is
Izzy hiding?

Twenty-Five

"There's a young man at the door." Grand's standing in the doorway still gussied in her town clothes, her face done up in bright shades.

"Oh." I sit up on the bed and smooth a hand over my hair where the pillow bunched it up on one side. "I thought I wasn't allowed to have any visitors."

"You're not. He's here to see Isabel."

Izzy's been painting, ignoring us, but now her face lights up and she looks at me. She points to the bathroom and makes a mother cat gesture—pretending to lick her hand to dab the paint off of her face. I act like I don't understand what she wants and say, "And is Izzy allowed to have visitors?"

Grand's lips tighten and she sets her jaw. "Someone told that boy about your sister. Whatever happens, it won't be my fault."

Izzy stops miming washing her face and turns to meet my eye as Grand wheels on her heel and stomps downstairs. The words hang in the air and then there's a *tap ta-tap* at the door. Everett's standing there stonily, hands jammed in his pockets.

"Hi." He's staring at me hard, but Izzy's beaming at him, the long-handled paintbrush in her lap smearing her t-shirt beige, and when he glances sideways at her his shoulders soften.

"Hi," I say. "Nice of you to pay *me* a visit."

Everett sighs heavily and rolls his eyes. "I had to tell your grandmother I was here to see your sister or she wouldn't let me in."

"Okay. So you're *not* here to see her?" Izzy's smile never falters as Everett sets his jaw, looks down at the floor and shrugs. He glances up at me again but then his eye catches on something in Izzy's painting and he takes a step closer to look.

It's the same painting—Izzy's just been adding paint over the top of what was there, blending the shadows and contours on Everett's face so they're softer, rounder, less like paint on a flat canvas. She touches his shoulder and he steps in even closer, both of them cozied around the painting. "This is... I've never..."

I snort and brush past them, stomp downstairs to yank open the refrigerator and stare in. Upstairs I hear Izzy's chair slide back, the water running, and when I go back up to the room she's propped up on her bed, furiously scrubbing her cheek with a washcloth beside a smear of blue paint. Everett points, but still she misses, and he

tentatively takes the washcloth and cleans her cheek with
a few quick swipes. Everett's head tilts to one side and
when I slam the door behind me he breaks their trance
of eye contact, then steps into the bathroom to rinse the
washcloth. He clears his throat, fiddling the washcloth flat
on the edge of the sink and says, "Your sister's hungry."

"How do you know?"

"She told me."

Izzy's smiling shyly, knitting her fingers together and
glancing up at Everett. I look around for her notepad and
see it's still on the easel next to her paints, flipped to a
blank page.

"She *told* you?"

"Yeah."

"What do you mean, 'she told you'?" He lifts his
eyes to me and suddenly Izzy's smile falters, her brow
furrowing. "You mean she spoke," I say. "Out loud. Words.
To you."

He stops smoothing the washcloth and stares at me,
wondering. "Yeah...?"

All the air in the room hits me hard in the chest, the
lurking shadows rushing at me from all corners. "Izzy," I
whisper, my blood coursing, acidic in my veins, and she
folds her arms, won't meet my eye. My head is swimming,
I could fall over with dizziness but I find the words, "What
else did she say?"

Everett sputters and Izzy stares at her footboard with
a steady, defiant glare. "She just..." he swallows, shifts his

weight from foot to foot, shrugs, and mutters, "Well, she sort of… basically, she said she's been… waiting for me." Splotches of red stain his neck and cheeks, but when he looks up he sets his jaw and directs his gaze at the wall.

The words thud into me and I nod jerkily, my voice coming out in a squeak. "I'll go make us some sandwiches."

Downstairs I yank open the refrigerator door again, grab the bologna and white bread, smack a piece of bologna between two pieces, repeat, then plop both sandwiches right on the dirty breakfast tray. I take my time smearing mayo and mustard on two more pieces and add the bologna before cutting the sandwich neatly in half, arranging it on a plate and carrying all of it upstairs. I drop the tray at the foot of Izzy's bed, then grab the plate and curl up against my headboard to eat my sandwich. Everett's crouched beside Izzy's bed swiping at her hands with a sudsy washcloth, and when all the paint's scrubbed off he goes back to the sink, rinses, comes back and wipes her hands again, then blots them dry with a hand towel. Izzy's sitting perfectly still, holding her hands palm up like the statue of a saint, and Everett picks up one bare sandwich, placing it in Izzy's hands. "Aren't you going to feed her?"

Izzy shoots me a withering glare as Everett takes a bit of the other sandwich, muttering, "I think she can do that herself."

"You sure about that? What about going to the bathroom? Did Izzy say anything about that? Did she tell you she needs her diaper changed twice a day?"

Everett stops chewing and pulls his eyebrows together, but Izzy takes off the top slice of her bread and throws it at me. It lands with a smack on the floor.

"Missed. You missed me, Izzy."

She lets out a shriek and Everett backs up against the bedside table as she throws the bologna, then the bread, both of which fly over my shoulder and land on my pillow. "Missed me again." I keep eating, Everett gaping, glancing between the two of us as I pop the last bite of sandwich into my mouth. I calmly peel the slice of bologna off my pillow, pick up the two pieces of bread, walk around to the bathroom, and throw them away. "If you decide you want another sandwich, you'll have to ask your new little friend to make it for you, Izzy." I stand up straight and look at them both like they're just children, not even worth a minute of my time, then turn on my heel and concentrate hard on not stomping downstairs and outside.

> *Hardly a betrayal. That day in the hospital*
> *when the words came out garbled, if only*
> *she had heard what I meant to say, had*
> *spoken for me instead of stepping back,*
> *letting those doctors declare me damaged.*
> *Then that first month here, the absence of*
> *mother and father all I could feel, I spent*
> *every minute fastening to this half-unfeeling,*
> *inhabitable numbness, weighing myself*

down against the helium of grief. I never
stopped calling out to her. It was she who
released me, severed the always-binding-us
tie. I know even now the words coming out
of my mouth won't align, gibberish pushing
her farther away from me and any shared
sense. But he reads Dickinson, listens with
a mind that can hear through the gushing
tumble, receives everything I say, takes it
in, follows each mismatched word up rungs
of understanding. How can she not see—a
deeper betrayal were I to write to him—to
let him hear inside his head the sound of my
true thinking only she should hear. Speech
is only one symptom of affection—silence
the stronger. I speak to him with my body
because he is outside of me enough to
need it, kin enough to comprehend. And we
might need him. Something is happening
that neither of us can control.

I pound and pound on Iain's door, but the windows
are dark, the door locked tight, so I loop around behind
the hotel to the pier and walk out to the edge. The sky is
slate, the wind thin and icy here next to the water, so there
can't be too many people paying for boat rides. I walk
back around towards Iain's house then keep walking along
the beach to where the docks are jostling with anchored

sailboats, sails strapped down and spindly masts jabbing the sky as the boats bob. Finally I see him, sitting in his boat, tinkering with the motor.

"Iain."

His eyes are muddy and flat when he turns around and they take a second to register me. "Oh, Ansel. Hello."

"You said to come by." He nods, messy curls falling over his forehead, then pats a seat and goes back to clanking around the propeller. I climb in and sit down, watching his knuckly, tan fingers slide inside a crevice to pull out a clump of seaweed. He flicks it overboard then wipes down the propeller edges with a rag, his hands making strong, smooth circles over the blades. I reach across to the cooler, flip open the lid and pull out a beer. "Want one?"

"No, thanks." He doesn't look up, so I pop off the top with the bottle opener and stretch out my legs on the other seat, leaning back and gulping down a big swig. Iain puts the rag down, clears his throat, and I can feel the wide pools of his eyes focused on me.

"You know, Ansel. I think you're a little young for that particular bevvy."

"You let me have one before."

"Yeah, but…" He looks at his hands, licks a knuckle, and tries to rub the grease from the crease. "That was before, you see. I wasn't—I was a bit out of my head."

"Well, maybe I'm a bit out of my head." I try to say it in a low, grown-up voice, scooting forward to touch his hand. He stands up suddenly and looks down at me, his muddy eyes sharpening.

"Ansel. Give me the bottle." He holds out his hand and I stand up, hide it behind me, walk up close against him.

"Take it, if you want it." There's a pause, and he seems to retract behind his eyes as his mouth tightens. He shakes his head and walks around to the motor again, turning his back to me and picking up the wrench to tighten a few screws. He wipes them with the rag and tilts the motor back down into the water.

"It was good to see you, Ansel."

"Yeah, well, I'm still here."

He puts the wrench down to turn all the way around and his hangdog face seems to lengthen, growing even sadder as he looks me hard in the eye. "I think you'd better go."

I swallow thickly, take a big gulp of beer, my eyes brimming, and all the blustering darkness of no one wanting me presses up against my skin so hard I want to scream, to hit someone, to tear someone or something into tiny bits, tinier and tinier until there's nothing left that I've ever loved or wanted or known. Shaking, I peel the label off the bottle, take another gulp, and because he's still silent, staring me down I say, "Lee's not coming back."

Iain stares at me for a long time, then reaches out and takes the bottle gently from my hands. "You come back sometime when you *are* right in the head. That nice girl I took out in the boat a few weeks ago—you tell her she's welcome anytime." My eyes spill over as I scramble out onto the dock and start running.

By the time I reach the fort, unroll the sleeping bag and crawl in, it's started to rain. The branches and leaves make a tattered umbrella where occasionally one fat drop falls through. The sky darkens to granite and pours forth harder as I pull the tarp over me, curling on my side and listening to the hard fast smacks of rain. Thunder rumbles far off and I think of Lee, of how she can make anyone want her by not wanting anyone.

I squeeze my eyes shut and imagine myself far away in a sweltering rainforest, brightly striped snakes coiling branches, monkeys chattering and swinging between trees, and all around me the million blinking eyes of knob-fingered bush babies straight out of my science book. I'm a famous photographer, standing under a tent in safari shorts and heavy boots, my face covered with the net of my pith helmet, but the face behind the net isn't my face, it's Lee's, and I remember her sitting on the edge of Iain's table—his hands cupping her jaw, his jaw hinging again and again when he kissed her, gulping her like a dying man swallowing water. And then they're not Iain's hands but Everett's—long and bony and white—and they're lifting to Izzy's face, cradling her head like a drooping rose. He dips his face to hers and they kiss and I squeeze my eyes shut harder, trying to think back to the jungle and the bush babies' big eyes, blinking.

Twenty-Six

The rain has stopped when someone is suddenly rustling into the fort and shaking me awake.

"Ansel." It's Everett, and in the light of his flashlight I see he's gotten his hands and knees muddy crawling in. "Your grandmother wants you to come home."

I sigh, sitting up and smoothing my hair out of my face, and Everett folds his arms, props them on top of his knees, looks at me, then looks away.

"So. Here we are…" I say, gesturing around at the branches, and Everett stares harder at the ground, picks up a twig and starts digging with it in the packed sand.

"You should have told me about your sister."

"Why?"

"Because you lied to me."

"No, I didn't. I just didn't bring her up."

"You told me she died in a car crash!"

"*You* said Liza Seeley told you she died with my parents. You did the talking. Not me. I just didn't correct

223

you."

"Ansel! It's the same thing!" He breaks the twig in half, throwing part of it at the branches as I slip out of the sleeping bag, roll it up, and sit down next to him on the tarp. He shifts away and I say before I can stop myself, "So, what—you hate me now?"

"No, I just..." he furrows his brow and starts peeling the bark off the remainder of the twig. "She isn't the only thing you lied to me about, okay? You should have told me you didn't paint. And—do you even like Dickinson? No—that's her. The art books, that's her, too. I mean, God, it's like everything I thought—"

"What difference does it make? You should have told me all kinds of stuff, like how your mom's never around and how you'd like me a lot better if I was some crazy, crippled mute!"

Everett throws the stick down, grabs his flashlight and starts to crawl out. When I catch his leg, he doesn't jerk away but doesn't come back—just stops halfway into the hole of the opening.

"Everett, please. I just wish you'd kiss me and tell me you still like me."

My voice catches, I can't help it, but when he crawls back in my eyes are dry. He sits down next to me on the tarp and stiffly puts his arm around me. I curl into him, breathing on his neck and kissing his collar-bone until his whole body softens. I smear my mouth along the vein on his neck and he shudders, drops his mouth to mine, and it's like we're starving—kissing and touching. His hand slips under my shirt and as I grab his wrist, push his hand down my shorts as he moans and bites me though my shirt. I pull my shirt off so his mouth can find me and wrap my arms around his head, rocking against his hand, sick with how much I need this rocking faster and faster until I arch with the breaking point and then his hand is fumbling with his shorts and I wrap around him and we rock, holding on as hard as we can until he cries out, falls against me. I hold him tight, trying to feel every inch of his skin against mine and wanting this touching with every cell.

He lies against me breathing until his breath is slow and even, then pulls away. When we put our clothes on and crawl out, Everett holds the flashlight and I pull his arm over my shoulder as we silently cross the highway. We're quiet for the twenty minute walk through the moonlit trees, but when we come up to the house he glances up at our room, tugs loose and shrugs away from me. My breath freezes, heavy in my chest, then heats to a quick simmer and I swallow hard to keep from feeling sick. There's nothing I can do to keep him.

"I'll stop by tomorrow," he says.

"Yeah, I might be busy, " I say. "Izzy might have more time for you these days." He stares at me, the shock of my words slowly tightening his face, and then his pale eyes flicker back up to the yellow curtain. He furrows his brow, kicks at the sand, and starts to say something. Blinking quickly, he steadies his gaze, looks away, nods and walks off towards town.

When I open the back door a paper bag holding three rolls of film falls out on my feet. I step inside, hiding the bag behind me, and Grand is standing at the stove in her floral housedress and grimy slippers cooking hamburger. "Well, hello."

"Hi."

She turns back to the stove and flips three burgers over, then scoops one patty on her spatula, walks over to the trashcan, steps on the pedal to open the lid, and drops it in.

"There's your dinner."

I don't say anything, and she walks around me to get two plates out of the cabinet, then two buns, lettuce, and pickles out of the refrigerator to build the hamburgers. She turns off the stove, carries one plate into the living room, sets it on the couch, and carries the other upstairs. I look at the trashcan, then pick up the bag and wait until I hear Grand come back downstairs.

Izzy's propped up against the headboard eating her hamburger and when I meet her gaze her eyes widen. She scans my hair and my mouth and then points to something on my neck. I look down to see my shirt's on backwards, inside out, and Izzy's pointing at the tag. I blush as I pull my arms in the sleeves to turn my shirt around, and Izzy puts her hamburger down, pushes the plate onto the floor with a crash. She pulls her legs over so she can turn on her side and sinks low into the covers as the pieces of plate rattle and come to a stop.

I pick up the plucuc, dump them with the last bite of hamburger in the trashcan, and get some toilet paper to wipe up the mustard and ketchup smears. Then I pull the camera out from under the bed and pour the film out of the bag onto the blanket. I open the roll of 400 B&W, load it, cock the camera so the film's pulled taut, and close the back, then train the lens around the room, stopping on the folds of Izzy's blanket, peaked and shadowed like an aerial view of mountain ranges. Stepping closer, I focus on the back of Izzy's head, on her shoulder and the hillocks and gulleys of the blanket and how they lock into place as I press the button with a quick click.

I swallow against the tightness in my throat and walk around to the other side of the bed. Izzy eyes me and the camera, a question flickering across her forehead. I focus on her hand on the sheet, on the overlapping stains of paint, stepping closer so I'm bearing down on her with the lens, on the lines of her fingers and map of paint colors rubbed into her skin against the white of the sheet. The shutter clicks a little too slowly, so I turn on the lamp and unscrew the shade. Izzy jerks her hand to her eyes, squints, and I step closer as she covers her face with both hands. My throat is burning and I wish I had a telephoto lens to zoom in even closer, focusing on the crossed line of her paint-smudged arms. Click, click.

Izzy grunts, pulls the pillow out from under her head

and tries to shield herself from the camera.

"What is it? Do you want something? Why don't you tell me, Izzy? Just tell me what you want." My voice starts to shake and I step closer, take a picture of the edge of the pillow and her eye behind it, the side of her mouth, her hair. She tries to pull the covers over her head, but I yank the blankets off, baring her to the chill, and click away on her pale, crooked legs as my eyes start to blur behind the viewfinder. Somewhere in this body is someone I used to know, someone who knew me from the inside looking out, and I bear down on her with the camera as if the lens is a microscope that can get me back inside.

Izzy grunts again and I'm crying, forcing out the words, "What's that? Sorry, can't hear you. You'll need to speak up." She shakes her head and hugs herself, shifts away from me, but the tears make me immune behind the lens of the camera. She can pull away from me all she wants, and I can't feel it. If the camera can't help me slip back inside her then I'll stay on the surface, record what there is to be seen in her left eye, the angles of her mouth and white-blond eyebrows aligning in the frame of the viewfinder.

My breath catches and I'm gasping, sobbing, the distance between the two of us vast as galaxies. Izzy turns to look at me sharply, tries to catch the strap to pull the camera away, but I keep it clasped against my face like a mask. "Want this? Just say so, Izzy. You're so talkative these days." She watches me, wondering, shaking her head slowly, then reaches down to move her legs, and buries her face in the mattress. I click away on the faint stains at the back of her hitched up nightgown, on the bedsore scars where I failed to care for her, and I keep clicking until the whole roll of film is used up.

> *How gravity fastens more to her live body*
> *than mine, how she pulls him to her like*
> *seed to plowed ground. No matter how his*
> *mind aligns with mine, it's the slotting of*
> *bodies he can't resist; she the undertow of*
> *a black hole, me the faint tug of a star.*

Twenty-Seven

Wednesday, July 31, 1974
7 days

It's early, but Grand is already seated at the table in a
tight, steel blue dress, her feet shoved into thick-heeled,
heavy shoes. I'm hollowed out from crying during the
night and I go through the motions of pouring milk over
two bowls of cornflakes and carrying them upstairs. When
I come back down Grand's flipping through a cookbook
and doesn't look up.

"Need anything from town?" I ask.

She clears her throat and puts her pen down
purposefully, taking a slow sip of her coffee. "I was under
the impression you're still grounded."

"Hunh," I say, pulling my sweatshirt from the back of
the other chair. All of the darkness inside numbs me like a
fog, and the words find my lips before I can think. "I was
under the impression you don't care what happens to me
or Izzy." Grand goes rigid, and the words keep coming,
I don't care, I don't care, and before I can think they're
forcing their way out into the room: "Did you mean to kill

grandfather?"

The air stands still, blood roaring in my ears. Grand inhales quickly and stands, takes two steps towards me and stops, the light in her eyes flashing then sucking down inside her like flame into dark coals. "How could you say such a thing," she seethes, her mouth quivering. "How dare you."

I stand there waiting for her hands to find my skin, my body so unfeeling the effort to move or shut my mouth is exhausting, and then a slow burn starts in my gut, the only thing I can feel as the words rise warm to my lips. "See, I was just wondering if you switched his heart medication with aspirin because you *wanted* him to die, or if you were just too cheap to keep filling his prescription."

My heart floods with hot, hammering blood, and Grand turns back to the counter, rubs a napkin over the edge of the sink with shaking hands. "You don't know the first thing about me," she says. "You and all the rest of this town. These doctors—they get paid by big drug companies to prescribe those stupid pills. Did you know that? Aspirin is just as good. Everyone knows that. Aspirin is just as good." She laughs, and looks out the window, shaking her head. "You don't know the first thing."

"Well, I know I'm not giving Izzy any more of your *aspirin,*" I say. The fog has burned off inside me and I'm standing in front of Grand, steady on my feet. "Izzy is my sister. She's mine to take care of. If she needs a doctor, I'm getting her one."

Grand turns to me quickly, her eyes glinting, triumphant. "Oh, you do that."

"What?"

She smiles broadly at me, looking me dead in the eye. "You call the doctor. Maybe he'll come out and decide she needs better care. Maybe he'll decide you need somewhere else to live, too. He'll arrange for that. But you can bet no one will be able to care for both of you—one of you a cripple and the other a delinquent. I'll tell that doctor why it's been so hard to take care of your sister—how you won't let me near her, how *she* won't let me near her, and Isabel half out of her head. There are places for the two of you. There are places where they can *put* you."

Grand steps across to the stove and pours herself a slow cup of coffee, takes a sip and looks back at me. "But I believe you were on your way out," she says, and my knees start to shake, I push through the back door, smack down the stairs, then take off running and crest the hill down into town. The image of Grand's eyes unfurls inside me like a dark rose and I keep running, only stopping when I see Everett's bike leaning against the light pole in front of the library. I push through the library door and walk the center row, looking down all the aisles.

"Need help finding something?" Mrs. Hammond asks, glancing up from her crossword puzzle.

"Is Everett Lloyd here?"

"He was waiting by the door when I got here this morning. Checked out a book and went across to

Pauline's, I think." She points across the street with her pencil.

I nod and step outside. The handlebars of his bike glint in the mid-morning sun and the warming street smells like sticky tar. When I push through the door to Pauline's, Everett is the first thing I see, hunched over a book behind an empty plate smeary with egg yolk. I step up close behind him and touch the nape of his neck. "Hey," I say, the word bursting from me too loud, and Everett startles, then turns his attention back to his book.

"Hi."

I stand there jittery, waiting for him to look at me, then slide onto the stool next to him as Pauline glances up from the end of the counter. She finishes jotting down the trucker's order, tops off his coffee, and cracks two eggs on the stovetop before stepping over to me.

"You want your breakfast usual or your lunch usual, Ansel?" I catch my breath, try to keep my voice steady and cheerful as I tell her just a hot chocolate would be great. She grins, looks between Everett and me and gives me a hard wink as she turns. I peek over Everett's shoulder at what he's reading, but he furrows his brow, marks his place with a straw wrapper, and closes the book back cover up. He takes a swig of hot chocolate, scrapes his fork over the last of the egg yolk.

"What are you reading?"

"A book."

"Yeah, I know," I say, and Pauline sets my hot

chocolate down with a big smile. I try to make my voice brighter as she walks away. "What's the book about?"

Everett clatters his fork, pushes his plate away. "It's just a biography of this artist."

Pauline glances over at us as she slides the trucker's eggs onto a plate and I put my elbow on the counter, turning my shoulder so she can't see my face. "I like art. I took Mrs. Lynch's art appreciation class last year. Who's the artist?" Everett sighs, pushing the book across to me so I can flip it over to read the title. "Oh, Chagall," I say, making sure to pronounce the name right: *shu-GAHL*. "I like him." Everett nods, then slides the book back around to the other side of his plate and drops it inside the messenger bag at his feet.

"Isabel wanted me to read some of it to her today."

"Oh." I take a deep breath and make my voice cheery. "Well, that's nice of you. I just need to drop off some film, and then you can give me a ride home." He nods, his face blank as he stands up and slings his bag over his shoulder. I chug the last of my hot chocolate, drop some change on the counter and wave to Pauline. Everett's already across the road righting his bike when I jog over and he squeezes the brake handles a few times before starting off down the street. I'm walking fast to keep up with him as we turn the corner, pass the hardware store and cross the street past the Watering Hole. Everett stops outside the door of the Quik Prints and stands there twisting the front wheel of his bicycle side to side as I push through the door.

The store smells like wet copper and the tips of matches and a slope-shouldered, white-haired man in an apron ducks out from behind a large churning machine. He steps up to the counter as I fish the roll of 400 out of my pocket and hand it to him. "I just need to get these developed."

He turns the film over, adjusting his glasses and looking at me hard. "This is expensive film. Where'd you get this?"

"Mr. Carson bought it for me in Fort Harmon, I think."

"Mr. Carson. So you're a townie. I've never seen you in here before. What's your name?"

"Ansel. Mackenzie." I glance over my shoulder and Everett's heaving on his handlebars, bouncing the bike on its front tire as he looks down the street and shifts from foot to foot. "Look, do I need to pay now?"

The man shakes his head, pulls out a long white envelope from under the counter and scribbles some things, then asks me for the last four digits of our phone number and tears a tab off the top of the envelope, drops the film in and seals it. "You're Ailene's granddaughter." He slides the tab from the envelope across to me and I shove it in my pocket, turning around to make sure Everett's still there. "They'll be ready tomorrow by five." I nod and he looks at me hard as I slip outside back to Everett.

"All set," I say, and Everett starts off down the street, pushing his bike beside him. I walk fast to catch up, then put my hand over his on the handlebar. He stops to look at my hand as I step under his elbow, wrap my arms around him and bury my nose in his chest. He stiffens, gives me a few quick pats on the back, and the air is thin in my lungs as I loosen my grip and duck away. "I think Izzy's painting today," I say. "I doubt she'll have time to listen to you read."

"I read to her yesterday while she worked," Everett says, his jaw tightening. "She said she liked it."

I ignore the word "said"—the way it dances like a lick of fire—and say, "Well, she was probably just being nice. That won't last long. She might have humored you yesterday, but I wouldn't count on it today. Izzy's not all that patient." I'm banking on her still being upset about me coming home last night with my shirt on backwards. Everett pushes his bike off again and I scramble after him. "You'll see. She gets tired of people pretty quickly."

He pulls his bike up short and I almost run into him. "Well, she won't get tired of me." He shoots me a glance sideways then sets his sights towards the hill.

I reach out to pat his shoulder, "I wouldn't—"

"She told me." He jerks away from my hand and pushes off down the road again, his voice tightening to a whisper. "She *told* me."

Grand is gone when we get home and I'm the first one up the stairs. I burst in to find Izzy reading the Dickinson book, her breakfast tray shoved crookedly down towards the foot of the bed. She's already got her arms up for me to drag her to the bathroom but when Everett walks through she drops them, turning her head quickly like she's just been slapped. The steely assurance drains from Everett as he glances between Izzy and me, the light in his eyes hardening to ice. I shrug, trying to give him a sorry-but-I-told-you-so smile as he turns, shakes his head, then thumps downstairs. The back door slams on its tight hinge.

I drag Izzy to the bathroom, dress her in shorts and a t-shirt, then heft her over to her chair and strap her in. She selects a blue from the row of tubes, touches the hard blobs of paint on her palette and uses her palette knife to scrape a clean space.

When I carry her breakfast tray downstairs I see Everett through the window, sitting slouched on the back stoop. I step outside, lower myself next to him, and he shifts his weight away from me as I put my hand on his shoulder. "I don't know what to say. She's really difficult sometimes—I'm sorry." He starts shaking his head before I'm even finished talking, turns the book over in his hands, flipping it open to the first few pages. "I can give her that book if you want."

He fans the pages with his thumb and then his jaw tightens and he snaps the book shut. "What is it with the two of you?"

"What do you mean?"

"You can't just—" He looks at me, shaking his head,

then shuts his eyes. He stands up jerkily, stomps inside, and up the stairs. I scramble up to follow him, but when I reach the bottom of the stairs the door to our room slams shut and I hear Everett's voice higher and louder than I ever thought possible.

"—just ignore me, after all those things you said yesterday, you can't just toss me aside because I'm in your way or you're bored with me or I cramp your artistic sensibilities—" There's the faintest sound, like wind through narrow leaves, silk rubbing silk, but when I take a few steps up the stairs Everett's talking again, much quieter this time, the panic still high in his voice.

"I don't know what I'm supposed to do. She—Ansel and me, we sort of—I didn't even know you existed, and then a few days ago, suddenly— out of nowhere, you're here—and I don't know what we—or you, what you think of me or if you expect—" The sound again, a little louder, like a broom on dusty floorboards, and I can almost hear words. I try to creep up the stairs but the voices have stopped, and then a bed creaks and Everett's reading, his voice steady and formal. I tiptoe upstairs and push open the door to where Izzy's sitting with her hands folded in her lap, her head tilted. Sensing me, she sits up straighter, grabs a brush and flutters it around her palette, then taps it to her canvas, all business.

"Everett," I say, but he's sitting at the head of Izzy's bed calmly unspooling the words for her and doesn't look up. I walk over and slide a hand along his arm, but he scoots away, doesn't stop reading. Izzy doesn't even glance at us when I sit beside him on the bed, but now when Everett looks up from the book his eyes are on Izzy, wide and wondering and a little afraid. I put my hand on his knee and his eyebrows knit together as he gets up, walks over with the book, and stands behind Izzy. He's stopped reading, and Izzy turns her head towards him. He looks at her, his eyes full of her, then flips the page and continues reading. I slide off the bed, grab my camera and a roll of film off the dresser, and walk downstairs, outside, around the house and down the dunes to the beach.

I pull off my shirt and shorts, wrap the camera in them, and walk into the water up to my ankles. I turn to make sure I'm facing the window before unclasping my bra and stepping out of my panties. The window is a glare of sunlight so I can't tell if they see me. I turn, walk bare-skinned into the water up to my waist, then duck under the crash of waves and imagine myself wiped from the planet, gone, erased, not a trace. I plunge as deep as I can, letting my whole body go limp, and drop in the green sifting light, but I keep drifting up and have to kick and kick to stay under water. I kick deeper, shoving hard with my arms until my belly grazes the sand, but the light is thick, sparkling, issuing from all sides, and the dark in my chest pushes against all that light until all it can do is rise, breaking through to air. My head crests the surface just as a wave crashes and I'm coughing, spluttering, bobbing between swells.

I turn to see the camera abandoned on the beach and swim for shore, then crawl out dripping, wringing my hair. The wind raises goose bumps and, standing there with air touching every inch of my skin, I feel suddenly wild, all body, the simmer in my gut flooding my muscles and making me strong, untouched and untouchable. I turn a few naked cartwheels, the air curling around me, icy and thin, and keep turning until most of the loose water's dripped off and I can pick up the camera.

I pull on my shorts and sit on the beach, then lay my shirt across my legs and nestle the camera lens between my knees. Cocking the film advance lever and clicking the shutter release, I cock and click, cock and click until the counter reads 36. I position the wide strap over my bare chest so most of my breasts are covered, glance up at the window, shake out my t-shirt, and set off down the shore towards the hotel. The sun blazes and my calves are scratchy with sand, the water dripping from my hair corrosive and hot.

A tiny laugh bubbles up inside me, and suddenly I see a new image of me in the rainforest. This time I'm naked, stalking through the jungle, silent and sleek. I walk in the tide line, closing my eyes to let the sun soak through my eyelids, lifting my arms out to my sides so the air swirls every crevice, the water crashing around my ankles, and I'm just a body feeling until I open my eyes and everything is sharp lines and angles, the world seen through a lens.

Neither of us can be the whole Eurydice,
the bride and muse in one. And given
the choice, it wasn't the body Orpheus
descended into Hades to reclaim, but
the constructed loved-one, the only way
anyone knows how to love. She claims him
with a body, but always floating nearby in
the quiet, how his mind drifts to me. She
grows wild, and this is her way of kicking
loose—as if some distance, some imagined
exotic could draw the restlessness from her
body like poison from a wound. She will
leave me. The first chance she gets. And he
will be here to take her place. How the paint
tells more of the whole story.

Twenty-Eight

Further down the beach people are sitting on blankets under staked umbrellas, so I tug the camera strap off and pull the t-shirt dangling from my pocket back over my head. Walking behind some sunbathers with the camera held to my face, I slide the viewfinder over the slack body of a young mother in a shirred purple one-piece, her hand lifted to her forehead in a silent movie swoon. None of the lines of her click into place so I turn the camera on the bunchy pink folds of the baby beside her scooping sand into a plastic cup and pouring it out into cone-shaped hills. Then the mother tilts her chin to look up at me and I drop the camera on its strap and keep walking.

I walk up to the pier just as an older gentleman and his grandson are climbing out of Iain's boat, their fishing poles and nets an awkward tangle. Iain waits, holding a cooler behind them, and their voices drift over to me on snags of wind, the boy suddenly pounding down the pier towards me, the net streaming over his head like a kite. I raise my camera, find something in the top half of his face and the flapping net, and hope the shutter speed is slow enough to blur just a little. The grandfather walks past and Iain's right behind him, eyeing me cautiously.

"Nice camera."

I start to respond, but then he's past me, rounding the front of the hotel. I walk down the dock and find the inside of the boat strewn with newspaper and torn comic book pages, empty soda bottles and chip bags. I scoop up as much trash as I can hold and make two trips to the trashcan at the end of the pier before Iain comes back.

"Thanks for that," he says guardedly, but something in the easy swing of his arms makes me think it's okay to follow him. He climbs in the boat, picking up a fishing rod and pulling the line taut, then fiddles the hook into its safety loop, cranks the reel, and sets the rod in the corner. "Gave it to you, did she?"

"Yes."

He nods, picking up another rod and fiddles it into order before leaning it against the other. "Been putting it to good use?" He glances at me, and I nod. He nods back distractedly, then cocks the motor up on the boat, leaning in to untangle seaweed from the propeller. I pick up my camera and step close, clearing my throat, and Iain looks up. I hold the camera to my eye tentatively and he smiles, shaking his head.

"No? Okay, sorry." I drop the camera and Iain laughs.

"It's fine, it's fine. Take your bloody pictures. It's only…

you're such a wee thing. Not the sorta bird I'm used to
seeing behind a camera."

"Well I'm sorry About yesterday."

"Ah," he swats at the air like he's waving off a bad
smell and tugs on the seaweed, then holds out a hand.
"Pass me that knife, will you?" I pull the bone-handled
switchblade off the dash behind the pilot's wheel and lean
across to him, careful so our hands don't touch. He takes
it, flicks it open, and I raise the camera to my face, framing
his shoulders down to where his t-shirt sleeve meets the
bulge of bicep, just above the tender crook of his arm.
I push the shutter and slide the lens down to his tan,
damp fingers moving with careful assurance, catching the
sunlight in glints.

We sit in the afternoon sun as Iain putters around the
boat stowing swimming gear, wiping down equipment
and tidying. I run the lens of the camera over him, trying
to catch the gestures that are him and only him, the way
he stands lost in thought looking shoulder to shoulder, his
long muscular arms slack at his sides, the fingers of his
right hand twiddling the air as he thinks. The curl that's
hanging down just far enough to nestle in the rim of his left
ear. The hot-iron-on-white-cotton smell that the camera
can't catch.

"I've got a 2:00 I'd better go collect," he says,
stopping his work long enough to lean back on his heels
and smirk at me. I try to get his whole body in the frame,
the way he rests his elbows on his knees with his forearms

dangling between his legs.

"Okay."

"You're wanting to come along, then." I click the shutter release and he cranes back to look at the sky. "Those are some dark clouds rolling in. Might be a short trip." I focus on his collar-bone, on the thumb-sized hollow below his Adam's apple, and click and click. He gives me the tiniest smile, shaking his head. "Lay me out two life vests." He climbs out to the dock and I wait for the boat to stop bobbing before crawling over to the side where the vests are kept and setting them side by side on the bench at the prow. I splash some water up to rinse a dingy shoe-print off the edge, then unsnap and fluff the seat cushions and switch out a damp one for an extra stowed in the side compartment.

When he comes back he's carrying the cooler behind a young couple holding hands, the man in khaki pants and dock shoes with a navy sweater draped around his neck, the woman in white shorts and a red checked button down, the sleeves rolled and the front knotted. She laughs, curling into the man as they walk up, then sees me and drops his hand, taking a step back as the man's face spreads with a slow grin. He dips his chin so he can peer over the rims of his sunglasses at me.

"Well, Iain. You've got a little helper." The man flashes me his white teeth and steps up to the boat. "And what's the little helper's name?" His eyes shift from my face, slide down, and I cross my arms over my chest, look away. The woman is staring at me icily and the man laughs.

I catch Iain's eye and he gives me a hard look, setting the cooler down stiffly and shaking his head in the tiniest no. I turn my back to him and wrestle the fishing poles into the boat as the man reaches his hand to help the woman into the prow. She steps in like a queen and settles herself, keeping her eyes low as Iain taps my elbow, muttering, "We'll see you when we get back, love." He's trying not to be heard by the couple up front, the man with one arm around the woman, his other hand on her knee trying to pull her onto his lap.

"I want to go," I whisper back.

"You can't, Ansel." He gives the cooler one last shove to wedge it into place. "That wanker tries anything I'll have to chuck him overboard, and then where would we be?" Iain settles a soft-eyed gaze on my face and with every pore of my skin I hold the feel of his eyes on me, let it seep deep down inside the way water into rock becomes part of the rock. He holds me in his wide hazel eyes and I float there for as long as I can, clinging to the seconds and hanging on. Then the man laughs again, Iain glances away, and I clear my throat and nod.

"You're all set, Iain," I say loudly. The man nuzzles the woman's neck as she looks away sulkily.

"Yeah, thanks for that, Ansel. We'll not be gone long." Iain touches my shoulder, then steps to the engine and pulls the cord without looking back at me. As I climb out and walk down the dock the man says, "Will the little helper be here when we get back?" and in the pause I can't hear how Iain answers.

> *Surrendering him, so slow she doesn't*
> *notice, trading his false acquaintance for*
> *some other version of herself, a body fully*
> *body, the sunlit-water-girl she can't help but*
> *be. No pretense, no costume of ill-fitting*
> *parts, but the her-version she's becoming*
> *that even I can't hope to know.*

Twenty-Nine

I drift around to the front of the hotel where they've set
up the tables on the grass to clear the porch for dancing.
When an older couple in golf shirts gets up, I watch for
a gap in the bustling waiters, then hurry across to their
recently vacated table and drape my legs over the arm of
a chair. I'm nibbling a piece of toast and reading the funny
pages when a waiter appears behind me. "Daddy says to
charge it to the room," I say.

"And what will you be having, miss?"

He slides a thin menu out of his green apron pocket,
and I take it from him gingerly. It's my first time actually
ordering from a menu, so when he comes back with a new
set of silverware and a glass of water I tell him the most
sophisticated-sounding thing I can find.

"French toast?"

"Yes. Anything to drink?"

"Um…" Something that sounds like a rich girl's drink.
"Earl Grey Tea?"

The waiter takes my menu and I settle in, the tightness in my chest starting to loosen. A sudden gust of wind flips one end of the tablecloth, knocking over my water glass, and I grab for a napkin that blows off as the sky darkens. The other diners hurriedly gather their sweaters and newspapers, stuffing their children into sweatshirts and shuttling them towards the hotel.

When my plate comes, big puffy pieces of bread covered in powdered sugar, the waiter asks if I want to move inside. I tell him I'll just eat quickly, and in between big bites I imagine myself in a beret eating at a little metal table under the Eiffel Tower. I have two bites left when a gardener on the other side of the lawn stands up and walks briskly away from the bushes lining the front staircase. A grey-haired woman in a navy dress is following him, waving some garden shears and yelling. It's Grand.

Truly, it's her, and what she's doing here I can't imagine. The gardener disappears up the stairs and she drops the shears on the ground, walks back along the bushes, leaning in to touch a branch, shaking her head as the wind tugs her hair, bowing her over. When the snooty man at the front desk hurries down the stairs, Grand's entire posture changes. She stands up ramrod straight, staring down her nose and wagging her finger, and he nods so deeply he's almost bowing, the wind battering the flaps of his green sports coat. He reaches out a hand to take Grand by the elbow but she jerks her arm loose, and now a man in a dark suit comes down the stairs, followed by another in a security uniform.

I shove the last few bites of my french toast into my mouth, wash it down with a swig of the flowery-tasting tea, and walk quickly away from the table. When I glance back the security guard and suited man are taking Grand by the arm as the front-desk man scurries back up the stairs. She's shouting, her words blanked out by the wind, as they lead her, struggling, around the side of the hotel.

As the first fat drops of rain start to fall, the waiters rush out to gather up the last of the dishes and I dash across the grass to peek around the corner of the hotel. The man in the suit is helping Grand into the passenger seat of a car painted with the large "C" of the hotel insignia. Pieces of what he's saying blow back to me in quick gusts. "I understand, Ms. Calvert—you'll have to—up to us," and he shuts the door, knocks twice on the hood, then steps quickly under the awning out of the rain. The security guard gives him a wry smile, shaking his head as he ducks into the driver's seat and starts the engine.

I duck back around the hotel, the rain drumming down, and run and slip up the edge of the staircase so I'm out of sight when the car drives by. When it's traveled a little down the driveway I take off towards home, running through trees along the cliff side, my camera bumping clumsily at my hip, the ocean behind me crashing like someone chasing. Rain pours through the trees, and I'm running so fast my feet barely touch down between bounds, crashing through the rain-thinned scent of salt, churning up the smell of wet dust and dead leaves. I get home just as the car's pulling away and Grand's clomping up the steps to the back door. As I run up the car slows, and the security guard rolls down his window.

"That your granny?" he calls to me over the drumming rain. I nod, and he smirks, "Isn't there any way you can keep her home?"

"Sir?"

He shifts in his seat, his smile hardening as he spits out the window. He motions me over and I step out from under the runneling gutter into the downpour close enough to the window to hear him. "I'm not trying to tell anyone how to live their life," he says, "But you better see if you can't keep your granny home more. Mr. Pritchett, he's pretty patient, and everybody understands, but she can't be over there every afternoon telling him how to run things."

"I'm sorry?" Can he mean Grand? She hardly leaves the house—at least, I never see her—but half the time she's in her room and the other half I'm not home.

"Look, we all understand it must be hard, but what's done is done, you hear?" The security guard seems to take my slow nod as a sign that I understand what on earth he's talking about, because he tips his hat and starts cranking up the window. "So keep her away from there. No sense in this thing escalating." The window seals and I step back from the car as he drives off. I slush through puddles to the back steps and duck inside just as lightning splits the sky and thunder crashes. Two plates and a knife smeared with peanut butter are piled in the sink, a pair of white gloves rest next to Grand's pocketbook on the counter. I unclasp her purse to find inside some wadded up tissues and a roll of breath mints. From the other side of Grand's door come sharp bangs and slams.

Everett pokes his head out of the door upstairs and I climb up, brushing past him, dripping.

"What was all that?" he asks.

I shrug, grab a towel from the bathroom to wipe the camera, and pull some dry shorts, undies and a t-shirt out of the dresser. Everett nestles back into Izzy's pillows and picks up his book. Cozy in his sock feet in the warm light of the bedside lamp, he draws his knees up as Izzy contentedly swirls a big brush over the water again and again until it looks moodier, cloudier, harder to see into too deeply. He clears his throat and Izzy stops painting to nod with a prodding smile.

"As if the Sea should part," he reads, glancing at me, then straightening up and reading louder. *"And show a further Sea—and that—a further—and the Three But a Presumption be—"* He smiles, scoots forward and reads more quietly, with more intensity, and it feels like a tunnel opens in the air between him and Izzy, making everything else in the room disappear. *"Of Periods of Seas—Unvisited of Shores—Themselves the Verge of Seas to be—"*

There's a blunt boom of thunder, a low rumble, and I drop my shorts at my feet, pull my t-shirt over my head and drop it, sopping, with a loud smack to the floor.

"Jesus." Everett flinches and sits up, quickly turning his back to me, the intensity between him and Izzy evaporating as she glances back. Her eyes catch on me and she looks and looks, her gaze steady, her expression inscrutable. In the dresser mirror, hair plasters my breasts like seaweed and I stretch languidly, walking slowly past Izzy, stepping so close past the bed I practically brush up against Everett. He startles to a stand, staring at the floor as I pass, then he grabs his shoes and bolts for the door, the book clattering from the bed as another crash of thunder shakes the house.

Izzy catches him by the wrist before he can escape, wrenching his arm so he has to turn and look at me again. His eyes stay glued to my face but his gaze widens to take in all of me, and Izzy touches the tender crook of his elbow with two fingers. He swallows as Izzy gently strokes his skin, then he slips free of her grasp, dashes down the stairs and is gone.

Slowly, slowly, Izzy turns to look at me.

"What."

Her expression is aware, alive, but impossible to read, and I slam the bedroom door, round on her, grab her by the arms.

"What? What is it? What are you thinking? I'm such a tramp, is that it? I'm such a pathetic, shallow, stupid…

that's it, isn't it? That's what you're thinking." She looks down at my hands when I shake her, then slowly rakes her gaze up my body, her cheeks flushed, her eyes shining. I give her another shake and she tilts her chin so she's aiming her line of sight straight into mine, but all I can hear is my own voice inside my head screaming *what, what?*

The quiet in my ears buzzes as I drop my hands from her arms and bite back tears. Izzy reaches for the long-handled flat brush, dabs it in the clump of green paint and the hair on my arms stands on end as she reaches across the inches of silent distance to touch the brush to my forehead. She runs the brush gently down the bridge of my nose, across my lips and chin, then reloads paint and continues the thin green line like a lick of cold fire under my chin, down my neck, along my sternum, between my breasts and down to my stomach, stopping just below my belly button.

Lightning flashes, followed by a quick crack of thunder, and the air feels charged with ions, the smell of ozone tinny in my teeth. Izzy reloads her brush with paint and draws a line like a belt around my hips, turning me so she can continue the line all the way around my body, the brush a chill, blunt knife carving me into neat, wet sections. I hear the *muck muck* of paint then feel a licking up my spine. Izzy parts my hair, brushes half over each shoulder, and continues the line past the nape of my neck, up into the hairline.

The air seems to gather close to my skin, the room's

silence vibrating, and I glance over my shoulder to see her slowly wiping the brush off with a rag, then dipping it in water and wiping until the brush comes mostly clean. Her movements are careful and choreographed as a ceremony as she dabs the brush in red, grabs me by the hip and turns me towards her. She wipes big licks of color on my right arm, then I close my eyes as she sweeps the brush over my left eyelid and down my cheek.

My ears are roaring with the silence of a caught, airy ocean, and behind my eyes a light is shining, the bright vibrations of my hearing opening to some new sound. Izzy slowly paints my shoulder and then there's a pause in the chill air and the brush touches my breasts, tracing sloppy circles. I flinch, and Izzy's free hand grabs me, holds me, so I stand with my eyes closed as she reloads the brush, circles my belly button. Then the water sloshes and the brush gently fills in my lips, lifts, then traces meandering lines across each shoulder until every inch of my skin is humming in the charged air.

When my eyelids feel dry I open them and Izzy's nodding towards the dresser mirror. As I walk slowly across the room, the buzzing in the air seems to slip in through my sinuses. I step in front of the mirror and see how I'm suddenly half-human, half-vegetation, my skin a cluster of climbing vines and rain forest flowers gaping their throats open. From the center of a large red hibiscus my left eye blinks like a lethal bird. I don't look anything like myself, anything like Izzy, nothing like anyone either of us has ever known or seen or been, and the shock of the me we've found together snags my breath, hitches my lungs. Izzy stares at me from across the room and when I turn to meet her eye I hear her voice ringing, ringing, sharp and cold as a metal bell inside my head. *Like this?* she asks, and I think, *yes, like this, Izzy, exactly.*

> *Why I never sounded, out loud, the words*
> *to her: she should hear me. Without larynx*
> *and vocal cord, the clumsy reed this body*
> *tweets, I should claim a corner of her mind,*
> *line her listening with our sixth sense. I can't*
> *make in sound the kind of sense she's used*
> *to, the kind I didn't used to have to make.*
> *Long ago car trips, when here was vacation,*
> *playing you-know-I-know. What crayon,*
> *what letter. If one didn't guess exactly, it*
> *was only the name that was off, the other*
> *concentrating hard on the color. Enough so*
> *we knew we knew, knife deepening clean,*
> *already-cuts. But now, so long since we felt*
> *the slide of the other's mind inside our own,*
> *muscular as a squirmy worm. Only occa-*
> *sional wisps of images, breaths of thought,*
> *never knowing if she sent them. Finally*
> *claiming her body for the both of us, seeing*
> *her as she wants to be seen and painting*
> *her fierce enough to withstand whatever*

the world holds, how like sympathetic
resonance my voice strikes the still string of
her listening. Finally, once again, sounding
inside her.

*   *   *

Thirty

The next morning Izzy's still sleeping when I roll over.
I hold the memory of last night in the center of my belly,
watching her chest rise with delicate, hitching breaths, her
arms crossed, wrists up, thrown over her eyes. I float my
thinking voice into the bright, live space between us, *Izzy,
Izzzzzzzzeeee, wake uuuuup,* and wait for it to wash up
and echo inside her. The room is a hive of silence—what if
we lost it? What if the line snapped or drifted, blew away
over night?—and then Izzy drags her arms away from her
eyes, smacks her hands on the mattress and sighs. She
glares across at me, flashes on an image of sitting behind
me, wrapping my mouth around and around with strips
of bed sheet, gagging me, and I throw a pillow across
the room at her and laugh. *Like that would do any good,* I
think, and she imagines my head encased in a snow hat,
then a ski mask, then a football helmet on top of it. *That
wouldn't work either, Izzy—you're stuck with me,* I think,
and we beam across the room at each other. Our skin

could break from holding in so much light.

I get dressed, then cart Izzy between bathroom and easel and carry up breakfast. When I walk back into the room she's staring at a new canvas, the blank rectangle inside her mind tracing quick pencil-less lines that dissolve and are replaced by other possibilities on top of them. I lay the plate of eggs in her lap, grab the camera off our dresser and train the lens around the room. Focusing on Izzy's beaded crystal flowers clustered in their juice glass, I pan back to include the frayed pages of her Dickinson book propped against the lamp base, the cord of the lamp trailing from the edge of the nightstand. I shift the camera so that the book bisects the frame, the flowers bumping the top left corner, the kinked fall of the cord through space taking up most of the bottom right, and click the shutter. Izzy glances at me, and then replaces in my mind's eye the lamp with an empty drainage bag, the lamp cord with tubing. "Izzy, gross," I say out loud, as she replaces the ruffled pages of the Dickinson book with one of her folded up diapers. She's grinning impishly at me, and as she turns the glass of beaded flowers into an orange prescription bottle of dusty aspirin I shut my eyes and push back with my thoughts, crowding out Izzy's still life with a bowl of fruit on a blue tablecloth, maybe a fly rubbing its legs together on the pulpy moon-surface of one apple cut in half. Then Izzy pushes back and turns the apples into pomegranates, the fly into a hole in the cut half where one seed has been eaten, and I think, *That's right*

Izzy—there's no going back now.

It's only 9:00 but the lights are already on in the Lloyd's house and when the door opens Mrs. Lloyd is standing in a faint slant of morning light, staring out at me through the screen.

"Why, Ansel," she says, holding it open for me, "What a nice surprise." She gestures me towards the kitchen where Mr. Lloyd is sitting with a glass of orange juice and the paper spread out between the two of them. He waves me into the empty seat to his left then struggles to his feet, leaning heavily on the table and stretching across to give me a kiss and pat on the cheek.

"Prettiest sight I've seen in a long time," he says as Mrs. Lloyd sets a glass of juice in front of me and settles into a chair.

"I'll pretend like I didn't hear that, Henry."

"Well, May, look at her."

They both smile at me and Mrs. Lloyd says, "I guess you have a point." She inhales and says brightly, "Everett's not up yet this morning, Ansel, but I'll have to wake him in a little bit if he's going to be ready for his mother when she gets here."

I choke on my juice and Mr. Lloyd reaches a hand around to thump me on the back. Coughing, I take another swallow and try to keep my voice steady.

"Everett's mother is coming?"

"Mmm," Mrs. Lloyd nods, arranging the salt and

pepper shakers, then pulling the table cloth taut, brushing it free of crumbs.

"Is Everett leaving?"

Mr. Lloyd snorts, and Mrs. Lloyd shoots him a pursed-lip scowl before smiling at me.

"Oh, I don't think so. Everett wanted her to see your sister's paintings?" and on this last half of the sentence her voice rises into a question as she cocks her head at me. "We didn't know you had a sister."

I concentrate on the tablecloth, drink my juice, and the silence stretches on. "I don't... talk about her that much." Mr. Lloyd folds his paper and reaches for a piece of toast, trying to look casual, but I can feel both of them waiting for me to go on. "She's paralyzed," I say, and Mrs. Lloyd nods with a look of concern as the silence lengthens. I shift in my seat, stretching the last bit of juice in my glass into lots of tiny sips.

Finally, Mr. Lloyd clears his throat. "I expect people usually ask a lot more questions once they find that out," he says, and I nod. "Well. Can't blame you for wanting people to keep their noses clear of your business." Mrs. Lloyd pats my hand and takes the empty plate of toast. She walks over to the counter, unruffles the bag of white bread and slots two more slices in the toaster.

The stairs creak and then Everett walks into the kitchen, his striped golf shirt tucked into khaki slacks, his still-damp hair lined with the tines from the comb. He stops and stares at me as I force a smile and Mr. Lloyd says, "Thought I was gonna have to go up there and check for a pulse." Everett stands looking at me and Mr. Lloyd continues, "Good morning to you, too, by the way."

Everett walks slowly up to the table, pulls out the empty chair and sits with his back partially turned to me. "Morning, Gramps. Gram. Ansel." Mrs. Lloyd sets a glass of juice down in front of him, pets his hair, and Everett flinches from under her hand, smoothes his hair carefully back into place.

"You look fine, honey. Why don't you eat something." She sets a plate in front of each of us, and Everett picks up a piece of buttered toast, looks at it, then sets it back down.

"Your grandma and I were just saying, we haven't had such a pretty early morning visitor in quite some time." Mr. Lloyd inclines his head towards me. "I expect your mother will be pleased to meet her, too."

Everett puts down his toast and wipes his mouth with a napkin. "She's coming to meet Isabel," he says.

The silence seems to buzz as the heat climbs my cheeks and I imagine dissolving—just melting into the linoleum to disappear.

Mr. Lloyd's voice has an edge to it when he says, "Well, I don't suppose she'll mind meeting someone new, but I *know* she'll want to meet the young lady you've been running around town with all summer." He reaches across the table to squeeze my hand, and I swallow, keeping my eyes on the tablecloth.

"Gramps? Stay out of it," Everett says, then pushes back his chair and steps out of the room. The silence is suffocating; I can't breathe.

"Everett Claude Lloyd, you get your—"

"Henry," Mrs. Lloyd says, inclining her head towards me. "Later."

Mrs. Lloyd sits down and she and Mr. Lloyd take turns asking me about school—what's my favorite subject and do I play any sports—until Everett walks back in and sits down between us like he's in an entirely different room, tugging his shirt so it blouses out evenly over his belt, licking his fingers and leaning over to rub at a smudge on his brown oxfords.

"Can I talk to you a second?" I mutter to Everett when there's a pause in the conversation, and without looking at me he stands and steps into the living room.

"What?" His eyes are distant, intentionally blank, and I feel myself shrinking inside my skin under his cool gaze.

"Izzy's not allowed to have visitors," I say.

"Your grandmother doesn't seem to mind when I stop by."

"Right, it's just... grown-ups. No one is supposed to know about her."

"Why?"

"Because. She could get taken away if people found out about her."

Everett furrows his brow and leans in close. "*Get taken away?* Are you listening to yourself? She's not *crazy,*

Ansel—she's a genius." His face flushes and he looks at his hands. "I think *you* don't want people to see her. I think you I don't know want her all to yourself." He raises his gaze again to stare at me hard, and then at the sound of a car outside he jerks backwards into the kitchen, bumping into the door jamb. He retucks his shirt and tugs it out, running his hands over his hair so it rests flat against his head.

"Calm down," Mr. Lloyd says, and Mrs. Lloyd places a hand on his shoulder as she passes into the living room. The engine noise gets louder, crests, and then fades, and Mrs. Lloyd walks back into the kitchen, shaking her head. Everett drops into a chair and picks up his juice, stares into the empty glass then sets it back down.

The phone rings and Mr. Lloyd mutters, "Here we go." Mrs. Lloyd shoots him a hard look before walking into the hallway at the bottom of the stairs to answer the phone. Her voice is high and bright, and when she calls for Everett Mr. Lloyd lets out a loud sigh. I pick the funny pages out of the folded pile on the table as Mrs. Lloyd crosses quickly to the sink, scrubs determinedly at the piled dishes. Everett says hello and then his voice drops low, flattens out, speaks in one-word responses. Mrs. Lloyd stops scrubbing the pot in her hands as Mr. Lloyd watches the door, slump-shouldered, his eyes flat and resigned. Finally Everett hangs up and when he walks back into the kitchen his shoulders are hitched up around his ears. Mrs. Lloyd turns around slowly, wiping her hands on her apron and clasping them together.

"That was my mother," Everett says, inhaling quickly, "She can't make it out today—she had a client pull out last minute of a show she's curating, so she's just really busy. But she said, you know, she really trusts my judgment, and I should just pick out the pictures I think are best." Mr. Lloyd stares at him, squints, and Everett doesn't meet his grandfather's eye as he talks faster. "See, they had a cancellation at a gallery in Fort Harmon and mother says if she can't find anyone else to fill it then Isabel can have the back wall for a couple of weeks." Everett's eyes are clear and bright, and no one else speaks. After a long pause he blurts, "It's a really great opportunity." He nods, carries his juice glass to his grandmother at the sink, then turns without making eye contact and walks quickly from the room. Mr. and Mrs. Lloyd both stare after him and then Mrs. Lloyd turns back to the sink, clatters a plate free from the pile, and rinses it in slow, methodical circles, around and around with the spray nozzle.

Thirty-One

I make Izzy's lunch and empty her drainage bag, then walk back down town. When I push through the door of the Quik Prints the man with the bushy eyebrows looks up from behind the clicking and shushing machine. "I said 5:00. You're early."

"So they're not ready?"

He glares at me steadily and steps over to the machine, gathers some prints into a handful and drops them in an envelope, then opens the machine to pull the negatives out and slot them into plastic sleeves. He seals the envelope, tosses it across the counter towards me, punches some buttons into the cash register and tells me the total.

My hands are shaking as I slide out the curved stack of glossy pictures. I sort through the images of Izzy and, noting how the exposure's all wrong on most, how only two or three came out the way I wanted, the familiar weight of disappointment sinks slowly into the center of my belly. I needed Lee's 28-150 telephoto lens to get the images I'd seen in my mind's eye, and all of these pictures can be divided into four piles: ones that are a lost cause, ones that are okay, ones that need a longer or shorter exposure and ones that need recropping.

"If they meet with your approval, you might consider paying," the man says.

My birthday money envelope is fat with the wad of twenties Lee gave me, and I pull out one crisp bill, laying it on the counter. "I have a question." Shuffling through the piles of pictures, I show him how I want to crop some and lighten or darken parts of others. He lays one red, chapped hand on the glass case with my change, lifting his glasses with the other hand as he leans over to peer at the prints.

"That's custom work," he says. "Cost you a pretty penny. Cheaper if you do it yourself."

"I don't... I wouldn't know how to do it myself."

"A camera like that," he says, nodding with his chin towards the Canon looped around my neck. "Don't you even have a dark room?" I shake my head, and he steps back to the machine, threads some negatives in, clicks the hood into place, and sets the machine running again, whirring and shuffling out wet prints. "Something else you needed?" he says, wiping his hands on a rag.

I shift from foot to foot and nod towards the heavy door with the red light bulb mounted above it at the back of the shop. "Is that your darkroom?" I ask. He squints at me, folds his arms across his chest. I want to grab my prints and run out of there, but I imagine Loo taking pictures in some war torn country as bullets fly by, remember the image of myself painted up like a mythological creature, and I take a deep breath to find my voice. "I was just wondering if maybe you needed some help. I could help, if you showed me what to do. You wouldn't even have to pay me. Or I could pay you—for lessons—if you don't need a helper."

"Pay me for lessons. If you're Ailene's granddaughter I doubt you have money to burn. Woman's in hock to half this town." He tugs a box off the back shelf and opens it with a box cutter, ignoring me. I pull another twenty out of my envelope and smack it down on the glass counter.

"Well, I've got this. How much of a lesson would this buy me?"

He straightens up and stares down at the bill, then holds it up to the light. "Where'd you get this from?"

"I sold some of my photographs," I say. "At a show I had with Lee Reeser down at the hotel."

"Probably stole it, and that camera you've got there, too."

"I didn't steal it," I say, my voice starting to shake. "She gave me the camera, and Nigel Fox bought two of my prints. He'll probably buy more if I ever have another show."

"Nigel Fox?" He laughs. "That man is so gullible—he'll buy anything."

My pride shrinks as I remember how Lee egged him on, how no one else looked twice at my pictures. All the light inside me sucks into the pit of my stomach and falters, a flame suffocating on a drowned wick, and I realize it's true—I'm no good—I'm not talented like Izzy. Shame crawls my neck, burning my ears, and I'm almost to the door when the man calls after me.

"You got that much spending money you should put some of it towards your grandma's grocery bill," he says, and as the words seep in the little guttering flame in my belly flares.

As if I would ever buy anything for Grand, ever spend any of my money on her. All the times I needed new clothes and had to wear ratty underwear to school, a little girl's dress to church, all the times Izzy got an infection and Grand waited to call the doctor until her fever was pushing 104°—never—nothing—not one damn thing. I turn, sweeping the store with blazing eyes. "Business must be really good if you're willing to let a paying customer just walk out of here."

He sighs, turns back to me slowly wagging his head. "You don't give up, do you?"

"Twenty dollars for four lessons," I say, my heart pounding.

He levels his chin and says slowly, "That twenty of yours can buy you two lessons, plus supplies."

"Deal," I say, holding out my hand for him to shake. "When can we start?"

He glances at my out-stretched hand over the top of his glasses and folds his arms across his chest. "I'm busy the next few days, and they're saying this storm—"

"You don't look too busy today," I say, taking a deep breath. "How about right now?" He squints at me, his white eyebrows bristling, then holds out his hand for the envelope of prints. Sliding the negatives out, he walks to the door in the back and steps inside. Three plastic trays—one red, one yellow, one blue—are lined inside a long metal sink, a large plastic tub brims with water at the other end, and the smell of thin, greeny chemicals singes my nostrils. He steps over to a tall machine, lifts a lever and pulls out a hinged plate with a rectangular hole in the middle, flipping it open like a paper-thin waffle griddle.

"Which image did you want to work with first?" he says. I find the one of Izzy's blankets peaked like mountain ranges, her face a blurry horizon, and hold the negative by the edges. He gently takes it from me and slips it between pins in the hinged plate, lining up Izzy's image with the hole as he checks it in the light, then slots the plate into the machine and flicks the lever so the accordion neck drops down.

"This is the enlarger," he says. I nod, and he squints at me. "Did you see what I did?" I hesitate, and he sighs heavily, flips the accordion neck back up, slides the negative out of the levered plate and hands them both to me. "You do it," he says.

I'm just starting back up the hill with two new canvases for Izzy when Everett skids up on his bike. He's changed into shorts and a ratty t-shirt and a few strands of hair have shaken loose over his forehead.

"You know, this is going to work out really well, actually. This way I'll get to pick the paintings that best speak to one another and mother will be pleasantly surprised. She's not expecting much, I know, but when she sees Isabel's work—she won't believe it." He's walking duck-legged, off the seat but still straddling the bar of his bicycle, and as we approach the house I walk faster—up the steps, through the screen door, and straight through the living room where the TV's blaring to an empty couch with Everett talking about the show the whole time.

"The end of the summer, a lot of times big buyers come from New York, and Isabel's going to have one whole wall that's all her own. She'll still be seen in the context of another artist, though—mother has Sylvia Hennison's sculptures in the same space, and they'll really compliment Isabel's impressionistic style."

Izzy finishes brushing back and forth over the water when we walk in, so I carefully take down the painting, set it under the window to dry and strap a new canvas to the easel. Everett's chattering away, convincing himself, and Izzy turns to me with an amused *what on earth* smile, as I roll my eyes dramatically and think, *Izzy, you have no idea.* She catches a silent laugh in her hand and Everett stops mid-sentence, glances at Izzy, then slowly closes his mouth. Izzy tilts her head at me and I replay Everett's blusterings about showing her work in a gallery. An *oh, I see* expression flashes across her face, and then she looks at Everett, studies him, turns back to me and shrugs.

"Izzy doesn't really care to show her paintings," I say.

Everett stares at me for a beat and then inhales sharply, turning to Izzy all in a rush. "No, Isabel, listen to me—an artist of your caliber—you have to show your work," he says, touching her shoulder, and Izzy shrugs his hand away. He looks back at me, his eyes wild with panic as he begins frantically gesturing, "I mean—Monet and Manet and Morisot, think of how they influenced each other—they never would have made such great strides in their work if they hadn't shown, if they hadn't let other artists *see*. My mother—she knows tons and tons of artists, she's helped launch peoples' careers, so you see she's really—she's an important resource."

The word "resource" makes his mother sound like an oil field, and the image of a tall, skinny woman with Everett's eyes and a black geyser shooting out of the top of her head flashes across our minds' eye. Izzy and I both laugh out loud and Everett looks between the two of us and sets his jaw.

Izzy examines her hands, picking at the paint drips dried on her skin, running her mind over the possibility of her paintings hanging on stark white walls. I remember the hotel gallery the night of Lee's show, all the well-dressed

retirees milling between pictures oohing and ahing, and
then I imagine Izzy's paintings in place of Lee's pictures
and Nigel Fox pacing restlessly back and forth in front
of them. "People sometimes buy paintings at this show,
right?" I ask.

Everett nods eagerly, babbling about how much
his mother has sold various artists' work for and whose
collections they're in, and I catch Izzy's eye and replay
some of the worst fights I've had with Grand. Izzy's face
flickers with concern as she sees for first time Grand in her
sea-green nightgown, one tuft of hair free from its curler,
Grand slapping me and shaking me, Grand dropping my
hamburger into the trashcan, Grand standing at the sink
and saying, "Oh, you do that." *Izzy, we need money. We
can't rely on Grand. We've got to have money if we're ever
going to take care of ourselves.* Izzy's eyes don't waver
from mine as they slowly sharpen with a clear light. She
holds my gaze and nods.

"Okay, Everett. You can have the ones that are already
dry."

Everett whoops, grabs Izzy's hand and drops into
a kneel, gushing about how this will be so great, you'll
see, mother will be so impressed, this will really change
everything, and Izzy shoots me a look.

"Everett. Izzy wants to get started now," and he says,
oh sure wow, sorry, it's just so great, though, isn't it? It's
like—and then Izzy glares at him and he shuts up. He sits
down on her bed, props his head on top of his arms on

the footboard, and Izzy turns back to her canvas, tilts her head back and forth, then swipes the first few wispy pencil lines onto the new canvas

I sit down on my bed and flip through the Izzy images Mr. Simms and I didn't have time to reprint, testing out the words *burn* and *dodge* in my head for what I'll need to do to the pictures as I make new piles. The afternoon slips by in companionable silence, Izzy sketching, me sorting, Everett watching, and when I head downstairs at five o'clock Everett follows.

"This next painting is definitely one of you, which is really great. Mother will be pleased that the works are cohesive in terms of subject and style, but with some thematic variance. That's something artists have to work for years to accomplish, but Isabel just knew from the beginning, didn't she? That's not to say she doesn't take risks, she does, I can see she's trying new things all the time, but the risks work, it's amazing, it's really like nothing I've ever seen before."

"Are you eating with us?" He nods, so I pull a fourth TV dinner out of the freezer, set the oven on 375° to preheat, then step into the living room to turn off the TV that's chattering loudly to no one. When I walk back into the kitchen Everett's looking at me intently, a little shyly.

"What?"

He shakes his head but steps close, touches my shoulder. "Thanks for your help. With Isabel." He gives my shoulder an awkward pat and then shoves his hands in his pockets and steps away. "How did you convince her?"

"Well, I didn't. I just told her we needed the money, and she agreed."

He smiles, says how it's funny, he was babbling so much he didn't even hear me say anything. His eyes are bright, soft, holding me in their blue-white beam as he laughs, but I remember how he ignored me at his grandparents' house, how I had to trick him into touching me once he knew about Izzy, and a slow simmer starts in my gut. I step up close to him and he backs away. "Well, there's no way you could have heard us." He gives a slow, puzzled nod and I back him up against the wall so that we're almost nose to nose. "Everett, Izzy and I don't have to stoop to *talking*."

His eyes are wide, blinking, a little scared, then he swallows, slowly steps away and heads upstairs. I stand in the kitchen, my heart hammering, and as I slide the aluminum trays into the oven, the hot air washes my flushed face.

When the timer dings I carry Grand's meal over to the table and knock on her bedroom door. "Dinner's ready." I can't hear anything inside, so I go back to the kitchen and put our three meals on the tray and carry them upstairs. Everett's scooted back against Izzy's headboard, watching her smear on the first few layers of under-paint, and he doesn't take his eyes from her when I walk in.

"You're going to have to move, Everett. That's where

Izzy needs to sit." He gets up and crams himself into the little school desk in the corner, his long legs hinged and tangled as a spider's underneath, and I drag Izzy over, settle the tray across her legs. Everett eats silently, glancing up sometimes to look between the two of us. Izzy shoots me a grin and we both laugh at the same time.

He drops his fork with a tinny clatter. "I'll need to get titles for the first four paintings, Isabel. I have to make the labels."

Izzy nods as she cuts up her chicken in gravy, chews, and inclines her head towards me.

"See for yourself," I say, trying to infuse boredom and pity into my voice. "Everett, the titles are embedded in the paintings."

His jaw tightens as he wiggles out of the desk and goes over to pick up the Medusa. "Which words?"

"All of it."

"But that's too long to be a title. *Even the mouths—of our various—envies are toothless and used to—exhaling—their coiled poisons—*? It's too long."

Izzy shrugs, dipping a piece of cauliflower into her gravy, and I say, "Izzy, would it matter if we just took the first fragment for the title? People could read the rest in the painting anyway." She chews, looks at the picture, shrugs, and cuts off another bite. I nod at Everett and he stares back.

"What," he says.

Izzy stops mid-chew, looks over at me with raised

eyebrows, and I open my eyes wide, saying to him very slowly, "The first fragment, Everett. *Even the mouths.* That's the title, okay?"

After Everett leaves, the house is quiet, darkened unnaturally by the late summer storm clouds. It starts to rain—fingernails on the window—then gathers to a hard downpour, endless bags of marbles emptying onto the house. Lightning flashes and thunder cracks, rattling the windows. I move the lamp so Izzy can see, and she keeps sketching, the rain a racket, her hand wispy as a faint breeze.

After a while the rain settles down to a light drizzle, a car door slams, and I scoot downstairs as the back door opens. Grand comes in, sopping wet in a thin floral dress, her hair dripping and falling out of the pins. Her heavy shoes clunk past me to her bedroom, and there's a fast heavy knock on the back door.

The security guard from the hotel is standing there with one thumb hooked in a belt loop, and he shoves a piece of paper at me. "Mr. Pritchett's had it, you hear? That woman shows up at the hotel one more time, I'm carting her in—I don't care who she is or how old." He turns, clomps down the stairs, ducks into his car and revs away.

I look at the paper, something official with Grand's name in big letters, only it says Ailene Calvert, not Mackenzie. There's the large C of the hotel insignia and a signature and a bunch of fancy language that swirls around the words "banned from the premises" in bold in the middle of the page.

I knock on Grand's door. Silence. I turn the knob, pushing open a crack, and something thunks hard against the door, knocking it shut. I wait a few seconds before pushing the door open again. One of Grand's shoes is lying on the floor by the door and somewhere inside the dark room she's breathing fast and heavy. I pull the door closed and go back upstairs.

Thirty-Two

Friday, August 2, 1974
5 days

Friday it rains all day, the wind gusting hard at the house. I sit on my bed counting our birthday money while Izzy reworks a painting of me standing at three-quarters view in front of a mirror, one hand raised to the rippling reflection. She layers on paint but keeps the reflection in the mirror semi-transparent, a hint of a skeleton showing through, the spine cracked down low towards the tailbone. She fiddles with the exact shape of the bones, sketching lines on top of lines, then growls and throws down her pencil and gives me a pleading look.

Now that I can feel her again inside me there's no point in keeping secrets, so I finish counting—$242 plus the $400 from Nigel Fox—then leave the money in seven rubber-banded stacks on the bed before unlatching the little panel by my headboard that leads into the crawlspace. I haven't been inside for years—not since the last time the doctor came and Izzy had enough medicine to sleep soundly. It's damp and hot behind the wall of our room, and water drips through the roof, softening the floorboards.

I grab a box and pull it into the light. Izzy turns her head to watch me sort through the baseball trophies and boy scouts' paraphernalia, including a metal lockbox that I lay out on the bed. I dig deeper, unearth a framed picture of a group of boys standing behind a canoe, then show Izzy the tall boy in the back row whose ears stick out. She squints, looks up at me suddenly, and I nod. "It's father," I say. She takes the picture from me, holding it gently in both hands. Her face is blank, unimpressed, and I don't feel bad for keeping his pictures a secret for so long. She hands it back to me, turns back to her painting, so I set the picture on the dresser and keep digging.

Further down in the box are carved antique frames, pictures of people standing in front of the C. Grand Hotel or next to a horse carriage or sitting primly on a bench in lacey dresses over high button boots. I'm putting them all back when my eye catches on a little girl standing in the center of the hotel staircase. A man dressed in a tight jacket, vest, and high-collared shirt holds her hand, and standing stiffly next to them is a short woman in a wide-brimmed hat, necklaces cascading down layers of lace. A rim of space radiates around the three of them, separating them from the other men and women in hotel uniforms, everyone facing the camera with solemn faces. I look closer at the little girl with the smug, prim expression, and her dark eyes are flat as bullet-holes.

My heart drumming, I slide the picture under my
bed, push the box back into the crawlspace and pull out
another box full of big envelopes marked "X-RAY, DO
NOT BEND." I unloop the red string lashing one envelope
shut and carry the x-ray over to Izzy, holding it up to the
light. She runs her finger along the ghostly rope of spine,
the vertebrae like knots tied tightly together, but her hand
stops and hovers at the tailbone, over the impossibly
intact bones. Holding the x-ray up closer to the light,
we're hunting for the breaks and damage we know must
be there when Izzy takes a sharp breath and points to the
typewritten name in the corner: "Mackenzie, Ansel."

I don't meet her eyes as I slide the x-ray from
between her tight fingers and slot it back inside the
envelope, then sift through the others, holding the
films up to the light until I find one of a spine that reads
"Mackenzie, Isabel" in the corner and carry it over to
her. This time the rope of vertebrae seems to bend at the
bottom, unraveling into fragments of floating bone. Izzy
peers closely, pulls me by the wrist so the light shines
through, then traces the bone slivers onto the canvas. I
stand there holding it for her as the rain drums down.

When Izzy's finished I put the boxes away, stack our
money in the lockbox and hide it under my socks in the
top drawer of our dresser, then head downstairs. There's
no sound from Grand's room this morning, the TV's silent,
and she's not in the kitchen. Finding again the envelopes

marked with Izzy's name and mine and grandfather's,
I sort through the indecipherable abbreviations on the
bills, the numbers jumbled as a code. I'm putting it all
back when I notice more envelopes marked with initials
and dates and pull out a bunch of official-looking letters
written on hotel letterhead.

"Dear Ms. Calvert," they all begin, followed by flowery
greetings and dollars earned for the month. They're all
signed "R. Pritchett, Manager, Calvert Grand Hotel" and
as they progress they begin to mention minor necessary
repairs. Later letters are less polite and more insistent: a
leaking roof, a wing they've had to close off, then visits
from the Department of Safety and reports on mold and
finally a letter from the Board of Health. Inside another
unmarked envelope is a sheaf of official documents. The
date at the top reads "May 14, 1949" the words "Calvert
Grand Hotel" written next to "Property." I flip through
page after page of numbers and columns of abbreviated
words, and at the back are two signatures: Ailene Calvert
Mackenzie and Robert Pritchett, Jr. There are also a
pack of rubber-banded bank statements and three
business-sized envelopes tucked inside, all addressed to
"R. Pritchett, Manager, Calvert Grand Hotel." Scrawled
across the front of each are the words "Return to Sender"
in watery black ink, and I ease the flap open, sliding out
a piece of yellow legal pad paper covered in Grand's
handwriting.

July 2, 1974

Dear Mr. Pritchett,

At this time I am prepared to buy back the Calvert Grand Hotel, built by my grandfather, Franklin Calvert, and left to me, the only child of Edward and Lydia Calvert, as my legal birthright.

An unfortunate misunderstanding led to the erroneous sale of the hotel two decades ago. However, I am now prepared to offer you $123,452.83 in cash for the sale of the hotel.

I am sure that you will want to return this important historical landmark to its rightful owner, the only living heir of Edward and Lydia Calvert. However, in the event that you are unable or unwilling to return the hotel to its rightful owner, you can expect legal action to be taken. My attorney is on constant retainer and ready to win recompense for the wrongful sale of the hotel.

I appreciate your cooperation in rectifying this heinous grievance against history.

Sincerely,

Ailene Calvert,

Sole living heir of Edward and Lydia Calvert,

and rightful owner of the Calvert Grand Hotel

I snort. Grand really is crazy if she thinks she has $123,000 laying around in a suitcase. I pull out the most recent bank statement and my stomach turns over. *Current Balance: $15,368.22.* Grand has all this money, has *had* money all this time and she won't even pay for groceries—but it's nowhere near the amount she offers Mr. Pritchett, and the other bank statements from previous months aren't much different—only slightly less. I'm folding up the most recent statement when I notice Grand's handwriting in pencil on the back of the page:

108,084.61

+ 15,368.22

123,452.83

I stop breathing, stare at that bottom number, and then pull out again the most recent letter to Mr. Pritchett. The number's right, $123,452.83, assuming there's really $108,000 lying around somewhere. I write down the most recent figures and hide the scrap of paper in my back pocket, then sit down and take every envelope out of every drawer. I sort through letters, bank statements with smaller numbers, court documents for me and Izzy, but after half an hour of searching, there's no sign of $108,000.

I'm putting the envelopes back when the Carsons' truck pulls up through the thick curtain of rain. Grand opens the passenger side, drops down and slams the door, bustling across the driveway in the downpour. The older Mr. Carson follows after her with an umbrella as she clomps inside, her hair wild and her eyes on fire. I step away from the stove as she stomps past and slams the door to her room. The silence in the house reverberates and then Mr. Carson clears his throat and taps on the screen.

"Hey there, Ansel," he says, peering in at me and shifting his tall, rectangular weight from foot to foot. He looks over his shoulder at the truck then glances towards Grand's room and leans low, whispering, "Mind stepping outside for a minute?"

I lay the spoon on the spoon rest and ease the back door closed behind me, folding my arms against the sudden mid-summer chill. The water's cascading off the clogged gutters by the front stoop, the rain so loud it's like trying to talk over a drum roll, and when Mr. Carson speaks all I see is his mouth moving.

"What?"

"Your Grand's been in some trouble," he says, wringing the umbrella over and over in his large, calloused hands. "I picked her up at the station. Seems she's been going down to the C. Grand Hotel and giving them a hard time like she owns the place."

"Well, she *did* own the place," I say, watching his eyes. Mr. Carson bows his head, looks at the crack in the doorway behind me and lowers his voice.

"That was a long time ago, Ansel. She don't own it no more. She's been acting crazy, saying she's gonna buy it back, when everyone knows she hasn't got the money and it ain't for sale. Some folks are starting to think she might *be* crazy. You're gonna need to keep an eye on her and let me know if she goes missing." Mr. Carson's eyes are the color of rain, fear and pity flickering through them. I nod, and he stands next to me watching the downpour.

"I don't mean to scare you," he says.

"I'm not scared," I say, "Grand getting carted off would be the best thing for me and Izzy."

Mr. Carson mutters, now, you don't mean that, and I say I do mean it.

"Then you're not thinking straight!" We're both startled, and Mr. Carson ducks his head, murmuring, "Ansel, if your grandma gets taken away pretty soon people will be coming around to get you, too. You're a minor, they can't just leave you out here all alone."

"What do you mean *people*—what kind of people?"

"State people, Ansel, and when they come around for you they're gonna find out about Miss Isabel, and then—I don't even like to think."

"I can take care of Izzy. She's fine. With Grand gone, what is there to find out about Izzy anyway?"

"That she exists, Ansel! That your grandma's been keeping a crippled girl in her attic with no schooling and, come to find out, not enough care. There are laws. People in this back-ass town keep themselves to themselves—we never ask no questions. We got used to the Calverts doing whatever they pleased a long time ago, and we know better than to meddle with any of their affairs. But state people won't care who your grandma is—and I don't know, but they're liable to cart Miss Isabel off to some state hospital."

The words *state hospital* start a chill at my nape that washes down my arms. I glance at the stairs but it's too late, I can feel Izzy sensing my fear, can feel her seeing the imagined dingy corridors and metal-barred beds, the stinging smell of antiseptic and bandage chalky with blood.

"They can't take her away," I say. "We're old enough to take care of ourselves."

Mr. Carson shakes his head. "You'd have a hard time convincing state people of that, especially with Miss Isabel being... well, sick as she is." He stares at me hard, his eyes suddenly steely as girder metal, and he speaks slowly. "Now, I mean to be of more help to you—I'll be checking in on you more, making sure you have what you need to take care of your sister, but if you and Miss Isabel want to keep living here you're going to need to keep your grandma around for appearances' sake, you hear?"

I nod, and the wind gusts against the porch, twirling my hair and making me feel small and cut adrift. Izzy and I are on our own. The air shifts thinly around me and even though, dimly, far off, I realize we always have been, I feel dizzy. Suddenly the sure, solid walls of this house and our lives inside it seem to dissolve like mist, and all that's left are Izzy and me floating in a wide white void. I lean my back against the solid support of the door frame and tell Mr. Carson okay, yes, I understand.

"Grand's not crazy," I say, but my voice sounds small in the guttering rain. "She's just used to getting her own way."

"Better keep her home all the same," he says quietly. He watches me carefully, then looks at his hands and wrings the umbrella. "You girls going to be okay out here? They're saying this storm that's coming through could get bad."

"We're fine," I say.

"You could all come out and stay with Clay and me just until—"

I snort. "Yeah, Grand would love that. "

Mr. Carson ducks his head. "Maybe I should board up these windows at least, check to see—"

"Thank you, Mr. Carson. We'll be fine. Have a good night," I say, turning on my heel and shutting the door behind me. The dark shadow of his body lingers in the window, then he steps out from under the eaves and walks across the yard in the grey downpour.

I close my eyes and wait for the world to steady beneath my feet, then go back inside and place one foot after the other across the kitchen and through the living room to tap my knuckles on Grand's door. No answer. The bathroom light is on when I push through, the tub is running, and a line of sopping clothes trails across the bedroom floor.

"Grand," I say, stepping into the bathroom doorway. She's standing in her slip, running a towel over her head. "Grand, you've got to stop," I say, and she turns, her face tracked with tears, and smacks the towel down on the floor.

"Don't you tell me what to do! I'm not nobody—people can't tell me what to do! I tell *them* what to do!" She's quivering, screaming as she turns to the sink and slams the medicine cabinet door, some of the cosmetic bottles on the back of the sink falling into the basin. She reaches across the sink and snatches up a pair of nail scissors, then turns to face me, the small points of the scissors poking out of her fist like a bird's beak. Her voice is an earthquake, low and rumbling. *"You get out of here."*

I turn and trip over my own feet, scrambling and stumbling upstairs. When I burst in, Izzy's sitting with her hands folded in her lap and she looks up at me, her eyes flickering with fear. *What do we do, Izzy?* I think, but all I can hear from her is a frantic airy blank like the sound of a teakettle whistling. She turns her eyes pointedly to her canvas, to the wispy lines that drift into the shape of me standing on a dock holding Izzy, our backs to the viewer, the two of us looking out to sea with two snakes, two rabbits and two birds huddled at our feet. I step close to Izzy and lay my forehead against hers. We shut our eyes as all around us the wind gusts, smashing into the house like an avalanche, a tilting into chaos that's gathering force and speed as it sweeps towards us.

I replay Grand's last words—*You get out of here*—and think, *yes, Izzy, we have to get out of here, soon, we have to go,* but Izzy flashes on me dropping her on her back at the shoreline, the water rushing up and choking her as it carries her backwards and the words *No no no* play over and over in her head as she shakes and clutches me, my throat clogging as I blink back tears. *OK, Izzy, OK, I'm sorry, we'll find a way to stay,* but I do the math and figure

$624 will only buy us groceries for a few months. We need more money, we need the show at Mrs. Lloyd's gallery, just a few more days. I hold onto Izzy and she nods her hot forehead against mine, *yes, stay here,* and then she squeezes my hands and lets me go. I take a deep breath and tiptoe down to the kitchen, ladle soup into two bowls, and carry them back upstairs. We sit on Izzy's bed and eat silently, swallowing the taste of salt and listening to the house around us. Izzy spoons in her soup without taking her eyes from the canvas, and when I wave a hand in front of her face she frowns, tilting her head to see around me. I clear my throat, try to sound bright and optimistic, and ask, "Why don't you like it?" but she shakes her head and keeps staring. Slowly the words *too still, too waiting* rise in my thoughts and when Izzy glances at me I put my toast down and swallow hard.

"What do you think is going to happen?" She shakes her head again and when I try to listen, her mind's quiet, her brow furrowed hard to keep me from hearing what she's thinking.

"Izzy—it's not fair. You can't just shut me out when you want to," I say, and she looks at me with surprise. The words *of course I can* flicker in my head and I stand up, drop my dirty dishes on the tray, carry her half-finished soup downstairs.

It's still pouring, but I duck out into the rain, the fast hard drops smacking into me. The water's high, lapping the cliff-edge, and when I slide down the dune I plunge in up to my knees. A wave crashes, catches me at the waist and pushes me back up against the cliff, but I push back, steady myself and look out.

Once, when we were just learning to walk, father brought me down here to the water alone. Izzy was in her highchair while mother and Grand tended steaming pots on the stove, but I had been crying and father lifted me out and carried me down. He sat me in the sand and waded in up to his still-knobby knees until a tall wave crested, crashed, rushed up, and knocked me over, scouring my nose and eyes and sliding me, squalling, several feet up the beach. Father picked me up before the wave could roll back out and held me against his chest, wading in up to his waist even as I kicked and screamed. "Shh. Look, Ansel. Just look," and I remember holding still long enough to watch the water lap around his waist. Now when I remember it, I think, *This is why I want to be grown-up—to choose when to pull the world close and when to keep it at a distance.*

When the water pulls back to my knees I kneel down, grab a handful of sand, and let it dribble from between my fingers, but there are no shells in such a high tide. Only on low tide days, when thin water creeps up all day leaving rings, might I find half a mollusk, the fingertip-sized shell water colored with sunset colors, orange fading to purple. I wade in up to mid-thigh and dig with my toes for sand dollars. Nothing. All that water and sometimes even it cannot resist stinginess.

Thirty-Three

I sleep fitfully, with our bedroom door wide open and one ear trained for any sound, so when I hear footsteps in the kitchen the next morning I bolt out of bed and pound downstairs. Grand's bedroom door slams and locks. I lay my ear against the wood, but all I can hear is the rustling of a dry-cleaner bag. The stove clock in the kitchen says 6:12 so I make cereal, carry it upstairs, pull Izzy into a sitting position and settle the tray over her legs.

The house is silent but not in the buzzing, expectant way it was the night I first heard Izzy inside my head. Everything feels sucked in, tensed, the glass in the window panes pulling in tight around us like a vacuum. One rough breath feels like it could blow everything apart. I sit down on the other side of Izzy's tray and make myself swallow a few bites of cereal. "What are you thinking," I say, but Izzy just shakes her head, staring into her bowl. We sit facing each other and then I get Izzy clean and dressed for the day and heft her over to the easel.

I settle her on the stool, adjust the belt to hold her in place and suddenly Izzy leans forward, hugging me, laying her head on my chest. I hug her back and stand there, my heart thudding into the side of her hot face, her heart thudding against my stomach, and I imagine the two of us curled up like the yin and yang inside our mother, the held-close protection we must have felt before we knew to feel. I hold her so tight I imagine our chests dissolving, each of us pressing into the other's center, and then Izzy pulls away, dabs a big brush with yellow and white paint, blots it on the palette and touches it to the canvas, filling in her skin with quick, controlled scribbles.

Her hot face. Izzy's turned away but the heat of her forehead still burns my sternum and when I grab her arm to turn her towards me I see her cheeks are pink, her eyes, if I'm really looking, slightly glassy. *A fever—Izzy—how long?* but she just furrows her brow and leans a little towards her canvas, blocking me from her thoughts. I pluck the brush from her hand, unbelt her, and she starts to struggle before seeing how determined I am, how I'm imagining already carrying her, clawing and scratching, over to the bed to check. She goes limp, turns her hot cheek to my shoulder, and hugs me tight. I lay her on the bed, pull up her t-shirt and strip off her shorts and diaper as Izzy looks away.

The skin around her stoma is a bright, stinging red, and I duck into the bathroom, wet a washcloth, then step back to the bed and dab around the opening. My breath clogs my throat as I wipe, and when the washcloth comes away pink with blood and puss my hands start to shake.

Izzy, how long have you had a fever? I ask into the silence, but she won't meet my eye, is keeping her thoughts airily blank. "Izzy, I need to know—you have to tell me," I say out loud, and she turns to face me, her eyes tired and sad. *A while,* she thinks.

"How long exactly?"

It's not your fault, she thinks, and before she can erase it, she flashes on the memory of falling from her stool late in the night, hitting hard and her bag breaking, urine spilling across the floor around her as she tries to pull herself up on her hands.

So long ago—a Sunday night, the one I spent at Everett's—almost two whole weeks. The air in my throat expands, choking my windpipe and my eyes sting. Izzy grabs my arms, *I haven't had the fever since then—only the last few days,* she thinks, and I shrug her hands off. *It's not your fault*, but I'm back in the bathroom opening the medicine cabinet and rifling bottles. *It is my fault, it is, but I can fix it*, I think, letting the toothbrushes and dental floss and nail scissors drop into the sink basin. *There's something here, antibiotic ointment and medicine, I'll figure out something,* but all the bottles are grandfather's aspirin except for the one of Izzy's antibiotics that we already used up, and I start to shake and slump to the floor in front of the sink. I'm crying, feeling Izzy's eyes on me, but I can't look at her, and my face is burning with all I the ways I've failed to make things right.

Come here, Izzy sounds across the silent room to me, but I shake my head and hug my knees. *COME HERE,* she insists, and I haul myself up, cross the room and drop down beside her bed. I bury my face in her pillow and she turns so that her breath is hot in my hair, her gaze burning into my skull, and then her hands cover my ears and she's kissing the top of my head.

Izzy, I can't do it. I'm not enough for you, I've never been enough, we need help, I think, and she kisses my hair and thinks, *I know. It's okay. I know.*

I clean Izzy's stoma and smear it with ointment, then carry her tray downstairs. It's Saturday, so I can't call the doctor today, and I know Izzy won't go outside to see him anyway. We'll have to get the doctor to come out here, somehow, and thinking about how Grand will react I suddenly remember to check her door. There's no key, so a locked door must mean she's still inside. I pull out the phonebook, find the doctor's number and think at the very least he can recommend someone to come see her—a nurse maybe—people have live-in nurses. That must be what Mr. Carson meant by "not enough care." I sit down at the table with a cup of coffee and pull out the envelopes about the hotel to distract myself. Numbers and signatures, pages of them—whatever made Grand think she'd be able to buy it back?—and then I'm shuffling the envelopes into place when there's a heavy, formal knock at the back door and my heart stops.

Not so soon. Not yet. State People. Is there time to run upstairs and hide Izzy? No—I'll sneak upstairs and drag her into the bathtub while they're busy with Grand. It can work. I won't let them take her. I steady myself and walk slowly to the door, praying that Izzy is listening to my thinking and knows to not make a sound. A single tall shape looms in the dingy window and when I open the door it's Everett, only Everett—a quick laugh bursts from me as I step back to let him in.

"Happy to see me?" he asks, his gaze still guarded from yesterday, and I nod with relief.

"Are you here to get the paintings?"

"I thought we'd go a few hours early tomorrow afternoon and hang them then. I just needed to talk to Isabel."

I lead him upstairs and Izzy turns with a start when Everett comes in, then the fear on her face flashes into a relieved smile. Everett looks between the two of us, but then his eye catches on Izzy's painting and he steps towards it, staring.

"What did you want to talk about, Everett?" I say, startling him out of his daze.

"Yeah, um… the opening starts at four, so we'll need to pick Isabel and the paintings up by two."

Izzy furrows her eyebrows and I say what she's thinking. "What do you mean, 'you'll need to pick Izzy up.'"

"For the opening. We'll need to pick her up early to take her to the opening."

Izzy and I blink at him as Izzy starts to slowly shake her head. "Wait, wait," I say. "Izzy's not going anywhere. She doesn't go outside."

Everett stares, and then all at once his features contort in panic and he rounds on Izzy, grabs her hand and drops jerkily into a kneel beside her. "Oh no, you *have* to go, Isabel, mother will insist, the artist has to be there, you *have* to go."

Izzy squeals and jerks her hands free. I pull Everett back saying, "Forget it, Everett, she's not going. She won't go."

"No, she has to, she *has* to. Look—I'll carry you downstairs, and we'll put a blanket over your head, see, so it'll be like you're never even outside." Everett yanks the bedspread off of Izzy's bed and flops it over her head. She shakes furiously, tearing it off and shoving it back at him. I can feel the panic in Izzy rising, her *no, no no* echoing over and over in my head.

"Everett, look, I'll go. I'll be Izzy—no one will ever know." Izzy's nodding furiously, and when I step close and put my arms around her she clings to me.

"You—no, you're not the artist—she'll have to answer people's questions about the paintings—it has to be the artist."

Izzy snorts and I laugh. "Everett, listen to yourself. *Answer people's questions?* Izzy doesn't talk to anyone but you, remember?"

"Well, she'll have to start, people will have questions and she'll have to…" but the panic in Everett's eyes is starting to sharpen into calculation, and I hold up my arms like a marionette, tilt my head and give him an exaggerated beatific Izzy smile. Izzy snorts and I can see in her mind's eye how it looks like I'm faking, so I close my eyes, imagine Izzy filling me up on the inside, and when I open them I can feel myself mirroring her smile and the airy artist's look in her eyes. Everett shifts uncomfortably, glancing at Izzy.

"I'm not sure… you won't know what to say about the paintings."

I roll my eyes and Izzy tilts her head to aim a look of exaggerated pity at Everett.

"I'll know what to say, Everett."

He furrows his brow, glances quickly at the floor, shifts his weight and then nods. "Okay then, fine, be ready tomorrow at two. We'll pick you up. I just hope I can get mother to wait in the car—maybe you should hide Isabel somewhere just in case."

Izzy shoots me an amused, incredulous look and I say, "Oh sure, I'll just stuff her in the closet."

"Great, okay, see you then," Everett says, too distracted to notice we don't even have a closet, and when he closes our door behind him laughter bursts from Izzy in bright burbles.

Thirty-Four

Sunday, August 4, 1974
3 days

The next morning Grand's soup from the night before is still on the table, the cold coffee pot from yesterday leeching the smell of stale coffee grounds. My knock creaks her door open enough to reveal rumpled bed sheets, piles of scattered clothes, but no Grand. I check the bathroom, then turn and bolt outside, scan the road in both directions and take off running. When I pass the garage the door's open and the light's on and there's Grand in her housedress, hunched over an open box in the back.

"Grand!"

She doesn't turn around. She's crouched over the boxes, rooting through them intently, and I tiptoe into the cool garage, into the smells of oil, rusty nails and rotten wood, where most of the space is taken up by the green LTD. Scattered at her feet are a pile of papers, and I ease closer, kneeling to pick one up.

"Don't touch what doesn't belong to you!" she hisses,

snatching it back, then she steps over to another box in the far corner, pulls the flaps open, and rifles through.

"Grand," I say, somewhere between a whisper and speaking, "You scared me—I didn't know where you'd gone." I keep my voice balanced, carefully light, don't let it tip into accusation, but she doesn't answer, doesn't even turn around. I watch her sifting through the boxes, lost in her own world.

"I'm gonna make breakfast now—you'll come in for breakfast, right, Grand?" She nods half to herself and doesn't look up, just keeps rooting through the box, pulls out a paper, reads, and drops it back in.

In the kitchen I empty the coffee pot into the sink, fill it halfway with water, and try to watch the garage as I dump the old grounds in the garbage, fill the percolator and set it on the stove. I get out the eggs and check out the window but I can't see her. I crack the eggs in the skillet and check out the window again. The eggs are frying when the door opens and Grand shuffles past me to her bedroom and shuts the door.

"Breakfast's almost ready." The house settles still and silent except for the sound of the eggs in the skillet. I slide two onto a plate and carry it upstairs, slide two more on another plate and put it at Grand's spot next to her cold bowl of soup, then make myself a plate and set it across from hers. I tap on her door then sit at the table and eat my eggs. The light at the windows breaks through the fast-moving clouds in sharp flickers and then the dark curtain of the storm clouds close and the first drops fall. The rain picks up to a drumming as I finish my eggs and watch for Grand.

After half an hour I think I'll go crazy watching her door. I call the doctor, but it just rings and rings, and I hang up, thinking about those boxes in the garage. I tiptoe over to Grand's door and hear faint sloshy noises of her taking a bath, so I bolt outside and through the pouring rain to the garage. I sprint to the back box, tear open the flap and find messy envelopes stuffed inside, some with sheets of paper half hanging out. My hands start to shake when I see the bank letterhead— a bank in Charleston— and I shut my eyes and kiss the envelope before slowly pulling out the letter.

Trust account for Ansel Mackenzie and Isabel Mackenzie.

Current Balance: $107,774.45. Interest paid for the month of April: $106.23.

I sink slowly to the cold concrete of the garage and stare at the sheet rattling in my hands, then pull the rain-smeared slip of paper from my back pocket. The numbers don't match exactly, but this was three months ago. I dig deeper in the box, grab three more random envelopes, then close the box flaps and tuck the envelopes under my shirt. I dash through the pouring rain back to the house, my heart vibrating in my throat like close thunder, then tiptoe through the front door and back upstairs.

"Izzy," I say, but she's beaming at me already and scrabbles for the envelopes, wanting to see for herself. *This is ours?* she thinks, looking up from the page with wondering eyes, and a laugh bursts from me. I wrap my arms around her and squeeze and squeeze and lift her a few inches from her stool and plop her back down and we're both giggling. *It's ours unless Grand spends it,* I think, and then Izzy freezes mid-laugh.

She can't, Izzy—it's ours, I think, but already I'm running my mind over the figures in her letter to Mr. Pritchett and how, our money or not, Grand sure seems to *think* it's hers to spend.

Izzy pulls her arms back in and picks up her brush, and I sit down on the edge of her bed hard. *We'll figure it out. We'll find a way to get that money,* I think, but Izzy keeps her mouth screwed up into a tight bow, her back rounded like a turtle's shell, and then neither of us is thinking anything, keeping our minds blank, blank, blank, wiped clean as a tide line for the other's sake.

A few hours later the rain's coming down in sheets, the wind gusting hard against the house, and one by one I gather three lamps and set them up by the window so Izzy can see. I train my camera lens over Izzy's hands, click a few frames of her brush and her hand and the angle at which they meet as the rain drums down.

A little after one o'clock I head down to the kitchen to take pictures. When my foot hits the downstairs landing, I glance back at Grand's room. The door is standing

wide open—empty—all the lights on and no Grand. I
check her bathroom, then turn and dash outside into the
downpour. The wind slams the door behind me, a hard
gust almost knocks me down, and I'm running through
the mud and splashing rain to the garage, praying *please
be there, please be there, please.* The garage door's up,
the car's gone, and before my thoughts can catch up I
take off towards the hotel, my feet catching and stumbling
underneath me. I'm yelling "Grand," running down the
road away from the garage when lightning flashes, a clap
of thunder dropping me to the ground. I scream, crawl
back to the garage, bend low and sprint back to the house
and up the stairs. I trail water across the kitchen to the
phone, drop the camera on the table, scan the yellowed
paper taped to the wall for the Carsons' number and dial.
The line is staticky and rings two times before the phone
picks up and one of the Carson brothers says hello.

"Mr. Carson, hello, it's Ansel—Grand's gone, I think
she's gone to the hotel."

There's another flash and a clap as the house goes
dark. I'm saying hello, hello into the handset and the older
Mr. Carson says, "In this weather?"

"Yes," I say, shivering, "She took the car. Should I go
after her?"

"Christ, no. Ansel, you sit tight, you hear? Clay and I
will be over to check on you two once this storm blows
over," he says, and I say all right and hang up.

The glow-in-the-dark numbers on the stove clock read

1:38 and after suffocating all day on the dragging hours, suddenly there's no time. I feel my way upstairs in the dark and stumble into the room. Izzy's eyes are wild with panic, and she's holding out her arms to me, her skin glowing ghostly white in the stormy dark. I unstrap her, and she's saying *no no no* over and over in our heads.

"Mr. Carson will find her, Izzy, it's okay." I hug her against me and drag her from her chair, carry her into the bathroom where Everett's mom won't see her and lay her gently in the tub. She's shaking, thinking the words *no no no no no*, and then she meets my eye and goes still. "What, Izzy?"

Thunder crashes, rattling the house in two ear-splitting beats, and a quick flash of panic like unchecked ocean water washes through Izzy before her mind goes blank. I search her face, but she grinds her teeth, lets go of me, clenches her fists and shuts her eyes. Izzy's panic thrums through my chest and I take a deep breath to steady us both, to break through the swirl of momentum rushing against us. *This is stupid,* I think. *I won't go. I just won't go.*

Izzy's breaths are coming in quick hiccups, but she shakes her head, thinking hard and steady the words, *No, you'll need this money. Go.*

You mean we'll *need this money, Izzy—*

Yes, yes—we, she thinks, her eyes squeezed shut, then she swallows, slows her breathing, and opens her eyes. She looks at me so intently the words *go go*

go pierce my skull like an alarm, *go go go go go* and
the panic of the words floods me, washes me into the
bedroom where I grab Lee's dress and a pillow, scoop up
some books and run back to the dark bathroom. Izzy's
watching me very carefully in the dim light as I slide the
pillow behind her head, and when I hand her the Dickinson
book she hugs it to her chest like a life preserver. I grab
a towel, rub it over my hair, peel off my wet clothes and
drop them sopping on the bathroom floor. As I pull on the
white dress another clap of thunder shakes the house.
Izzy flinches, fastens her eyes on me, and I'm saying I'll be
back soon, Izzy—I won't be gone long.

When I turn around I scream. Everett's in the bathroom
doorway, wide-eyed, a painting in each hand, and
annoyance flickers across his face. "It's okay, my mother
is meeting us there—are you ready?"

Izzy looks between the two of us, then her eyes lock
on me and she hugs the book tighter to her chest. She
holds my gaze and a kaleidoscope of emotions flicker
across her face—soft-eyed tenderness, smooth-cheeked
forgiveness, then chin-clenched determination—and she
nods once, reaches out and slowly draws the shower
curtain closed between us. Everett glances nervously
between me and the bathtub, then pulls the blanket off
Izzy's bed and carefully stacks the paintings in its folds.
He pulls off his parka and wraps it around the blanketed
bundle; then between the two of us we pick up the pile of
paintings and carry them with heavy, careful steps down

the stairs. Everett pulls open the back door and we both pause.

"She'll be okay?" he asks.

"Well, she's not going anywhere." I force a laugh but the words hang heavily in the thick, thunderous air. Everett and I stare out into the rain where his grandfather's car is pulled right up against the back steps, deep tracks gouged in the sand all the way up to the house. We find a still moment together, listening to the silence of Izzy upstairs, taking one last deep breath, and then Everett nods, nods, as if convincing himself, and we plunge into the racket of rain, hustling the wrapped paintings between us to the trunk, then jump into the warm, dark car and slam the door. We're sealed in together, the rain a muffled pounding on the canvas hood. Everett looks at the house one more time, then turns the ignition and throws the car into reverse. He pulls away and all I can hear is Izzy's silence inside my head like a slow leak.

Thirty-Five

The rain is coming down so hard Everett is hunched over the steering wheel with the wipers on high. He bounces down the dirt road out to the highway and turns left towards Fort Harmon. I crane back to look towards the hotel, but the view outside the windows is like the view from a submarine—grey water coating the windows, the car seeming to bob and float in space, hard drops of rain hopping as they hit the road.

Everett squints through the windshield, his knuckles white on the steering wheel, and then he peels one hand free to quickly fiddle with the radio dial. *Definitely nasty out there, folks. If you don't have to go out in it, I sure wouldn't. The National Weather Service is calling this a tropical storm but they have issued a flash flood warning and as they continue to monitor this developing storm system they advise all southern coastal residents*—Everett twists the radio back off.

I shut my eyes and try to imagine Izzy, the bright, airy

light of Izzy filling me up inside, but the thought of her fading farther and farther behind me tightens my ribcage. I listen for her, but all I can hear is a loud void, the sound of Izzy blocking me out, and to slow my heart I imagine I'm coming home instead of leaving. I imagine pulling up to the house and running through the rain up the porch steps, into the empty house, bursting into the bathroom and pulling back the curtain to find Izzy grinning up at me. I pull her out of the bathtub and we laugh about all the money we made, then curl up on Izzy's bed together to wait out the rain. In the morning Mr. Carson brings Grand back and that buys us a few more days until we can figure out what to do if she gets taken away for good. When I've played the whole sequence out in my head and we still haven't reached Fort Harmon, I play it over again with different details. This time Izzy's annoyed that I didn't leave her more books. This time I start telling her in my mind about the show even before I get home.

When we reach the gallery Everett pulls into the alley next to the building and we lug the paintings under the overhang around to the front door. The gallery is a high-ceilinged white rectangle, one floor-to-ceiling window lining the street side. Scattered around the concrete space are molten statues of beheaded and dismembered nudes in various contortions, and Everett and I weave between them, carrying the paintings with short, quick steps to the back of the gallery where a floating wall hides the coat racks. Two women with dyed black hair are popping out

the legs on card tables, and one shoots us a lazy glance.
Everett ignores them, intent on quickly unwrapping the
paintings and propping them along the wall. He pairs
his Orpheus with our Castor and Pollux, leaving Izzy's
Pandora and my Medusa at the other end of the wall.
He slides two hooks along the strip of metal they hang
from and balances a painting in place, then steps back,
squinting at the image of his dreamy-eyed Orpheus. He
knots the wire so that the painting hangs a little higher
and then quickly hangs the other three, nudging and tilting
them into exact alignment.

"Everett, it doesn't have to be perfect—I'm sure Izzy
wouldn't care," I whisper, and Everett says quickly,

"Mother will care."

The two women are pouring wine into glasses,
arranging them in rows on the tablecloths, and when one
glances back at us, says something to the other, they both
smirk. Everett ignores them, digs into his wallet and slides
out four hand-written labels, then affixes them to the wall
next to the paintings with a surgeon's care. He steps back
and looks at the whole arrangement, then inhales deeply
and beams.

"They look great," I say, and they do—like four dark
blue windows on the wide sweep of white wall. I stare at
them hard, burning the image of them into my mind so
that Izzy can see what they look like as a group, displayed
for all the world to see. Everett nods, and then his gaze
turns inward and he glances at his watch. A shadow of

worry drifts across his forehead as he looks to the front door, checks his watch again and finally walks across the gallery to where the two women are laying out cheese trays.

"Have you seen my mother yet?" he asks.

The taller woman who's been glancing back at us has dark eyeliner drawn thickly out to points like Cleopatra, and she turns to the other woman, asking with exaggerated excitement, "Any sign of her highness tonight, Jackie?"

The other woman smiles thinly and shakes her head, and then Cleopatra turns back to Everett with widened eyes. "Sorry, pet, I don't suppose she'll be gracing us with her presence this evening." She laughs, and Everett blushes, sputters, saying, no, she's definitely coming, she's just running late. Both women laugh again, high-pitched and exaggerated and Cleopatra says, "Honey, in this weather, we'll be lucky if Joe Homeless wanders through tonight." Everett flinches, shakes his head, then walks jerkily back over to the paintings and shifts Izzy's Pandora a millimeter to the right, a millimeter to the left. The rain lashes the front window and I wander between sculptures, trying not to think of Izzy lying in the cold porcelain of the bathtub, the dark house around her rattling with thunder.

The door opens and two women dressed in black burst in, dripping water and blustering with laughter—

"Never one to let a little rain keep me home, but— "

"I thought we were going to blow off the road!" and then a few more people shove in behind them as the silent shell of the gallery fills with voices ricocheting off the bare walls. Everett stands rigidly beside me and people mill between the sculptures, tilt their heads, then wander over to the wine and cheese and stand around the table lifting plastic glasses between thumb and finger. After a while a few people walk past us to get their coats, and then two pause in front of Izzy's paintings, then two more. A woman in an emerald green dress with numerous braids wrapped in a high pile of head scarf is making sweeping motions with her pinky next to the Castor and Pollux painting, tracing the arc of the horse's neck as it sweeps into the hair of the Izzy in the picture. The brash chatter drops down to semi-hushed tones, and slowly everyone in the room shifts, clustering in front of the few feet of wall space. Snippets of conversation wash over to me from among the low murmur.

"—Almost hallucinatory, the way the lines shift and sweep among figures—"

"Well, yes, obviously the color, and the floating figures reference Chagall, but—"

"I wouldn't say Picasso, no, everyone always wants to say Picasso, but let's not forget—"

"Clearly very talented, but can we really say—"

"—Not a *little* self-consciously allegorical?"

"Well I, for one, think there might be something—"

"*What's* the name, again?"

Everett is beaming beside me, his eyes flitting from face to face and then he steps into the crowd to point out something in the Castor and Pollux. I walk over to another cluster of people standing in front of the Pandora and Medusa, and a man in a deep purple jacket leans close to read a tag.

"It's called *Even the mouths,* so we can't know for sure, but this one has the longer hair like the boxer in the twin allegory over there, so you have to assume…" His mouth twists into a smirk and a woman next to him leans close to the painting.

"Oooooh, you're right—"

"Again, I can't say for sure, but—"

"Not exactly the Bobbsey twins, are they?" one woman says, and the group chuckles, then shifts their attention to the Pandora where another woman with dark-rimmed glasses is bent, squinting.

The heat climbs my cheeks as I hustle over to the table and chug a ginger ale. It never occurred to me how Izzy and I—all of our ugliness would be here on display, bared to the eyes of everyone—and I trade my empty glass for a full one, taking long gulps against the lump in my throat. My chest starts to burn as I imagine Izzy seeing all of this, listening to their speculations with a smug smile—but then, none of this was her idea. She didn't care if anyone saw her paintings—she just needed to release the images inside her head, to find in paint the little-seen versions of who each of us is, or might be—and as I swallow the last gulp of ginger ale I remember the bright light in her eyes when I turned from her, how it sharpened to panic before she closed her eyes and changed the *no no no* in her head to *go go go*.

She told me to go, but she didn't care about showing her work, didn't care about any of this, she was scared, and even though we need the money, why didn't I just call the whole thing off, stay with her, the two of us curled up on our beds in the honeycomb light of our room? She told me to go—why did she tell me to go? The tether in my sternum twists so tight I'm gasping for breath and my eyes start to sting as I look around for a clock. Everett is gesturing and a few of the people around him chuckle as I approach.

"Everett," I whisper, and he steps forward saying, "This is the artist." The crowd draws away, forming a moat of empty space around me. The room goes absolutely silent, and then people start talking at once, stepping forward to take my hand, shake it, talking to me slowly, loudly, as if I don't speak English.

"So fascinating—you're a twin?"

"—Just love how you use myths to make the personal allegorical."

"The decision to mix media—"

"—Your next pieces?"

I smile, nod, but when I pull inside myself to listen for Izzy suddenly all the voices seem to reach me under three feet of water, everything swirling, dizzy, hard to focus on, and then Everett's taking my hands and pulling me over to a chair. I sit down heavily and his fingers reach my cheek. I focus on him, on the look in his eyes like nothing I've ever seen, like I'm something that might bite or evaporate, and I know then that he's almost forgotten I'm not Izzy.

"You're so pale," he says, touching my jaw with the tips of his fingers. "Are you okay? Do you need anything?" I shake my head and watch the rain coat the windows, thinking how he's never looked at me so close with so much light in his gaze, the irises of his eyes starbursts of white on blue.

He's never looked at me, never really seen me—it's been Izzy all along he's been looking through me to find, and suddenly everything crystallizes and solidifies, bodies and wisps of conversation pulling into sharp focus around me, and the silence of Izzy in my head is like a white horn blaring above the din.

"Everett, let's go, I want to go."

He jerks back, his eyes focus on me and he looks around. "My mother should be here any minute," he says. "I just have to wait for her."

"Everett, I can't hear Izzy," I say, my voice breaking, but then the woman in the green dress is pulling him by the arm, lining him up with the Orpheus painting where he smiles shyly. The minutes drag on between shuffles of bodies as the door gusts open and closed and then the crowd has dwindled down to me and Everett and a few others. Everett is nodding, smiling between glances at his watch, when I tug on his sleeve.

"We have to go, please, we have to go now."

His smile falters and the woman talking to him turns aside to slide on her coat. His eyes are very wide and bright, and I pull him down to eye level. "Everett, your mom isn't coming, okay? Let's just go. Let's go get Izzy."

He swallows, nods, casts his gaze around the gallery, pausing to look at the paintings one last time with a glow of steady pride, and then we're ducking out the front door without even a backward glance, running in the slashing wind across the street to the parking lot. We're already soaked when we shut ourselves inside the dry shell of the car. Everett watches the rain drum down, then furrows his brow, cranks the key, and pulls out into the heavily gusting wind, the trees around us flapping and bucking and swooning towards the ground.

Thirty-Six

The car is suspended in air, the wind buffeting it sideways, rocking us like a tramcar held high on wires, and we can't go fast enough to get home, get home, get home. We crawl down the blank highway, but the closer we get to Cumberland the harder the rain gathers so that we can't see anything out the windshield even with the wipers frantically jerking back and forth as high as they can go.

The radio is crackling over and over *tropical storm upgraded to hurricane status, take shelter, class one hurricane, take shelter* and Everett says, "I'm pulling over."

"No! We have to get home."

"Ansel—"

"Where are you going to go? It's just open highway— we'll blow away if we stop. Just keep going."

Everett shakes his head, clenches the steering wheel, but he keeps going, creeping the car forward over the invisible highway. I'm listening as hard as I can for Izzy, but all I can hear is the screaming air buffeting the car and Everett has to jerk the wheel to keep us on the road. The minutes tick by as he keeps saying, I'm pulling off, and I say we're almost there, we're almost there. I try to go back to the dream of returning home, to the idea of running up the stairs and bursting into the bathroom and seeing Izzy, but all I can hear is empty air and the weight in my chest sinks deep, feels anchor-heavy. *Izzy, I'm coming, I'm coming, hold on, I'm coming.* She told me to go, she was scared, and then she didn't let me see what else she was thinking—did she know, did she know this was coming? I press my nose to the glass, and the image of her last painting rises to my mind's eye—the two of us standing on the dock with pairs of animals at our feet like refugees waiting for Noah's Ark—and I remember how she thought, *too still, too waiting.*

No. My breath catches in my throat—she didn't know. She couldn't. A hurricane—but she'll be fine. I strain forward, trying to see anything as hours pass, years, half of my life passes tilting forward in my seat squinting into the grey erasure of rain. Izzy.

Finally, finally, a green exit sign appears dimly in the thunderous blur outside and Everett steers onto the exit for town. I grab his sleeve.

"This isn't the exit for the hotel—the exit home."

"We're getting off here," he says and steers the car through sheets of rain and gusting wind, through the empty streets of town and grey pounding down all around us.

"Everett, what about Izzy?" He's peering intently through the window opaque with rain, and then we're turning when he leans in, squints, and slows the car to a stop. Water is rushing down Main Street, burbling and gushing like a river loosed from a dam. Everett takes his foot off the brake and as the car noses forward the water rises, clattering against the undercarriage, pushing the car backwards a few inches. The tires catch, dig in, and Everett guns the engine. We jolt a few inches forward and then the water deepens, it's up to the doors, rushing against the grill, breaking around the sides of the car and rushing past us, and Everett stomps on the brake. The current carries the car and sweeps it back and sideways, and then the left tire catches ground and we swing to the left and catch more ground and stop. Everett's eyes are clenched shut, and when the car lurches to a stop he leans forward, lays his forehead against the steering wheel.

I'm sputtering, "It's okay, it's okay, we'll just get out here—we can run, it's okay." Everett opens his eyes, stares at the water, and then he turns to face me. His eyes are wide, fear-whitened, and he shakes his head.

"Everett," I say, but then the pit of my stomach goes cold and suddenly I know he can't do it—he won't go. It's just me—I'm the only one—he would leave her. For all his bedside tending, for all his swooning and wooing, Everett would leave her there—my sister.

"Izzy," I say, and I yank the door handle, shove hard out of the car and then I'm running as fast as I can in the thick, blinding air, sprinting and slipping down the street when the wind blows me off my feet. I hit the ground hard, sliding on the soaked, gritty asphalt, my hands and knees stinging. I get back up and I'm running, then sloshing, wading down Main Street and I duck under the metal awning for the Stop 'n' Shop. The street signs are wobbling, there's a wrenching sound and a piece of awning pulls loose and goes bouncing, tumbling through the air and disappears with a flat smack into the river of Main Street. The wind is coming at me hard from the side and the water is up over my knees, it's like trying to run in a dream, twigs and leaves whipping past me in the slashing rain. I grab a sign pole, pull myself up to it and hold on, then wade a few steps towards a parking meter and lean and grab on, pulling the rest of my body through the dense water and wind. I'm inching my way up Main Street, inching and listening for Izzy but all I can hear is shrieking air.

I make it to Pauline's then pull myself towards the edge of the building. I blink and gasp as the rain slaps icily into my eyes, my face, and I can just make out the door for the bathroom at Red's garage flapping back and forth. I crane forward into the thick air, the water is gushing and slamming into me, it's up to my thighs, and I'm reaching for the flapping door to pull myself closer to the building when it smacks into me. Pain screams up my left arm and I gasp, buckle, then catch myself and stay standing, shutting my eyes around an exploding star. My breath comes fast, I'm breathing through teeth, and I slip and struggle and push through the rushing water around the edge of the garage until I can see the road home.

I'm wading, stopping again and again to dig in my feet against the torrent, my arm tucked up against my chest, the trees bobbing and swaying and bending so far over the tops seem feet from the ground. I slosh my way out of the deepest water and claw one-handed up the hill. The water is still spilling thinly in quick surges past me down the hill to where it gathers force, gushing down Main Street. Leaves and twigs whip into me and I'm crawling, digging in with one hand as I crest the hill home. *Izzy, Izzy, I'm coming, I'm almost there,* and I stand for the last long slog across the yard. I stagger to my feet, but I'm turned around, the wind has blown me, I've come too far, somehow I've come too far, I've missed the house, and I'm staring down into water—water and a roof and a few windows.

Water and a roof and a yellow curtain—*our window, it's our window, and the house is drowning*—and then I'm running in water up to my knees, up to my chest, *no no no no no,* swimming, my arm flaring with pain so sharp I'm gasping, swimming to the house that's somehow sideways, tilted, teetering underwater on the edge of the cliff and only the top part showing. I'm screaming Izzy, Izzy, Izzy, but I can't hear her and now I'm floating, gasping as the water surges and smacks and drives me under, and I bob back up as the water shoves me against the back of the attic. I bob and go back under and claw with my right arm around the edge of the house and then surface at the bedside window that's tilted, half underwater, and pound on the glass. The house shifts under me, dips lower in the water, and I catch my feet on the edge of the window sill and tug. The window's locked—we keep the windows locked, why do we keep the windows locked?—and my breath is bursting in my chest, heaving, I'm sobbing, sobbing, looking around in all that water for something. *Izzy, listen to me, I'm almost there, I'm right outside, I'm coming.* A dark shape bobs a few feet away, *oh God,* my heart, but it's a branch, *just a branch.* I duck under, kick hard, come up, grab the slime-slick bark, then kick and float the branch back to the window and pound and pound on the glass until it cracks and I break all the big shards loose and slip inside.

Our beds are floating, clunking against the far wall under the window, Izzy's paintings turning slowly face down in the caught water of the room. The bathroom door is still closed, and I'm clawing and fighting my way through chest high water, my breath strangling in my throat, *get to the door, get to the door, in there, Izzy.*

The door won't open—I shove, but my feet keep slipping out from under me and I push as the water shifts and swirls, *in there, Izzy.* Dimly, dimly in the dark a shape floats above the bathtub, I'm churning through the water closer, Izzy, the scream in my throat, I'm to her, I'm touching her, the cold skin and my clogged throat *Izzy Izzy Izzy, I can't hear.* I shake her and she's white, wax-white and so cold, she's so cold, my mind's a blank, her lips blue and she's not speaking to me, Izzy. The darkness inside me blooms and expands, the cold vertigo of knowing it's just me, just me cut adrift from everyone who's touched me and named me and known me, just me and suddenly it's hard to tell the dark from light—it's that blazing, and when it sweeps inside it erases all I've kept hidden, bleaching blank any me I've ever known with its blinding beam.

Izzy Izzy Izzy Izzy Izzy. Her eyelids flutter, *Izzy,* she twitches, I hold her and her eyes open, her blank eyes flare with panic, her hands scrabbling to my shoulders, clamping onto me and the water in my throat, I'm choking and crying, I can breathe again, Izzy. She's clinging to me so hard, shivering, her fingers stinging as they dig into scrapes and cuts on my shoulders and I turn towards the door, my arm screaming. I slog with Izzy's legs trailing by my side and it's easier now, the water doesn't slow us so much, we're just floating, we have all the time we need, we'll make it, and then the house shifts, the roof sinks closer to our heads and I lose my feet as Izzy screams.

I'm trying to keep our heads up but we're too heavy—we duck under and I try to loosen Izzy's arms. She clings to me and when our heads crest the water I say, "Izzy, listen!" We're spluttering, coughing, she's

clinging so tight, and I scream again, "Izzy, listen to me!"
Our heads are under water, I try to pry her arms free,
and she's screaming in my head *don't don't don't don't*.
Suddenly I imagine loosening her arms and shaking free,
floating away alone to the window, leaving her to sink
in the sinking house, and I push the thought away but it
resurfaces—prying her arms loose, floating away alone. I
let the darkest part of my heart speak and I know *once I
might've, once, a long time ago, I wanted to leave you, but
not now, not now,* and then I know it's Izzy imagining this,
not me, and I scream over the image in our heads, *Izzy,
no, I wouldn't, I'm here, listen to me.*

    We bob up, but Izzy's holding so tight in a chokehold
I can't catch air and when we dip back under my lungs
are bursting, my vision starting to fog, and I imagine what
I want to do, hard, trying to burn the image into her head:
me loosening her arms enough to shift her onto my back
and then the two of us swimming, my right arm, her left,
and me kicking, the two of us together getting to the
window and getting out.

    Our heads crest the water and we're coughing, we
can't breathe, I wheeze *Izzy, I promise*, the image of us
swimming together floating in our heads. Her gaze clamps
on mine as I push the image in through her eyes. She
looks at me hard and her arms loosen.

    I duck under the water, come back up under the
hoop of her arms so she's on my back now and I can
see the window—Izzy's pushing with her left arm and I

with my right. It's so hard to coordinate our arms—we keep dipping under water and we're trying to make both arms stroke with the same strength and my lungs are screaming. A bed blocks our way and we flop onto it as it sinks, we go under, swallowing water, my feet tangling in the sheets. I kick hard, we break the surface, choking, coughing, and then we take two strong pulls across the water to the dresser floating on its back. Izzy grabs one handle and I grab the other and the dresser sinks a little as we pull open the top drawer, but Izzy's hand finds the lockbox and mine opens it and Izzy grabs the money and wraps her arm back around my neck. Then we turn as the water shifts, splashes over our heads, but the window, it's there, we can make it, and we each grab onto the window frame. The glass shards dig hot into our hands but we pull and pull ourselves through and we're out, we're swimming, our arms working together smoothly and I kick hard up and away from the house as the water pushes us under.

We bob back up and Izzy's gasping in my ear. I kick as hard as I can—the water wants to swallow us but I kick away from it—and we bob our way out of the yard, up the slope to where my feet catch sand, I dig my toes in and our arms pull us across the water to the edge of the bowl of land. The water's to my waist, then my knees, and I climb up under some trees, we claw our way up and over the crest of the hill where water sloshes over our heads down into town, but it's solid here and we dig into the brush, lying flat as we can on the ground beneath the trees.

We lie face down in the sand as branches dip and brush our backs, lying there breathing, breathing, and we let ourselves tumble into breathing.

Later, when we open our eyes, it's raining softly, the water lapping gently under us. Izzy splutters and I roll her over so that she's staring up into the grey sky. Her eyes are wide, wondering, and as we reach across our bodies to hold hands, watching the clouds shift and break overhead, I can hear the perfect sound of Izzy breathing.

Outside, she thinks. *Yes,* I say, smiling, and close my eyes.

Epilogue

Tuesday, August 6, 1974
1 day until birthday

Someone is carrying me, and when I look down it's Iain walking woodenly in puppet maker clothes. I laugh and snap his suspender, then notice that my fingers are jointed wood like an artist's dummy. I'm a puppet now too, and the relief floods me as I reach to hug Iain, but I only have one arm. He carries me into his house and sets me on the table next to a legless Izzy who beams when she sees me. *I've never made a puppet like this before,* Iain says, *I'm not sure how she'll turn out.* His brow furrows, and I say, *she'll be great, you'll see,* and Izzy nods as he takes a deep breath, gets his screwdriver, and scoots Izzy's wooden waist over to a pair of wheels from a roller skate. He's sweating, and he screws her into place then sets her upright and she's smiling, spinning around the workshop popping wheelies. He looks embarrassed, saying *I told you this wasn't a good idea* and I say, *what are you talking about, this is great.* Izzy wheels over and Iain picks up a pair of big scissors, cutting the strings from our hands and elbows, my knees and feet and back. Then he sets me on my feet, and I have to find my balance with only one arm. His eyes are sad, but I'm making Igor sounds, lurching forward with my empty shoulder, and Izzy can't stop laughing as we wave and coast towards the bright, wide-open doorway.

There's a knock at the front door and we hear Iain get up from the couch to answer it. Heavy footsteps plod across his kitchen and the older Mr. Carson opens the door. He stands in the doorway to Iain's bedroom staring at Izzy and me crammed into the twin bed. The first of the morning light is seeping in thinly from under the shade and I sit up as Izzy sighs, nestles deeper in, her cheek against my neck.

"That doesn't look comfy for neither of you," he says, and I wince when Izzy accidentally nudges my left hand. "It's hurting," Mr. Carson says, hooking his hat on the doorknob and coming over. He kneels down, gingerly unties the cloth sling, unwrapping the bandages until the splints fall out. I try not to show the pain on my face as he gently turns my arm. "This is damn-near idiotic," he says, sliding his fingers up my forearm, and then Iain is in the doorway with a cup of coffee, watching.

"I've been working on her, but she won't budge," Iain says. Mr. Carson exhales noisily, gently wrapping my arm back up, and I can't help but gasp when he squeezes the splint back into place.

"You see there," he says, "you need a hospital," and Izzy reaches her arm across my shoulder, burying her head in my chest at the word. *No hospitals.*

"No hospitals," I say for the both of us "Anyway, It's not even swollen. It would heal if you'd stop taking the splint off all the time."

"Ansel, we don't even know if that bone is set right so it can mend—you need an x-ray," he says, as Iain comes barefoot into the room in jeans and a white t-shirt, saying,

"Truly, listen to reason now, love."

"After they took Grand from the hotel the night of the storm, didn't you say there were social services people asking about me? And wasn't it you who said if they found out about Izzy they'd take her away to a state hospital, too?" I feel Izzy tense at the words *state hospital* and when I say them again even Mr. Carson flinches. "Just think, Izzy—maybe you could be in the same *state hospital* as Grand—I bet they put the loonies and cripples all in one big room together—it could be a family reunion, and hey, maybe they'll let me visit, oh, once a year or so."

Mr. Carson sighs, shakes his head. "We could take you to a hospital in another town, use false names, pay cash," he says, but I don't drop his gaze.

"No way—people think Izzy and I drowned—it's better they keep thinking that."

"People in this town care about you two," Mr. Carson says. "They deserve to know you're okay."

Izzy flashes on the image of Everett's face, but all I

can think about is getting the money from him for Izzy's paintings.

"Later. Once everything's blown over with Grand."

He shakes his head, muttering, paces in front of us with his hands on the small of his back. "And what about Miss Isabel? Don't you think she needs a doctor?"

"She's seeing a nurse this afternoon," I say. "Some woman Iain knows is coming out from Fort Harmon. She'll get Izzy fixed up, and I'll have her take a look at my arm too, if that's what you want." Izzy's drainage bag pulled loose during the storm, and with the fever she was already running she agrees we'll have to risk it. But my arm isn't going to kill me, and walking into a hospital to get an x-ray is out of the question. No hospitals.

Mr. Carson sighs, stands up and looks hard at Iain, smiling, leaning in the doorjamb. "And how long are you prepared to sleep on your own couch?" he asks accusingly. Iain shrugs, takes a swig of coffee and smiles at us both.

"I've slept on worse," he says, "though I can't pretend the two of them aren't cramping my busy bachelor ways." When he winks at us my insides go soft and Izzy pokes me, giggling.

"Oh, right," I say, "That get-up, go-to-work, come-home, eat-and-sleep daily whirlwind of social activity you'd be able to maintain if *only* we weren't here," I say. He grins, cheers me with his coffee cup, then drinks the rest down and walks back into the kitchen. Mr. Carson picks up his hat and points it at us accusingly. "That arm may never heal right, and then you'll be crippled the rest of your life," he says. Izzy snorts and Mr. Carson flushes as he realizes what he just said.

"I hear there are worse things that can happen to a person," I say, and Izzy laughs. "Anyway, Izzy's arms work fine, and it's about time she started taking care of her catheter herself."

Mr. Carson hangs his head, spins his hat brim in his hands, saying, "Clay and I should be the ones to look after you girls. It should have been us all along." He seems to shrink a little as the words hang in the air and I can't bring myself to tell him how insistently the wide-open world and all the unlived-out-there is tugging us. The light of how many still-to-come summers waiting to wash over Izzy, wheeled up in front of the all-glass windows of some tall apartment, painting, her body slowly aging and filling out with finally enough food and the exercise of shuttling herself between the meeting of her own body's needs. The nurse who stops by to check on her the months I'm away somewhere—twining through some incense-crowded, open-air bazaar or climbing the whitewashed, ocean-dizzy staircases of a cliff side village, trekking through the loose dust and heat-blurred horizon of mud huts, or shivering prow side, gliding between jagged hunks of glaciers— somewhere so far from Izzy I fear the tether will snap and dissolve, but it doesn't, it won't, now that what draws me to her is the closing of an orbit, the homing that spins me out and away so far I can hardly breathe, before pulling me back to her side where I find my footing.

I tear my eyes from Izzy's beaming, sneaky smile and don't tell Mr. Carson that there are years still between who we are and who we will be, but we'll never become those women living in Cumberland.

"Maybe we'll see you again," I lie. "If things don't work out for us in New York."

"This friend of yours—you sure she's willing to put you up?"

At the mention of Lee my stomach tightens, and I can see in my mind's eye the camera turning and sinking in the water-filled shell of the kitchen, settling, silted over on the sandy floor, lost to the dark unending openness of ocean. I swallow against my fear of all we might lose and can't predict in the coming years and force a smile. "She's coming next month," I say, "Lee says she can get me an under-the-table job in a photo lab, and she thinks she might be able to find some shows for Izzy."

"Shows," Mr. Carson huffs, "you know how expensive it is living in a big city? Can't get a cup of coffee for less than a dollar. *A dollar!* I'm thinking maybe those state people have it right—you two are too young to be out on your own."

"Our birthday's tomorrow," I say, "Sixteen. That's how old Iain was when he left home."

Iain takes a step into the room and freezes just as I'm saying this. Mr. Carson turns slowly towards him, sending him a long withering glare. Iain hitches his shoulders, palms open, and Mr. Carson sputters, "Well, there are papers—doctors you'd have to see, letters people would have to write on your behalf. The judge would want—"

"So it is possible," I say, and Mr. Carson blanches.

"Only in extreme circumstances, Ansel."

"Izzy and me, we're nothing if not extreme," I say. Izzy's tracing something with her finger on the belly of my t-shirt, and I shift a little so she can reach past me to grab her sketch pad off the floor. I get up to give her room to work as she pulls herself up on the pillows, takes the pad and starts to draw. "And besides," I say, but Izzy looks up at me and holds my eye, so I don't say what we're both thinking.

> *I could give back my half of her life, but*
> *finding how my mind exists partly inside*
> *her, how she exists partly for me, I can*
> *finally find my edges, risk a little of myself*
> *to the wider world. What my voice sounds*
> *like—now that it's once again half hers. Half*
> *or less than half, the world crowding in,*
> *taking more than its fair share. Or my voice*
> *rushing out to meet the world, blue ever*
> *outward and the changing space between*
> *our bodies, the poles we call between.*
> *Frequencies lengthening, flattening over*
> *distance, but always cast out and received,*

always tugged and released within this sphere. Light and dark balancing, and this grey in between will be boundless, ever-reaching, borderless as seas.

Acknowledgements

The definition of "cumber," used as an epigraph courtesy of Douglas Harper, Online Etymology Dictionary.

Emily Dickinson poem excerpts reprinted by permission of the publishers and the Trustees of Amherst College from THE POEMS OF EMILY DICKINSON: READING EDITION, edited by Ralph W. Franklin, Cambridge, Mass.: The Belknap Press of Harvard University Press, Copyright © 1998, 1999 by the President and Fellows of Harvard College. Copyright © 1951, 1955, 1979, 1983 by the Presidents and Fellows of Harvard College.

Many thanks to the following for early reads and helpful input: Rachel May, Rebecca Rotert Shaw, Emily Danforth, Jonis Agee, Carole Levin, Hilda Raz, Grace Bauer, Judy Slater. For writerly support and (in some cases,) years of encouragement: Miles Waggener, Amy

Ratto Parks, Natalie Peeterse, Cara Lustgarten, Nancy Willard, Eric Lindbloom, Eamon Grennan, John Murray, Susan Ginsburg, Liz Usuriello, John Sibley Williams, Mike Gannon, Nancy Michaels, and most especially, Leigh Gannon Feld. Thank you, Genevieve Williams of Gen Proofreads for excellent copy-editing. For answering my questions, thank you Mark Gilbert, Mary Helfenberger, and Gary Mills. For the cover image, thank you Mike Retelsdorf, the beautiful Catie Miller, and the talented, ever-patient Mike Gannon. A hundred thousand thank yous to Kevin Atticks, Kimberly Babin, and the editorial board at Apprentice House.

About the Author

Megan Gannon was born in Chattanooga, Tennessee and is a graduate of Vassar College (BA), the University of Montana (MFA) and the University of Nebraska-Lincoln (PhD). She also served as a Peace Corps volunteer in The Gambia, West Africa from 1998-2000. Her poetry chapbook, *The Witch's Index*, was published by Sweet Publications in 2012, and her work has appeared in *Ploughshares, Pleiades, Gulf Coast, Third Coast, The Notre Dame Review, Verse Daily, Poetry Daily,* and *The Best American Poetry 2006*. She lives in Omaha, Nebraska, where she is currently at work on her second novel.

Apprentice House is the country's only campus-based, student-staffed book publishing company. Directed by professors and industry professionals, it is a nonprofit activity of the Communication Department at Loyola University Maryland.

Using state-of-the-art technology and an experiential learning model of education, Apprentice House publishes books in untraditional ways. This dual responsibility as publishers and educators creates an unprecedented collaborative environment among faculty and students, while teaching tomorrow's editors, designers, and marketers.

Outside of class, progress on book projects is carried forth by the AH Book Publishing Club, a co-curricular campus organization supported by Loyola University Maryland's Office of Student Activities.

Eclectic and provocative, Apprentice House titles intend to entertain as well as spark dialogue on a variety of topics. Financial contributions to sustain the press's work are welcomed. Contributions are tax deductible to the fullest extent allowed by the IRS.

To learn more about Apprentice House books or to obtain submission guidelines, please visit www.apprenticehouse.com.

Apprentice House
Communication Department
Loyola University Maryland
4501 N. Charles Street
Baltimore, MD 21210
Ph: 410-617-5265 • Fax: 410-617-2198
info@apprenticehouse.com • www.apprenticehouse.com

CPSIA information can be obtained at www.ICGtesting.com
Printed in the USA
BVOW01s1341160414

350804BV00003B/164/P